Note to Reader: the publisher wishes to apologise for certain pictures that appear out of sequence within the storyboard of *MirrorMask*. Below is a list of correct pictures, with a note in each case as to where they should appear.

STORYBOARD FRAME

DELETED

p17, bottom left picture box

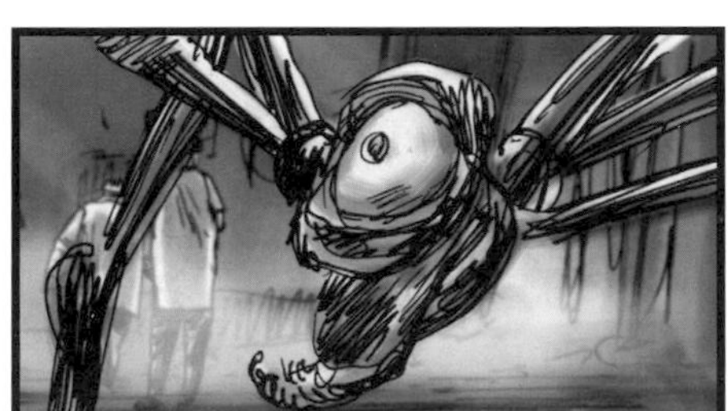

p73, picture 3

p76, picture 4

p79, picture 6

p106, picture 6

p125, picture 6

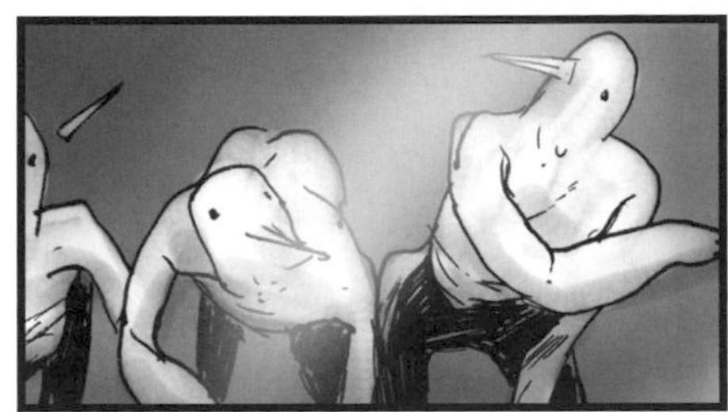

p184, picture 5

p184, picture 6

p187, picture 1

p204, picture 1

p204, picture 2

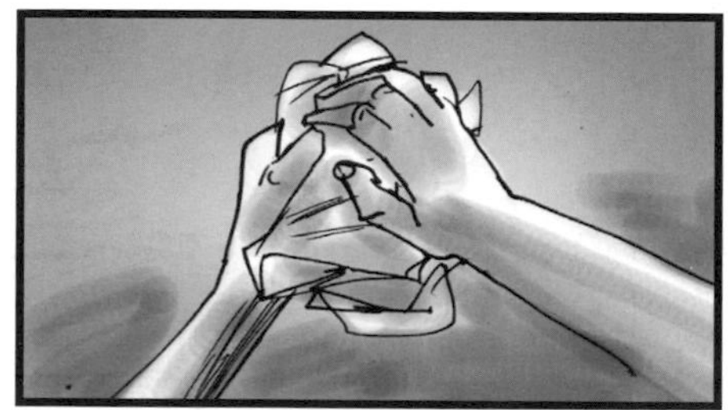

p204, picture 3

p204, picture 4

p204, picture 5

p204, picture 6

p247, picture 6

MIRRORMASK

Also by Neil Gaiman

AMERICAN GODS
STARDUST
SMOKE AND MIRRORS
NEVERWHERE
GOOD OMENS (WITH TERRY PRATCHETT)

Illustrated by Dave McKean

THE DAY I SWAPPED MY DAD FOR TWO GOLDFISH
THE WOLVES IN THE WALLS
CORALINE

The Illustrated Film Script of the Motion Picture from The Jim Henson Company

NEIL GAIMAN AND **DAVE McKEAN**

review

This book is a work of fiction. The characters, incidents, and dialogue are drawn from the author's imagination and are not to be construed as real. Any resemblance to actual events or persons, living or dead, is entirely coincidental.

Jim Henson
THE JIM HENSON COMPANY

First published in Great Britain in 2005 by REVIEW

An imprint of HEADLINE BOOK PUBLISHING

1

Cataloguing in Publication Data is available from British Library

ISBN 0 7553 2829 9

Printed and bound in Great Britain by CPI Bath

HEADLINE BOOK PUBLISHING
A division of Hodder Headline
338 Euston Road
London NW1 3BH

www.headline.co.uk
www.hodderheadline.com
Designed by Dave McKean @ Hourglass

For Lisa Henson, who gave us the opportunity;
and for Jim Henson, whom we would love
to have met

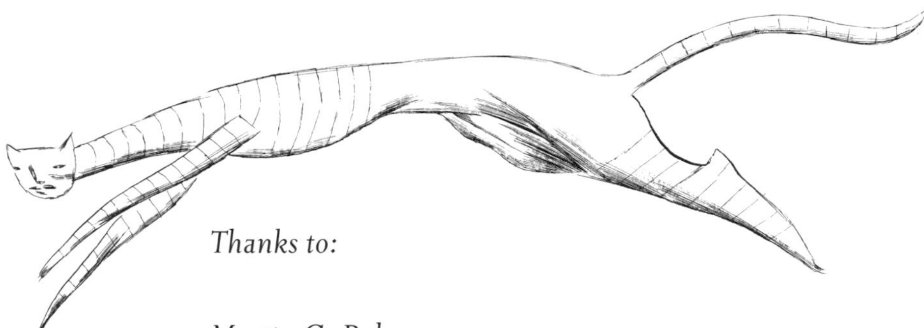

Thanks to:

Martin G. Baker
Terry Gilliam
Merrilee Heifetz
Lisa Henson
Ian Miller
Simon Moorhead
Michael Polis
Antony Shearn
Mark Spencer

A very special thank you to Jennifer Brehl

and

the late Jim Henson

MirrorMask. *An Introduction.*

Somewhere in North London, as I type this, Dave McKean is hard at work on *MirrorMask*. He's sighing and frowning and working extremely long hours, just as he has for the last eighteen months, compositing shots and solving problems. Dave designed and directed and composed every shot in *MirrorMask*. The finished film has to be delivered at the end of this month. If there's one thing he doesn't have time for, it's writing introductions.

So this is the story of *MirrorMask* according to me.

It was the summer of 2001. The phone rang. It was Lisa Henson, and she wanted to know whether I thought Dave McKean would be interested in making a fantasy film for them – something in a similar vein to *Labyrinth*. Although, she said, *Labyrinth* had cost Henson about forty million to make twenty years earlier, and, while the funding for a new film existed, there wasn't very much of it: only four million dollars, which is a lot of money if you come across an abandoned suitcase full of cash in a hollow tree somewhere, but won't get you very far in the world of fantasy film-making. She had seen Dave's small films and loved them. Did I think that Dave would be interested? I said I didn't know.

Obviously, said Lisa, she couldn't afford to pay me for writing a script. Maybe I could help a writer come up with the story . . . ? I told her that if Dave said yes to directing it, I was writing the script, and that was all there was to it.

Dave said yes.

I had half an idea, and I wrote it down and sent it to Dave. A girl from a travelling theatre, who found herself kidnapped into some kind of fairyland by a fairy queen. An unreliable Puck-like guide. A girl forced to become or to pretend to become a fairy princess, while a real fairy princess was forced to try and pretend to be human. I called her Lenore – I knew I wanted one of those names that meant "Light" and Lenore seemed like a wonderfully theatrical sort of name for a young lady to have.

Meanwhile, Dave had had a dream, and on waking decided it might be the basis for a good film: a mother in the real world who is extremely ill, a world of masks, a girl who had to wake the sleeping white queen, a white queen and a dark queen, a balance that was shifting and breaking. He sent me an e-mail, describing the dream, and his idea for a film, and several other ideas he had had for the feel of what he wanted to convey.

I wondered whether we could combine the two ideas. Lenore seemed like a theatrical name, but not a circus name, so the girl became Helena (a name that still meant "Light").

In February of 2002, the Jim Henson Company sent me to England for two weeks. To save money, and because we both thought it an excellent idea, Dave and I stayed in the Henson family house in Hampstead. It hadn't been redecorated since Jim Henson died, and everywhere we were surrounded by his world. In a cupboard in the lounge we found a video of an early edit of *Labyrinth*, more than three hours long with the voices of the puppeteers doing their characters rather than the actors, and we watched it in the evening over a few nights, to help put us into the mood. Dave had a pile of art books with him, books on surrealism and sculpture, books filled with imagery that he thought might come into play in the story.

Dave McKean and I had worked together very happily for about sixteen years at that point. It had always been easy. This wasn't.

Mostly it wasn't because Dave and I wrote, we discovered, in completely different ways. He plans it all out, and writes every idea down on little cards, needs it to all be done before the first word of script is written; whereas I'll talk about it to the point where I'm ready to start writing, and then I start writing and find out the rest of it as I go along. These methods of working are not entirely compatible. That was half of the problem. The other half of the problem was that Dave knew what he could and couldn't do, in order to make a film with the money that we had, and I didn't.

"I want to do a scene in Helena's school," I'd say.

"Can't do it," Dave would explain. "Too expensive. We'd need the class, and a teacher and kids as extras," and then, seeing my face fall, he'd add, "but we can make the world crumple up like a piece of paper, if you want. That won't cost us anything."

Still, Dave's certainties were reassuring. It's often easier to make art if you know what your boundaries are. In the case of *MirrorMask*, I wrote down in the basement kitchen, where it was warm (right now I'm writing this in the kitchen of a borrowed house, which goes to demonstrate consistency, I think), while Dave mostly worked several floors up, where there was light and a grand piano.

Our touchstone was something Terry Gilliam had once said about his wonderful film *Time Bandits*. He said he wanted to make a film intelligent enough for children, but with enough action in it for adults. And so did we.

I started writing.

Dave would suggest things that would, he hoped, be easy and relatively cheap to make in the world of computer animation – twining shadow-tentacles or formless black bird-shapes.

Several times during that week, Dave would go off and do a first draft of a scene on his own, to show me what he meant, and I'd fold that in – the first drafts of the Giants Orbiting sequence, the monkeybirds and the scene looking for the dome in the dream-lands were all Dave's, for example, as was the Librarian's Origin of the World speech, which Dave wrote long before we started writing the film. I'd tidy them up, and noodle with the dialogue. He for his part would look over my shoulder at the dialogue I was writing on the screen and point out whenever I was starting to sound like Terry Jones writing *Labyrinth*, and then I would try and make it sound a bit more like me writing *MirrorMask*.

Henson had mentioned they thought there should be goblins in it somewhere, owing to their having sold the film we were making to Sony under the working title of "Curse of the Goblin Kingdom", so every now and again I would insert the word "goblin" in front of a character's name – "Goblin Librarian" for example, while the character who doesn't have much of a name in the current script apart from "Small Hairy" was called "Dark Goblin" in that first draft. Dave took a jaundiced view of this practice. "They'll want to see goblins," he'd warn me. "And there won't be any goblins. It'll lead to trouble." I thought we'd probably be all right.

Neither of us were sure whether or not we were really making a film until the day Terry Gilliam came round to the house for a cup of tea. He looked at the sheet of paper we had covered with lines and scribbles to tell ourselves the shape of the film. "*That*," he said, "looks like a movie."

Ah, we thought. Maybe it did, at that.

The unreliable juggler character was called "Puck" in the first draft, and we knew we needed a better name for him. It was the second week in February, and we were surrounded by posters and signs telling us it was nearly Valentine's Day, so we called him Valentine. It was a slightly more flamboyant name, and he suddenly seemed, to both of us, a slightly more flamboyant character.

We sent the script off to Henson, and we waited, nervously. They had comments, of course, extremely sensible ones – they wanted more ending and more beginning.

Dave sent us pictures of characters and moods and places, to try and show the kind of things that he meant: how the White City would feel, what Valentine would be like, all that. The strange thing about looking at those pictures now, for me, is that they make complete sense. I can see exactly what Dave meant and why he sent them. At the time they came in I looked at them and wondered how they could possibly relate to the script we'd written.

Dave knew, though. Dave always knows.

Now, my theory about films is that it's probably safer to assume that they won't happen. That way, when, as you expected, they don't happen, you won't find yourself with six months of free time you have to fill. So while we did another draft of the script, and while Dave sat down and carefully storyboarded the entire film (the same storyboards you'll see in this book), and while Henson seemed quite certain that it really was going to happen, it seemed easier to assume that at some point someone would wake up and see reason, and that it would never happen. Nobody ever saw reason.

What you're waiting for, in the world of film-making, is a "green light". It's like traffic lights – the green light means it's a go. Everything's happening. You're making your film.

"Do we have a green light on *MirrorMask*?" I'd ask. Nobody ever seemed quite sure.

And then it was May 2003, and I was in Paris, at the end of a European signing tour. Dave phoned and said, "We're having a read-through of *MirrorMask*." I got on the train to London and found myself sitting in a small room at Henson's London offices, where a bunch of actors sat around a table and read. I was introduced to Gina McKee and Stephanie Leonidas. Brian Henson read many of the small odd creatures (I was particularly impressed with his reading of The Chicken). I scribbled on the script some more, cutting bits, adding lines, and feeling pleased whenever something that I'd hoped was a joke actually got a laugh from the people around the table.

After the reading Dave and I asked Lisa Henson if we actually, finally, honestly and truly had a green light for the film. She tried to explain that this film wouldn't work like that, and no, we didn't, but it would happen, so not to worry. We worried anyway.

And then, more or less to our surprise, Dave started shooting.

I wasn't there for most of it. I thought it wouldn't happen, and, by the time I realised it was actually happening, I could only be there for a week.

A film crew is quickly bonded, through adversity and madness, into something between a family and a team of soldiers in a foxhole under fire. There's never enough time before the light goes, never enough time to retake that last shot, never enough money to throw at the problems and make them go away, the trumpet player in the circus band still hasn't arrived, and tomorrow's shots in the hospital won't be what Dave's planning because the fish-tank he's planning to shoot through will leak, and then the tiger barb fish will start eating the neon tetras. . .

Because I wasn't there, I will never understand why the cast and crew T-shirts that Dave made have "Smell my lime" on them. Dave's explained it to me, but I think you really had to be there.

They shot the film in six weeks – two weeks on location, the rest of the time in front of a blue screen. They finished in July 2003. And then, once they were finished, Dave started making the film. When he began there were fifteen animators, and Max. Now, fifteen months later, there's just Dave and Max.

I'm writing this in October 2004, and Dave says he's nearly finished, and I believe him. I've seen most of the film cut together and am continually delighted by how far it is from what I'd imagined it was going to be, just as I'm delighted when actors who performed in front of a blue screen suddenly get to see what they were really doing all along.

I've now had eighteen years of being astonished by Dave, and you'd think I'd be used to it by now, but I'm not. I don't think I ever will be.

Neil Gaiman
October 2004

A note on the text:

A script for a film is like a detailed architectural plan for a house. After the plans are made, a lot of people are going to go out and build it. And then, at the end, it becomes obvious that the tree in that place is going to cut off all the light to the kitchen, and the table is really going to have to go, and that the tiles were a great idea in theory but in practice they make it look like someone threw up on the wall . . . So you write your script, and then you make your film, and lines get changed in filming, and then things get changed in editing. Some scenes get cut because they're too long, others because the film is too long.

In the old days that – whatever went out into the cinemas – was the film.

Now, of course, you get the DVD, with as many extra scenes as can be found popped on to satiate people's insatiable curiosity.

In *MirrorMask,* for example, Dave had originally planned, and shot, the opening in split screen, with Helena on the right and whatever her mother was doing on the left. It was beautiful, but in ways that we hadn't expected, it didn't really work: it felt too distancing, made Helena seem too bratty, made it harder to like or care for either of them. Dave recut it and reshot it a little, which also resulted in changing the opening credits from happening over the entry of the circus performers (as originally written) to animated credits earlier in the film.

What I've tried to put together here is the completest script possible. I've left in the full versions of scenes which were filmed but edited down.

As I write this, the film is still being finalised: Dave is still editing, eliding a line here, moving a scene there. We've tried to indicate what made it and what didn't.

Neil Gaiman
October 2004

STORY BY
NEIL GAIMAN & DAVE MCKEAN

SCREENPLAY BY
NEIL GAIMAN

STORYBOARDS BY
DAVE MCKEAN

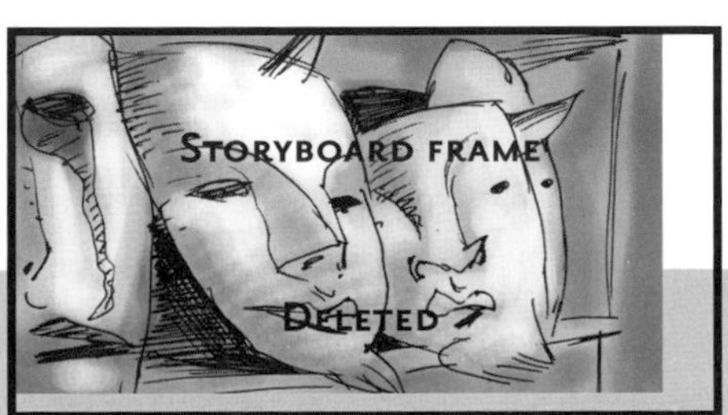

LOCATION: INTERIOR, EXTERIOR.
Description of action.
CHARACTER NAME.
Dialogue.

Deleted *action* or dialogue.

INT. CAMPBELL FAMILY CIRCUS. CARAVAN – NIGHT.

Silence. Split screen: black on the left. We see a black line drawing of a street, towers in the distance, a sun face in the sky.

HELENA AS WHITE SOCK
(ad lib)
I am the queen of everything in this part of town, I am queen of the city and queen of the towers and queen of the little wiggly things, and everybody who looks at me says oh, she is such a wonderful queen, and she is so normal and not ever embarrassing at all and she goes to a school and stays in one place forever and has nothing to worry about except . . .

Suddenly a black sock (on the other foot) jumps into frame.

HELENA AS BLACK SOCK
(in a different voice)
Ah but I am the queen of evil, and I must warn you, you cannot escape my cunning use of . . . black magic markers!

The sock/foot is holding a black magic marker and stabs the white sock with it, leaving little black marks – we hear sock screams . . .

and as the drama of white and black sock puppets continues, the action begins on the right-hand side of the screen, and . . .

Camera flies over animated circus

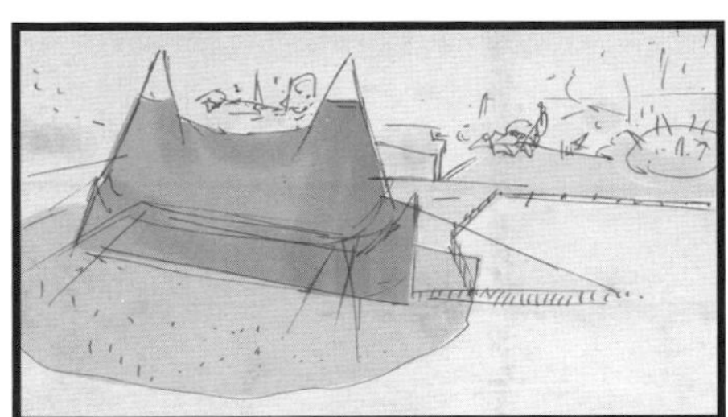

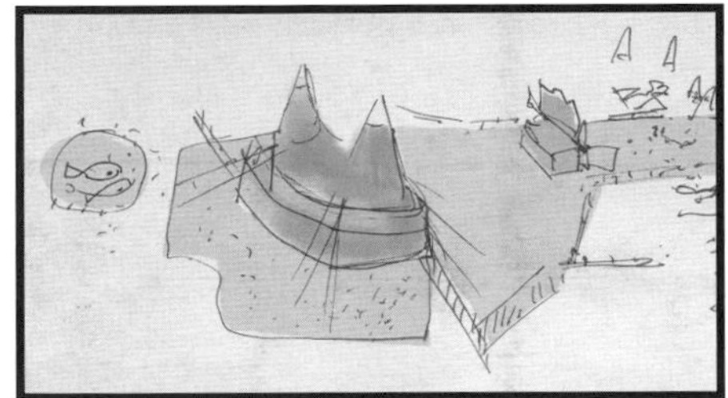

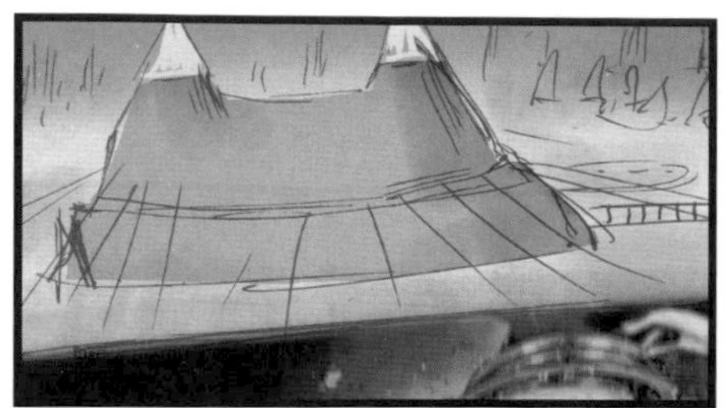

Camera flies over animated circus to:

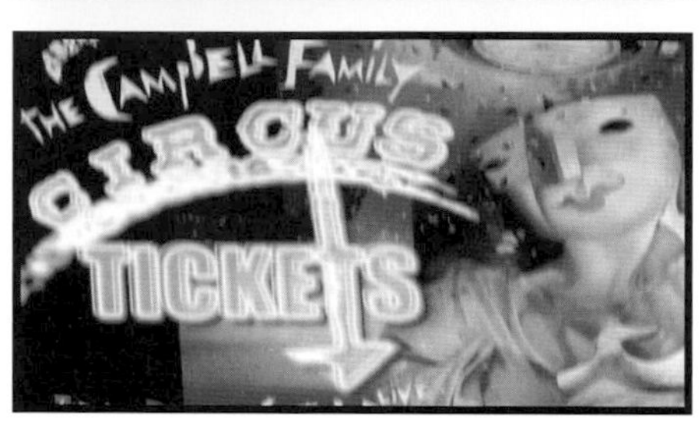

EXT. CAMPBELL FAMILY CIRCUS.
TICKET BOOTH – NIGHT.

Fireworks in the skies above the big top. We pan down to find . . . JOANNE CAMPBELL, in her mid-thirties, in the ticket booth, taking money, handing out tickets with a rote "Thank you – Enjoy the show" to the few people left in the line. She is not happy about something.
Posters and signs say "The Campbell Family Circus: The Greatest Little Show On Earth!" And that's where we are.

PINGO, a silent clown, goes past.

JOANNE
Pingo? Have you seen Helena anywhere?

PINGO spreads his hands in a "search me" expression.

JOANNE (CONT'D)
That girl . . .
(she bites back whatever she was going to say)
Can you take over here for a couple of minutes?

PINGO shrugs,

then sits down in the ticket booth.

The customer at the head of the line says:

CUSTOMER
Two adults and two kids, please.

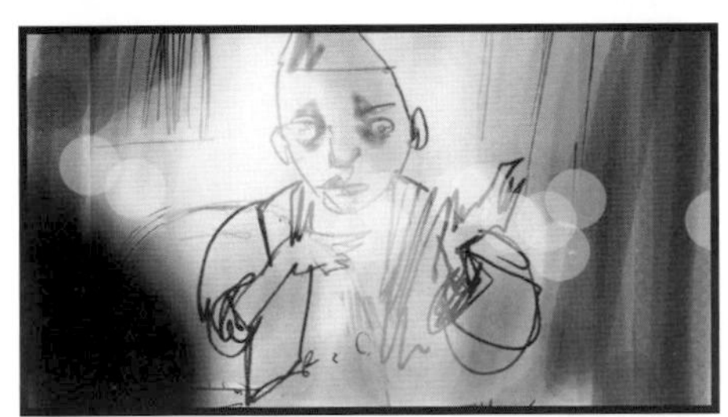

PINGO begins to mime to them on his fingers how much this will be . . .

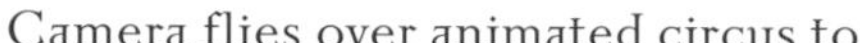

Camera flies over animated circus to:

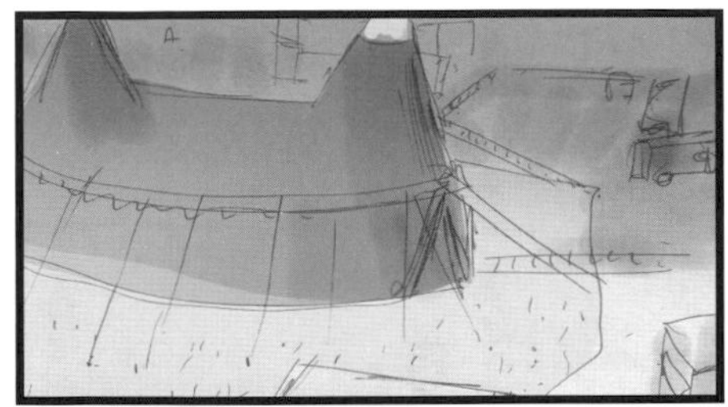

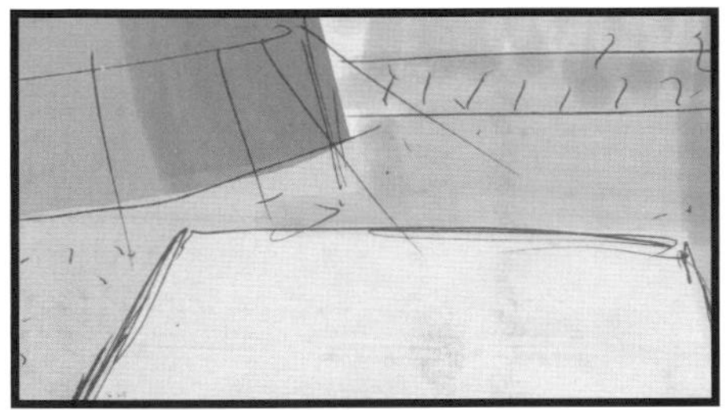

INT. CAMPBELL FAMILY CIRCUS.
CARAVAN – NIGHT.

The socks again, but now a kind of Harlequin doll is hanging by the neck from a piece of string between them. The two socks are taking it in turns to hit the doll, swinging it on the string . . .

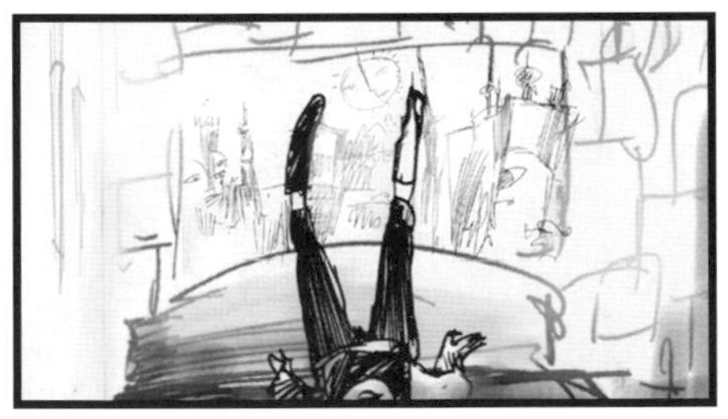

HELENA
"Aha, Mr Valentine, I knew you'd come to save our city," "Well, I am a very important man," "You'll be a very dead man in a minute," "Well, I think he's a very brave . . . well, moderately brave, Mr Valentine."
"Now then, I suppose you're going to turn us into mice, or three-legged chairs or something?" "You may think I'm a hard-hearted black sock, but under this woolly exterior is a naked pink foot."

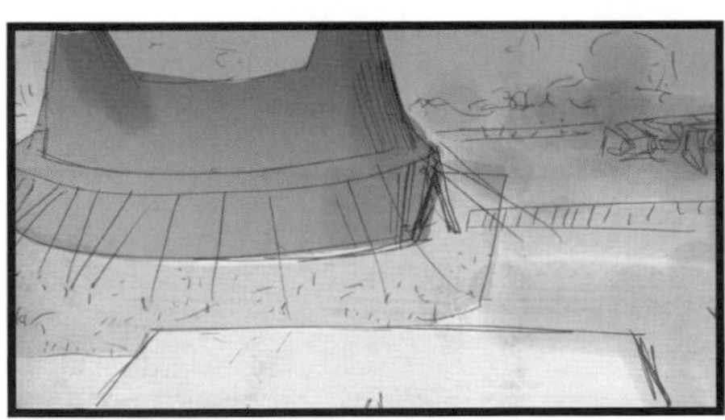

Camera flies over animated circus to:

INT. CAMPBELL FAMILY CIRCUS.
BACKSTAGE – NIGHT.

Bustling with people getting ready to go on for the initial "chari-vari" – the march around the stage. The ringmaster is JOANNE's husband, MORRIS CAMPBELL, with his top hat and cane, and he waves at JOANNE as she goes by.

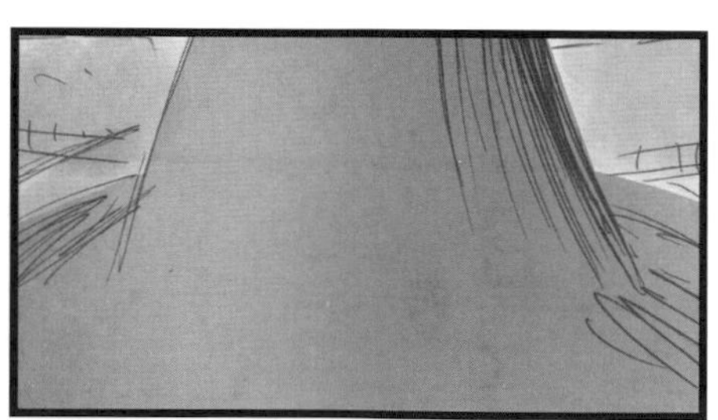

JOANNE
Helena. She's not back here yet, is she?

MORRIS
I thought she was up front with you . . . hang on, if you're here, who's selling tickets?

JOANNE
Pingo.

And before MORRIS can complain, JOANNE is out of the big top and out on the heath, heading for the caravans. She looks angry.

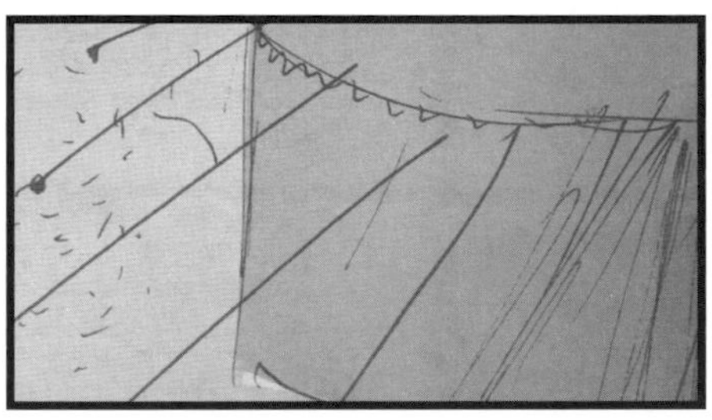

Camera flies over animated circus to:

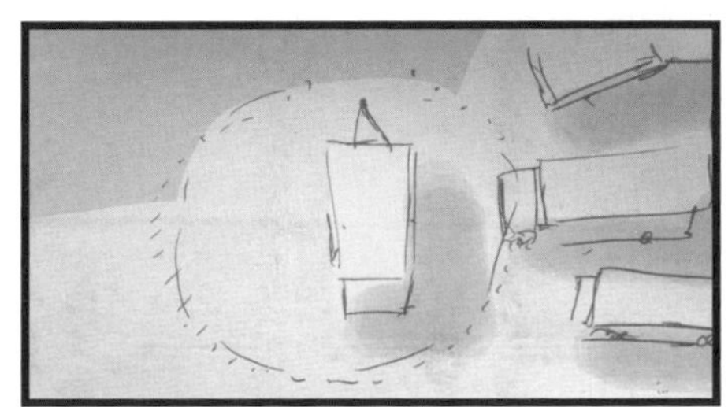

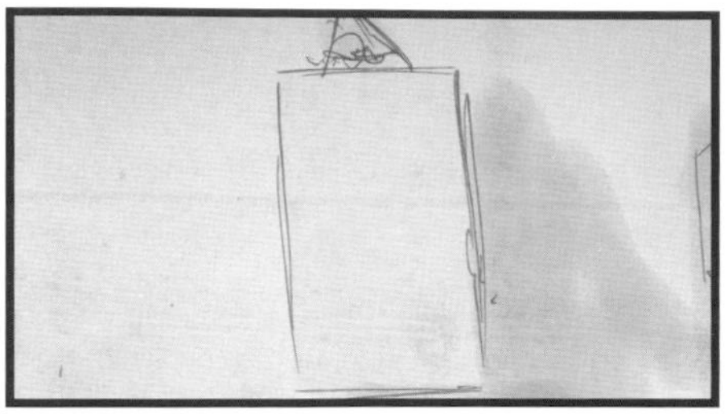

INT./EXT. CAMPBELL FAMILY CIRCUS. CARAVAN – NIGHT.

There is a loud bang on the door of the caravan.

JOANNE
Helena! Open up! There's three minutes to go, come on!

In the caravan, we tilt down to find that HELENA is lying upside-down on a sofa with her head down, staring up at her socks on her feet sticking up in the air. She tuts loudly and does a gymnastic back roll off the sofa, bounces to her feet and does not open the door. What follows is an argument, not a conversation:

HELENA
I'm drawing.
She takes a black felt pen and starts making lines on a sheet of paper.

JOANNE
Oh come off it . . .
(she looks through the window of the caravan)
Oh my god, you're not even dressed yet, you're not a kid any more, I shouldn't have to do this any more . . .

HELENA
(to herself)
Don't care. Not listening.

JOANNE rattles violently at the door. Circus music starts in the background.

JOANNE
That's Eric started playing already . . .

HELENA
(loud enough to be heard)
I don't want to go, I feel like an idiot, I look like an idiot.

JOANNE
Oh not again, not now, I'm not going to have this conversation now! You don't look like an idiot, nobody looks like an idiot . . .

At this point, a MAN ON STILTS wearing a large surprised bird head, a tutu and leading a stuffed rabbit on wheels walks by. He signals "time" to JOANNE.

JOANNE (CONT'D)
(to the MAN ON STILTS)
Yes, I'm coming.
(bangs on door)
Helena!

HELENA
It's just stupid. It never ends. Helena juggle, Helena sell the popcorn, Helena smile for the punters . . .

JOANNE
Your dad keeps this circus running on charm and peanuts, it's his dream –

HELENA
Exactly, it's his thing. Why should I suffer for it?

JOANNE
You're not.

Scowling, HELENA starts to pull on a costume, fast as a quick-change artist.

JOANNE (CONT'D)
All those kids in there,
the ones who buy your popcorn, the ones who've been cheering you since you were old enough to be thrown through the air,
they want to run away and join the circus.

HELENA
Great. They can have my job. I want to run away and join real life.

JOANNE
Please, Helena, just try to be reasonable –

HELENA
Okay! I'm getting dressed! You don't have to shout at me!

JOANNE
(shouting)
I'm not shouting!
(pulling herself together)
You are going to be the death of me –

HELENA
I wish I was.

They're both a bit shocked that this has been said. JOANNE is rubbing her forehead, as if her head hurts.

JOANNE
You selfish little – If you knew what it takes your dad and me to keep this circus going –

HELENA
Like you ever stop telling me?

JOANNE
Real life . . .
(she starts to walk away, then she turns back and says)
Fairy queens and magic socks, Helena? Real life . . . you couldn't handle real life.

JOANNE runs out, leaving HELENA. We see a few of the drawings, a fantasy city, creatures, masks. Now we move out of split screen. She wipes away a tear, corrects her hair, and, with a finger, she flicks the dangling Harlequin puppet with her finger, while imitating her mother –

HELENA
"Real life. You couldn't handle real life" – silly cow.

And then HELENA runs out of the caravan and –

EXT. CAMPBELL FAMILY CIRCUS. TENTS – NIGHT.

Across a patch of waste ground. We find her reflected in a puddle on the ground. She pulls on the last of her black-and-white costume as she goes, and runs into the tent.

INT. CAMPBELL FAMILY CIRCUS. BACKSTAGE – NIGHT.

JOANNE is putting on her diamond costume.
HELENA runs up to the front, to be next to her father. He is furious –

MORRIS
Helena Campbell. What have you been saying to your mother?

HELENA
Nothing.

MORRIS
Later.

But we can hear the band going into the opening theme.
MORRIS shouts to the assembled company –

MORRIS (CONT'D)

Big smiles, everybody . . . and –

INT. CAMPBELL FAMILY CIRCUS.
RING – NIGHT.

A crash of cymbals, a burst of light, and the Campbell Family Circus takes to the ring for the opening march around the charivari. The show is cheap and small. . .

The Credits roll over a Montage of the acts of which we see a few moments –

A MAGICIAN rolling glass spheres up and down his hands –

FRED THE STRONG MAN ripping a phone book in half then balancing HELENA high on one arm –

STILT WALKERS . . .

WILLIAM THE DOG and his TRAINER – WILLIAM is walking on his hind legs, and then steps onto a skateboard . . .

BALANCE ARTISTS . . .

PINGO the clown pours a pail of – not water, but glitter – over an irate MORRIS in ringmaster garb, then flees . . .

Three FINNISH TUMBLERS doing a routine –

We finish on a PYROTECHNIC ARTIST, doing his act in a kids' paddling pool filled with six inches of water, breathing fire and holding burning sticks like an astonishingly low-budget version of the Cirque De Soleil "O". . .

The Credits end.

Now we see the ringmaster, MORRIS CAMPBELL, ushering on a lovely woman, actually JOANNE, dressed in a costume that sparkles wherever the light touches it. It's half white, half black.

MORRIS

Ladies and gentlemen, boys and girls, let me hear you put your hands together for the very lovely Joanne!

She has a domino mask on, which is mirrored. She begins a Spanish web routine, climbing and performing on a rope. FRED THE STRONG MAN holds and twirls the rope.

The small but enthusiastic audience claps . . .

INT. CAMPBELL FAMILY CIRCUS.
BACKSTAGE – NIGHT.

MORRIS is throwing off his ringmaster coat and pulling on a coat, a hat, and a mask, assisted by HELENA – who has on a similar costume of her own.

A roar of applause from out front . . .

MORRIS
Right. That's our cue. . . Get your mask on, Helena, love.

He picks up a backstage microphone. HELENA puts on her own mask.

MORRIS (CONT'D)
(into microphone, as ringmaster)
And now, ladies 'n' gentlemen, boys 'n' girls, all the way from darkest Peru, the world's finest jugglers, Raymondo and Fortuna!

The MUSICIAN strikes up the juggling music. As MORRIS and JOANNE pass one another backstage, she winks at him, and his face lights up. He mouths "I love you!" at her.

HELENA looks heavenward, unimpressed by her parents' love for one another.

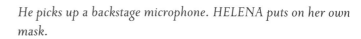

**INT. CAMPBELL FAMILY CIRCUS.
RING – NIGHT.**

And now HELENA and MORRIS are out onto the stage. They start to juggle with clubs, tossing them back and forth to one another . . .

INT. CAMPBELL FAMILY CIRCUS.
BACKSTAGE – NIGHT.

The juggling music is muted. The three FINNISH TUMBLERS are ready to go back on next, killing time. One of them is reading a Finnish newspaper.

JOANNE has taken her mask off, and, quick as she can, is pulling on a gorilla costume.

PINGO
(strange wave hand mime)

JOANNE
Yes, I realise . . .

PINGO
(strange wave hand mime)

JOANNE
I know, I know, I shouldn't let her get under my skin, she's just . . . very good at it.

PINGO
(strange wave hand mime)

JOANNE
Well, that's easy for you to say . . .

Suddenly she stops, with the gorilla costume only half-zipped-up and she sways . . . one hand goes back to her head. She's in pain.

PINGO looks concerned. Nearby, FRED THE STRONG MAN runs over.

INT. CAMPBELL FAMILY CIRCUS.
RING – NIGHT.

MORRIS has pulled out a bunch of bananas.

MORRIS
Hey, bambino, you want to joggle the bananas?

He throws HELENA a banana and she throws it back, as they start a juggling bananas routine . . .

HELENA
Uh-uh. No way. You know what you get if you joggle the bananas?

MORRIS
I don't know. What do you get?

HELENA
Gorillas!

MORRIS
Gorillas?

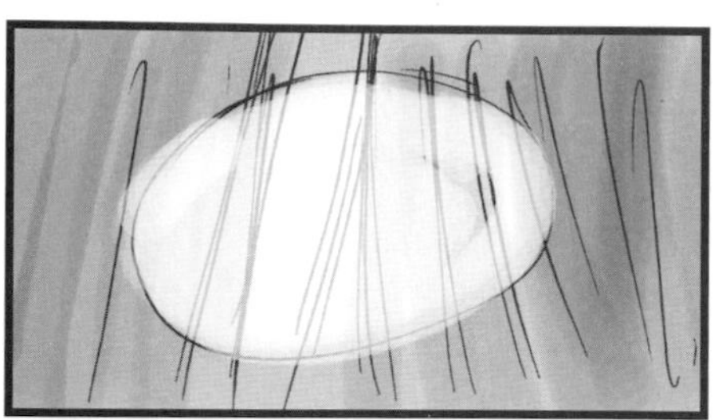

This is obviously the cue for the Gorilla to come on – musically . . .

Looks between MORRIS and the MUSICIAN/Bandleader, who keeps busking.

MORRIS (CONT'D)
Did you say "gorillas"?

Still no gorilla.

MORRIS (CONT'D)
I'm sure you said "gorillas"!

And finally here comes the gorilla running across the stage.

He grabs a banana, the MUSICIAN/Bandleader goes into chase music, and the gorilla runs into the audience chased by MORRIS and HELENA.

In the audience, kids are laughing . . .

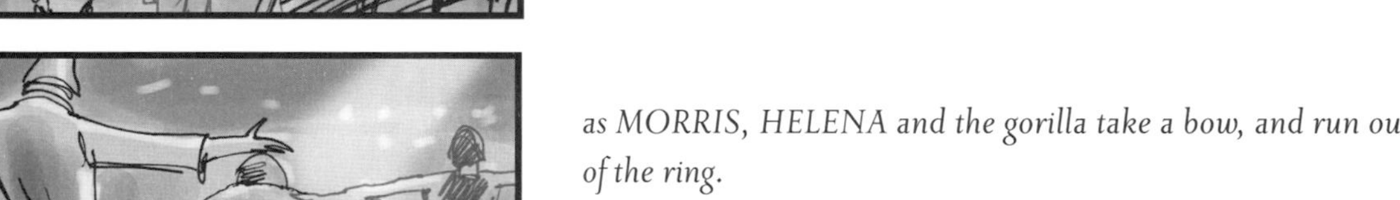

as MORRIS, HELENA and the gorilla take a bow, and run out of the ring.

INT. CAMPBELL FAMILY CIRCUS.
BACKSTAGE – NIGHT.

The FINNISH TUMBLERS bounce and tumble their way into the ring . . .

MORRIS turns to the gorilla.

MORRIS
Joanne – you were cutting it a bit fine. You had me worried there, love . . .

The gorilla pulls off its head, revealing FRED THE STRONG MAN.

FRED
It's not Mrs Campbell, Mr Campbell, it's me. She's over there.

We follow MORRIS's gaze around the backstage of the tent, ending on . . . JOANNE, slumped in a chair, looking pale and pained and almost unconscious. . . Her hand on her forehead. She's in pain and barely conscious.

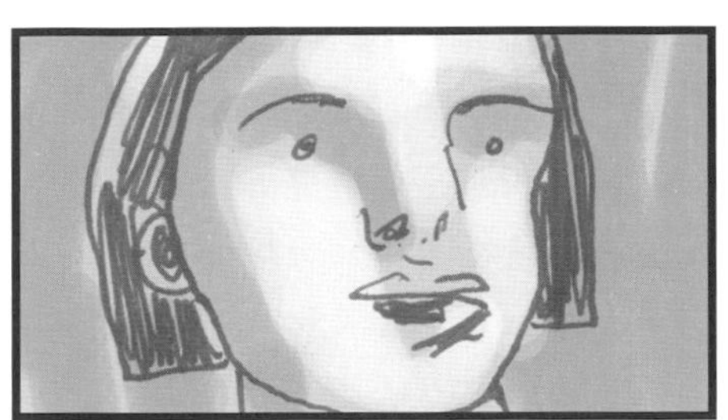

HELENA
Mum?

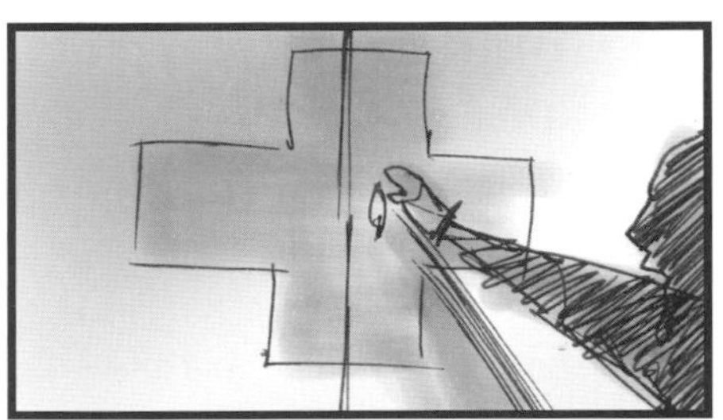

Cut to:

EXT. CAMPBELL FAMILY CIRCUS. TENTS – NIGHT.

The flashing lights of an ambulance – and the ambulance pulls up behind the circus tent. In the background the circus music – and thus the circus – continues.
The ambulance door is pulled open, and, on a stretcher, JOANNE is slid inside.
HELENA's standing by the open ambulance door, and her face has an expression on it of pure heartbreak.

The door slams, the ambulance pulls away, and the circus people stand, their mouths open, watching it go, getting smaller as we move away.

Cut to:

EXT. TOWER BLOCK – DAY

In Brighton. Morning. The tower block looks almost ready for demolition

INT. TOWER BLOCK. AUNT NAN'S FLAT. HELENA'S BEDROOM – DAY.

A caption: Ten Days Later is written on a drawing of a cityscape, done by Helena. We look at the drawings on the wall . . .
We can hear a television on in the room next door. And an elderly woman is talking mostly to herself . . .
A drawing of a skyscraperlike tower. It has an eagle's foot at the bottom (just like VALENTINE's tower, which we will encounter much later).

From out of shot we can hear a television – muted, the sound of canned laughter. Her bedroom is tidy, but the room itself is pretty grotty. The walls are covered with HELENA's drawings of buildings, which form a sort of panorama – a cityscape around the room. While from next door AUNT NAN'S monologue continues . . .

NAN
Something quintessentially French. . . I've never been to France you know, love. Your late Uncle Bozzy, he'd say I don't know what they've got that we haven't got, Nan my girl, and how do you fancy a trip to Frinton? Oh, five letters, begins with a P, poodle, prince, I've nearly got it . . . Paris? That's never five letters. I went to Monaco, though, when Sophie was ill, and your late Uncle Vernon needed someone to saw in half. Well, I started out as a box-jumper dear, so it was practically second nature to me.

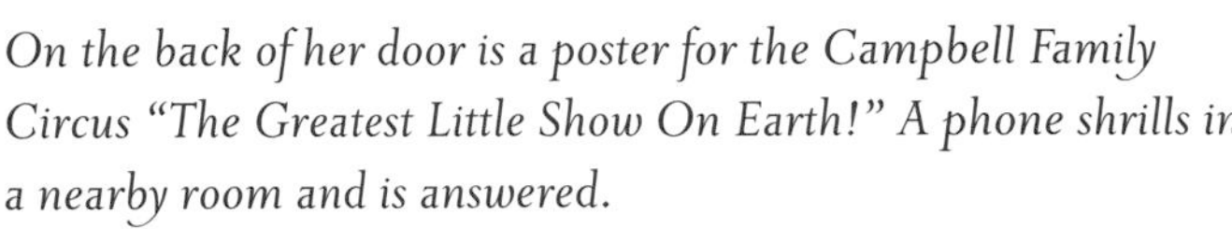

On the back of her door is a poster for the Campbell Family Circus "The Greatest Little Show On Earth!" A phone shrills in a nearby room and is answered.

HELENA writes "Mum, get well soon" on the bottom of her drawing of the tower. She folds it over.

NAN's monologue is ended by the phone ringing. She lowers her voice, so although we can hear voices, we can't hear what's being said any longer.

HELENA puts down her pen. She looks a lot more sober and sad than she did before.

HELENA takes her piggy bank from the shelf, and, with a knife, opens the bottom and starts shaking out money, angrily.

Taking the picture with her, she gets up and goes into the lounge . . .

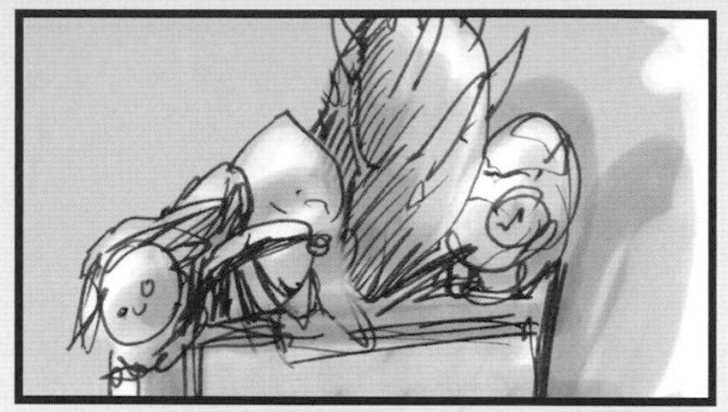

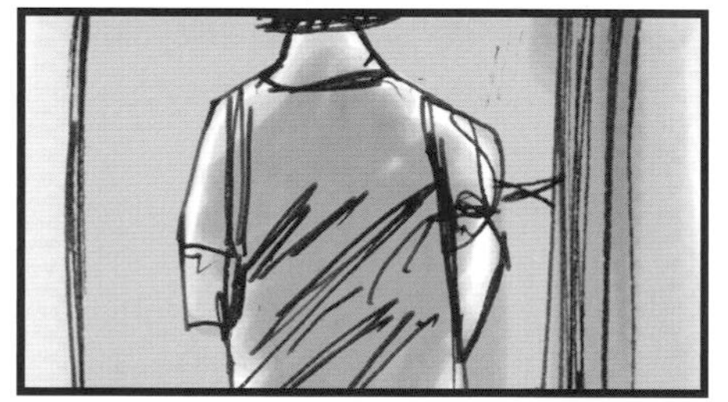

INT. TOWER BLOCK. AUNT NAN'S FLAT. LOUNGE – DAY.

HELENA comes in. Her AUNT NAN (actually her great aunt) is sitting in her chair watching the TV with a fine critical eye. She's watching a game show, and is talking on a cordless phone.

NAN
. . . I don't mind taking you two in, while everything is up in the air for you, and a meeting is a meeting and there's nothing I care to say about that even if I wanted to, but I've told him I have to draw the line at animals. And I'm not feeding them. If your lot come over here, I'll say "lovely to see you," and I'll go upstairs and have a coffee with Mrs. Greenberg. She's got a cafetière.

She clicks off the phone.

HELENA
Was that Dad?

NAN
On the phone? That was your dad, love. You should watch this. It's educational.

She uses the remote and turns up the TV.

HELENA
I told you to let me talk to him, if he called.

NAN
He's not going to be able to keep them happy for much longer.

Audience applause on the TV.

NAN (CONT'D)
There you are, that was educational, wasn't it?

HELENA
Keep who happy?

HELENA looks hurt and worried.

NAN
Oh, your dad'll sort it out. Not to worry. You give my love to your mum.

INT. TOWER BLOCK. CORRIDOR – DAY.

HELENA, still carrying her drawing, runs down the corridor.

She presses the button for the lift. Nothing happens. No light goes on.

HELENA
Oh come on!

INT. TOWER BLOCK. STAIRWELL – DAY.

HELENA runs frantically down a stairwell. It echoes.

EXT. BUS STOP – DAY.

The tower block in the background.

HELENA runs, exhausted, out of breath, towards us. She's running towards the bus stop, as the bus pulls up.

INT. BUS – DAY.

DRIVER
Hullo, love. I wondered where you were. It's been getting so I can set my watch by you.

HELENA
(panting)
Sorry – Lift was – it was dead –

She stops, breathless.
The DRIVER rings up her ticket.

HELENA takes her seat. At the back, a COUPLE not much older than she is are kissing, fairly passionately.

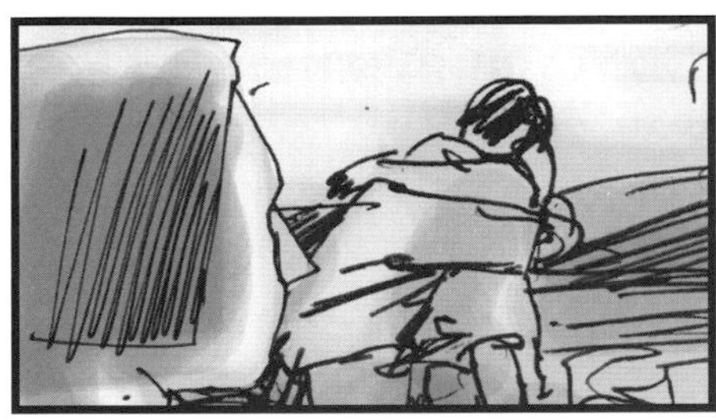

She glances at them, then looks away, making a face. For a moment she looks like she's going to cry.

EXT. HOSPITAL – DAY

HELENA runs towards reception.

INT. HOSPITAL. LOBBY – DAY

Tropical fish glide about their tank. HELENA comes in.
The RECEPTIONIST smiles at HELENA.

RECEPTIONIST
Hey!

She reaches under the desk, hands HELENA a hairbrush.

HELENA
Does it look that bad?

The RECEPTIONIST nods sympathetically. HELENA brushes her hair.

INT. HOSPITAL. CORRIDOR – DAY.

A NURSE enters with a clipboard.

NURSE
Helena Campbell. Isn't your dad here with you? I've got papers for him to sign.

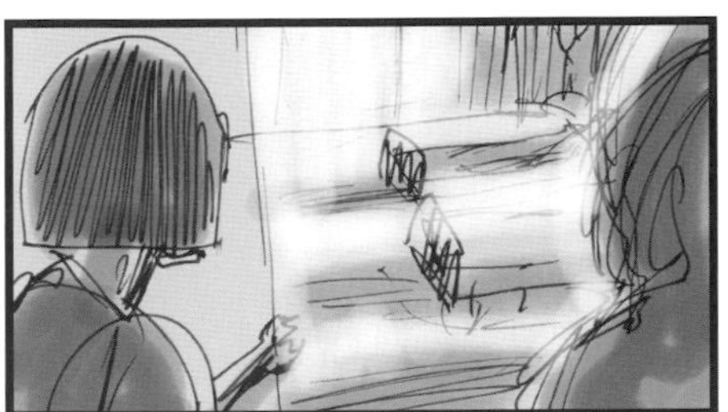

HELENA
He wanted to come, but there was stuff he had to do. It's just me.

NURSE
Your father was meant to be here. I happen to know Dr Witherspoon left him a message.

HELENA
He's at the bank. He had to see the manager this afternoon.
The NURSE doesn't believe it for a moment. They pause outside JOANNE's hospital room.

NURSE
Listen. She appreciates you coming in, but I don't want you tiring her out.

HELENA
What do you think I'm going to do? Take her dancing?
And with that she opens the door.

INT. HOSPITAL. JOANNE'S ROOM – DAY.
It's a small ward, with four beds in it. Two are empty, or their inhabitants are away. One has JOANNE in. The other has a VERY OLD WOMAN who, when she sees HELENA, takes a bowl of grapes from her bedside table and rests it on the covers in front of her, and starts to eat them.
Burt Bacharach muzak plays over the hospital radio: "Close to You."
JOANNE is asleep as HELENA comes in, her pale hands on the blanket. On the wall there are nine of HELENA's "Get well soon" drawings.

HELENA sits by the bed. She puts her hand down on her mother's hand. JOANNE's eyes open. She's very weak.

JOANNE
Helena . . .

HELENA
Hello Mum.

JOANNE
No Dad, then?

HELENA shakes her head. She shows her the new Get Well Soon card. It's a self-portrait of Helena, with her eyes crossed.

HELENA
Here.

JOANNE smiles, weakly. Helena puts the picture up next to the other nine.

JOANNE
They'll phone him, I expect.

HELENA
How are you feeling?

JOANNE
I'd rather be joggling bananas.
How's your dad?

HELENA
He's fine. I think he is going to have to quell a mutiny.

JOANNE
I told him they should keep going.

HELENA
He wasn't going to go to Scotland and just leave you here.

Where's your fruit? I brought you fruit yesterday. She didn't take it?
(indicating the old woman)

JOANNE
They've put it away. I mustn't eat anything today.

HELENA
Why not?

JOANNE
(lying)
It's just routine. How's Aunt Nan? You aren't being a bother, are you?

HELENA
She says it's a delight to have a young face around.

JOANNE'S eyes start to close. The VERY OLD WOMAN in the next bed is staring at them and obsessively eating grapes. JOANNE doesn't say anything. She's tired. HELENA reaches out and squeezes her hand. HELENA tries to get the conversation going again.

HELENA (CONT'D)
Aunt Nan says she'll be down on Saturday.
(pause. She's hoping JOANNE will say something, but she doesn't so HELENA continues)
She lost her teeth yesterday. I said to her, if Mum was here, she'd find them, she's amazing at finding things. She said, well, if your mum can find them she must be a miracle worker.

JOANNE
They'll be staring her in the face. Things you lose always are.

HELENA
They were in the fridge.

HELENA (CONT'D)
(beat)
Mum, you know. I didn't mean . . . what I said.

JOANNE
There was a little girl, and she had a little curl right in the middle of her forehead. When she was good . . . she was very, very . . .
(she stops, exhausted)

Her eyes close, in sleep. HELENA would sit beside her, but the NURSE is leaning in through the door, and she nods at HELENA, who gets up and kisses JOANNE on the cheek.

EXT. TOWER BLOCK – DAY.

HELENA walks back to the flat.

INT. TOWER BLOCK. AUNT NAN'S FLAT. LOUNGE – DAY.

Helena comes into the flat to find a meeting in progress. Some of the circus people and musicians from the opening scene are all sitting around the lounge in civilian dress. Commanding the room is MORRIS, her father. The argument has been going on for some time. One of the drummers is drumming with his fingers on a surface.

MORRIS
All I'm saying is that with a little time we can be back on the road, and I think we can be better than ever –

MAGICIAN
It's been ten days. That's fifteen shows we've missed. I don't see why everything has to grind to a halt.

HELENA
(whispers)
Hi Eric . . . can I get through please?

MORRIS
I can't leave Joanne right now.

FRED
It's for her we're still here, Mr Campbell. You know that. But it's too late in the season for most of us.

MUSICIAN
I've been busking. In the tube. At my time of life.

FRED
Eric's got a point.
If we knew that the circus would be back on the road in, let's say, a week, I'm sure we could all find stuff to hold us over till then.

ACROBAT
It's a big if. We can't hang around forever.

FINNISH TUMBLER
We are going to Quebec, my sisters and me. We are rats sinking the leaving ship.

HELENA catches MORRIS's eye. The DRUMMER is really starting to tap on the table now.

HELENA
Dad. Can I have a word?

MORRIS
(to drummer)
Please, Stian!

STIAN
Oh, sorry boss.

(to Helena)
Of course, love. If we can hold those thoughts, ladies and gentlemen.

He and HELENA move off to the side.

HELENA
Dad. You were meant to be at the hospital today.

MORRIS
You told them about the bank manager?

HELENA
Yes, Dad. They want you to phone Dr Witherspoon.

MORRIS
Now?

HELENA nods. MORRIS goes into the bedroom.

HELENA looks at the circus people. They look back at her. It's all very awkward.

PINGO the clown runs his hand up his face, replacing a frown with a smile.

The MAGICIAN gestures at HELENA. She looks. He passes one hand across another and produces a small ball, then, in the same hand, held between his fingers, another, then a third. Then he drops one.

MAGICIAN
Sorry.

HELENA
It was good till then.

PINGO the clown says

PINGO
Maybe this'll be a blessing for some of us. I know you always wanted to get off the road.

HELENA
Not like this.

Nobody says anything.

HELENA (CONT'D)
It's his dream.

FINNISH TUMBLER
Dreams take you only so far, darling. After, you need cash.

MORRIS comes back in, looking a bit shaken up.

MORRIS
Your Mum's going to . . . they're operating tonight, so . . .
(he doesn't know what to say)

EXT. TOWER BLOCK. ROOFTOP – EVENING.

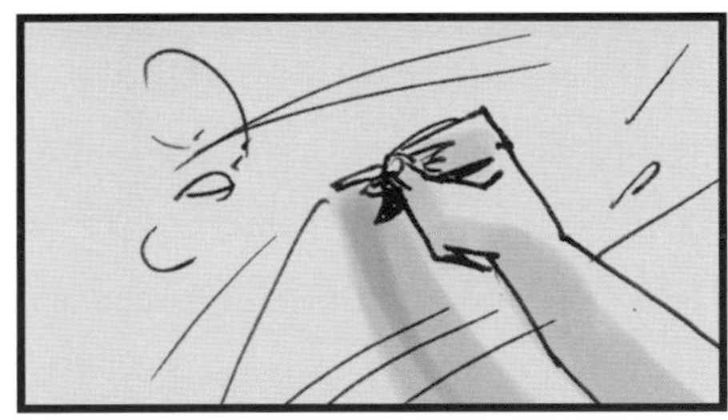

Several hours later. Angry slashes in chalk. HELENA's drawing out her frustration in her secret place. A chalk drawing, on the concrete roof, in coloured chalks, of a tall thin building. HELENA draws, her lips pressed together. She has a metal biscuit tin open beside her, filled with chalks and pens and little toys. There's a noise behind her.
It's MORRIS. He's come through the door onto the roof, pushing it open.
We can see a few chalk drawings by HELENA, on the surfaces of the roof.

MORRIS sits down next to her.

MORRIS
Eh bambino. That's nice. What's it called?

HELENA
It's just a drawing. It's not called anything.
(pause)

Mum says you should have taken the circus on to Scotland.

MORRIS
She's not the only one. What do you think?

HELENA
I don't know, Dad. Everybody at the hospital knew Mum's operation was tonight and nobody told me.

MORRIS
They didn't want you to worry.

HELENA
Should I be worried?

MORRIS
No, no, I'm sure she'll be fine.

HELENA
I mean, you said before, it's just an operation, and then she'll be up and about again.

MORRIS
Well . . . kind of depends on what they find tonight really, love . . .

HELENA
What do you mean, what they find?

MORRIS
You see? Now you're starting to worry.

HELENA
I wasn't worried until you told me not to worry.

Pause. She watches him.

Anyway, you're worried. You only do that when you're worried.

MORRIS takes his hand away from his face.

HELENA (CONT'D)
I wanted to see her tomorrow, can I still go and visit tomorrow?

MORRIS
We'll . . . have to see . . .

He's trying to be both honest and reassuring, and is failing at both.

HELENA
I still haven't said sorry, not really sorry, not so she believes me . . .

She's crying. MORRIS hands her a hankie.

HELENA (CONT'D)
I shouldn't have shouted at her. It was all my fault.

MORRIS
Don't say that. It's not your fault. These things are not anybody's fault, love. They just happen. It's just . . . life.

HELENA
It's just stupid.

MORRIS
It's um, it's just freezing. Come on. We'll catch our deaths up here.

He and HELENA run to the door and go through it. For a brief moment we see, as it closes, one of HELENA's drawings of a window on the back of the door.

INT. TOWER BLOCK. AUNT NAN'S FLAT. LOUNGE – EVENING.

The rain is coming down in buckets. AUNT NAN is watching the TV. She keeps up a commentary on what she sees on the screen. A TV laugh track plays in the background. HELENA and MORRIS sitting, both in their own worlds.

NAN
See her? She was in that comedy. Where she was sharing a flat with that other one. I don't know what she's doing in this rubbish. She used to be funny.

Lightning flashes outside. The TV reception dissolves into static. HELENA is staring off into the distance.

NAN (CONT'D)
Penny for your thoughts, girl.

HELENA shakes her head: nothing to think, or that she can say. She gets up.

HELENA
Good night, Nan. 'Night, Dad.

NAN
Good night, love.

MORRIS
Sweet dreams.

INT. TOWER BLOCK. AUNT NAN'S FLAT. HELENA'S BEDROOM – NIGHT.

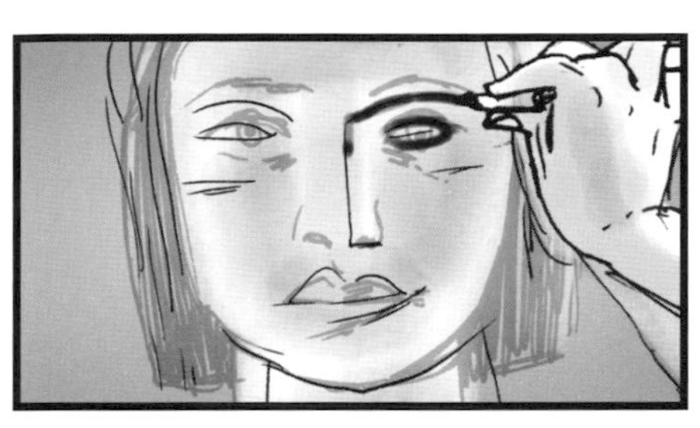

HELENA lines her own face up with the drawing on the mirrored door of her wardrobe. She draws dark lines around the eyes of the drawing, and then smudges them out with her hand.

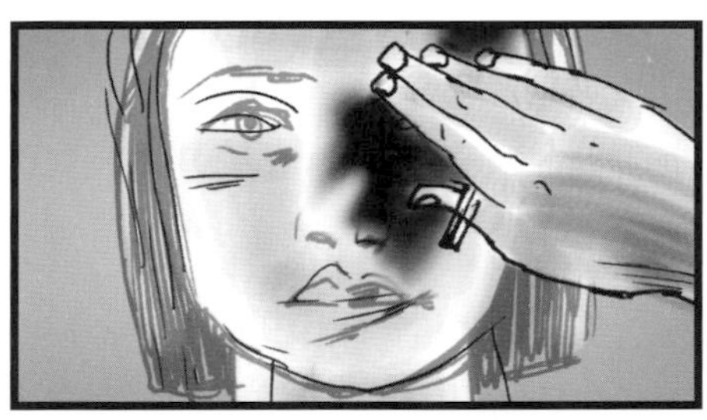

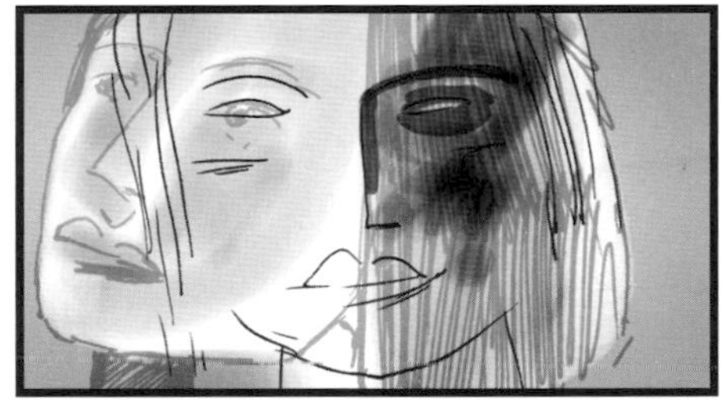

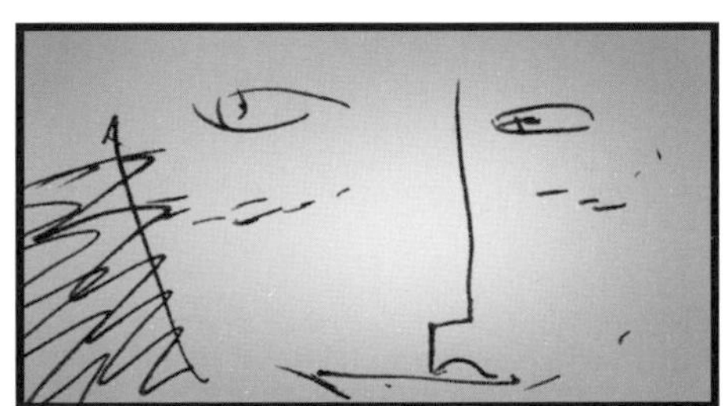

She lies down in bed, pulls the sheets up around her. Lights out. The lightning flashes outside the window.

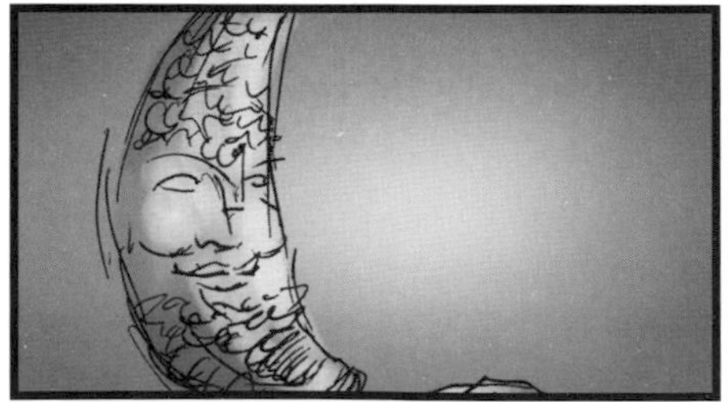

We look around her room, at all the drawings she's got arrayed about the walls, then back to HELENA, with her eyes closed. There are toys in the bedroom.

Dissolve to . . .

INT. TOWER BLOCK. AUNT NAN'S FLAT. HELENA'S BEDROOM (HELENA'S DREAM SEQUENCE) – NIGHT.

A confusion of images – curtains blow, shapes ooze and re-form like puddling chalks in the rain. HELENA pulls open the curtains.

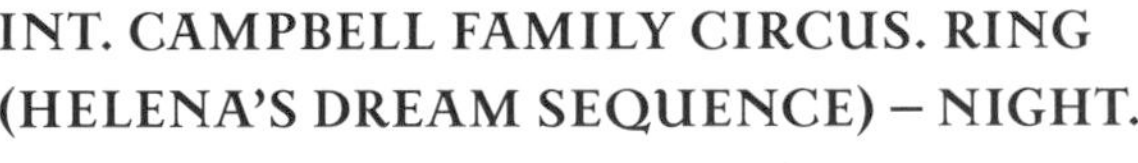

INT. CAMPBELL FAMILY CIRCUS. RING (HELENA'S DREAM SEQUENCE) – NIGHT.

JOANNE is wheeled on a hospital trolley through the middle of the circus tent, past the show.

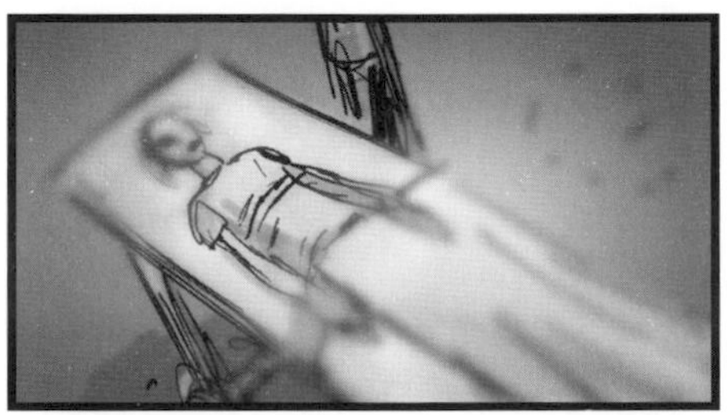

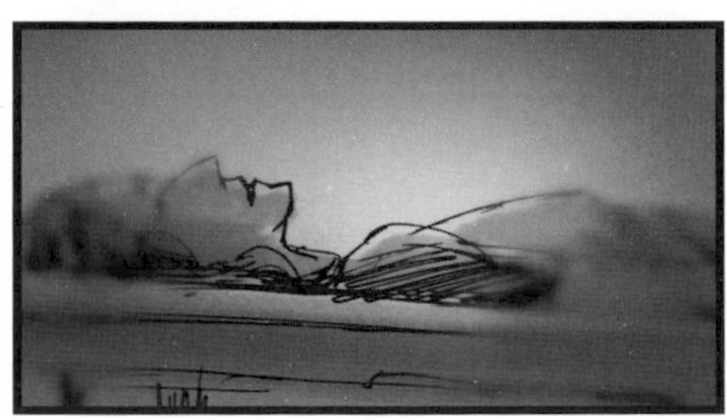

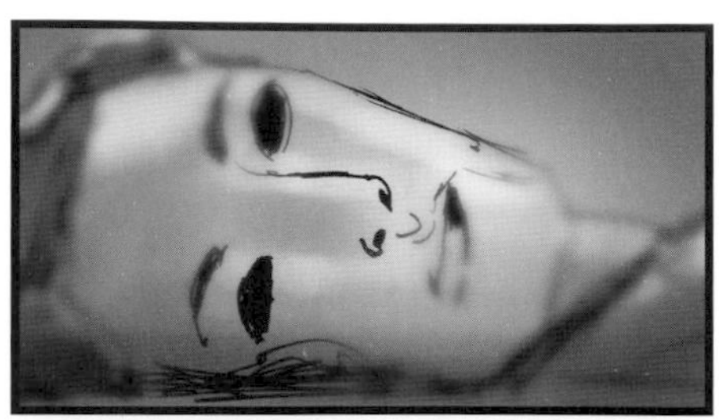

As she passes us she opens her eyes: they are quite black.

EXT. CAMPBELL FAMILY CIRCUS. TENTS (HELENA'S DREAM SEQUENCE) – NIGHT.

HELENA runs past the puddle once more, her reflection dancing while HELENA runs . . .

INT. CAMPBELL FAMILY CIRCUS. BACKSTAGE (HELENA'S DREAM SEQUENCE) – NIGHT.

Now HELENA's backstage at the circus. Backward footage: she appears to put her hands up to her face and smear them over it, smearing make-up on . . .

INT. CAMPBELL FAMILY CIRCUS. BACKSTAGE (HELENA'S DREAM SEQUENCE) – NIGHT.

HELENA looks out of the mirror at her own reflection.

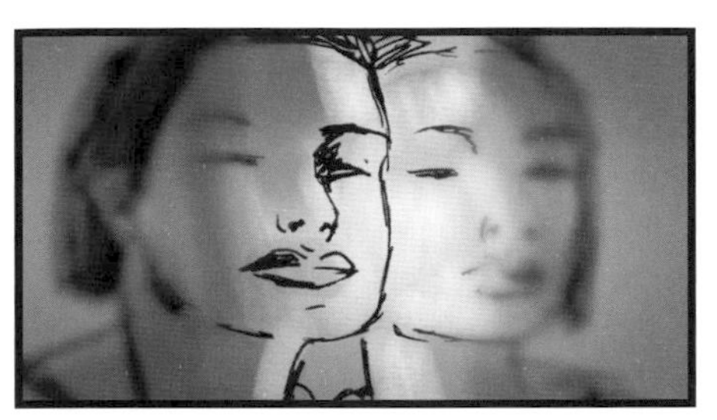

Then the reflection smiles and shakes its head, while HELENA stares, unsmiling.

**INT. TOWER BLOCK. AUNT NAN'S FLAT.
HELENA'S BEDROOM – NIGHT.**

HELENA's eyes open very suddenly. Everything's normal. The storm is over . . .
For a moment we feel like everything's normal again. And then the music starts . . .
A violin tune is playing in the background – something haunting and strange. It sounds like it's coming from somewhere nearby.

She gets up. (She's wearing an overlong T-shirt as a night dress.) She puts on her slippers.

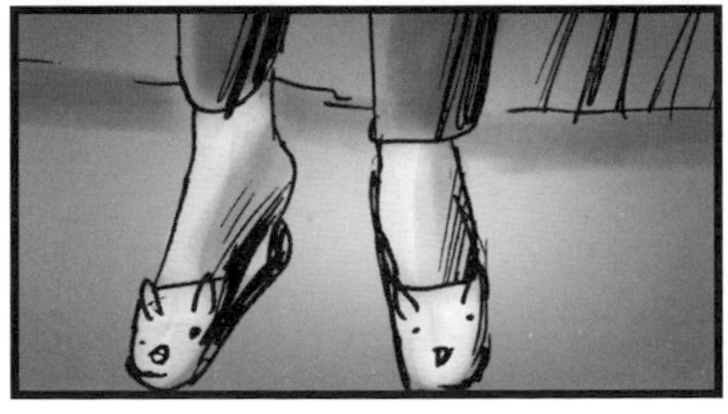

INT. TOWER BLOCK. AUNT NAN'S FLAT. HELENA'S BEDROOM/LOUNGE – NIGHT.

We follow her out of the bedroom and through the lounge.

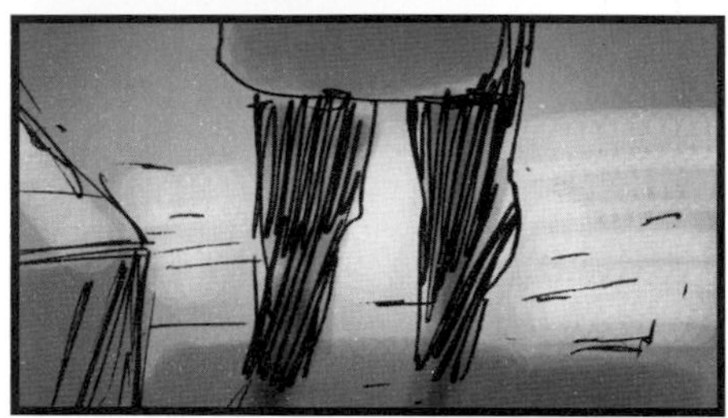

She clicks the light switch but the light does not go on. She picks up a torch and turns it on.
The violin music is louder, now.

INT. DREAM CORRIDOR – NIGHT.

HELENA's out in the corridor – we've followed her out of the flat.

HELENA hesitates. She's not sure if she should head down the corridor or go back to bed.

The music draws her on.
She reaches the end of the corridor. She walks down several steps and through a door . . .

EXT. TOWER BLOCK/WHITE CITY – NIGHT.

And, without entering a lift, steps out onto the lawn at the back of the tower.
She is, although she doesn't know it yet, in a city on the other side of reality.

It's more or less daylight – there's no sun in the sky, just a general white glow. She puts her little torch in her pocket.
In front of us the violin player, whom we recognise as ERIC, the MUSICIAN/Bandleader from the circus, is playing a circus-like tune on his fiddle. His face looks oddly masklike.

Further away from us are two jugglers, VALENTINE and BING. Both of them are young men, both good-looking, both wearing masks. BING should remind us a little of PINGO, the clown in the circus.

They are juggling balls of light of different colours, in time to the music, while VALENTINE keeps up a commentary.

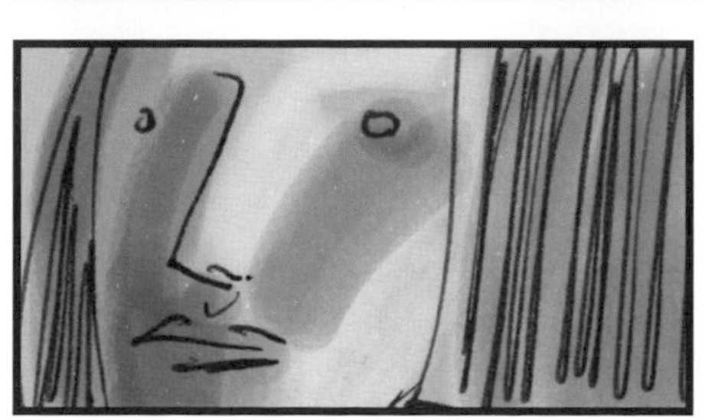

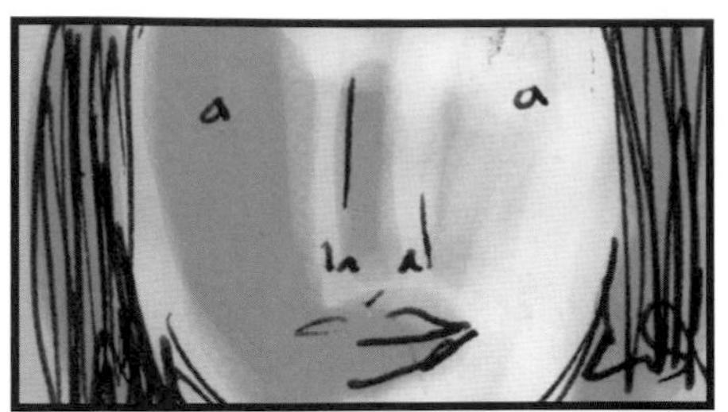

VALENTINE
Now we'll go to five balls – and now to me . . .

They start juggling balls back and forth.

HELENA
Eric?

VALENTINE
Quiet please! We must have perfect silence while we rehearse.

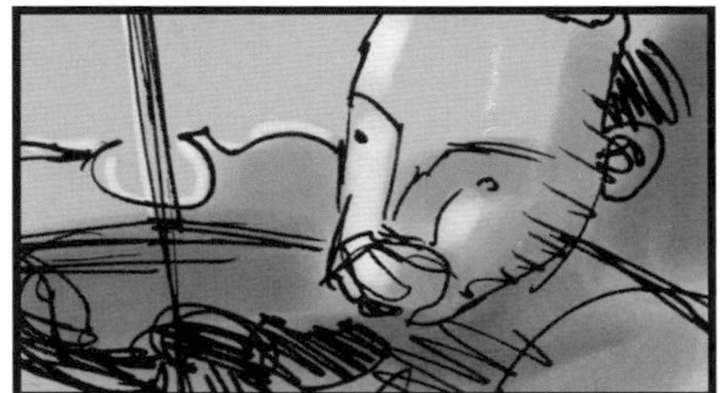

HELENA looks up at the MUSICIAN/Bandleader. There is something a bit odd about his face. He keeps playing. He looks at her, though.
He winks.

HELENA
Eric? Is that you?

He shakes his head.

HELENA (CONT'D)
It is you!

VALENTINE
Can we also not distract our accompanist if we don't mind? Some of us are rehearsing over here.

HELENA
(ignoring him)
Eric? What are you doing here?

Long shot:
A DARK SHADOW is gliding slowly across the world towards them.

The jugglers keep juggling. VALENTINE pays HELENA no further attention, but BING smiles at her as he juggles.

BING
Don't mind him. My name's Bing. What's yours?

HELENA
Helena.

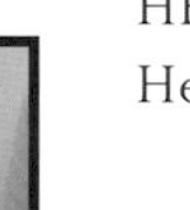

BING
What's wrong with your face?

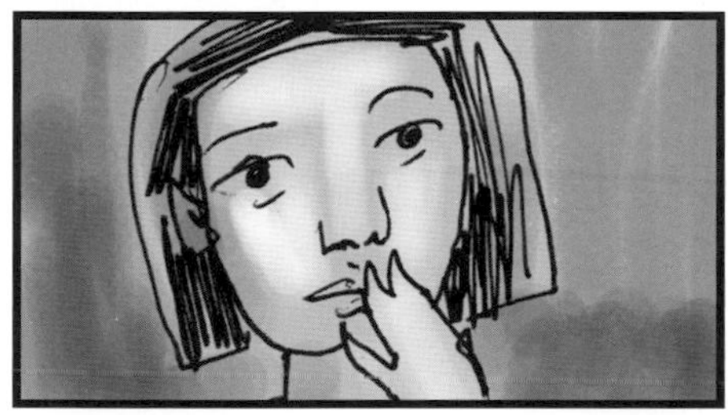

HELENA
My face?

She touches her face. The music is ending.

VALENTINE
– catch the last ball, and we stop. Bow. Then we say can we have a brave volunteer, blah blah blah.

Hey, you, *(pointing at HELENA)* you can be the brave volunteer.

HELENA
What?

VALENTINE
And it's music, Maestro, please.

MUSICIAN/Bandleader
(dreamily)
I know lots of songs. But they all sound a bit the same.

BING
Come on, we need a bit of 'ooh dangerous, creepy creepy' music . . .

MUSICIAN/Bandleader
(dreamily to HELENA)
I know you. Or somebody like you.

VALENTINE
Come on, Maestro, this is our big finish.

The MUSICIAN/Bandleader *runs his bow over the strings – and the edge of the shadow touches him, like a black flame.*

Instantly he carbonizes – turns into a black, man-shaped mass.

VALENTINE (CONT'D)
Not what I had in mind.

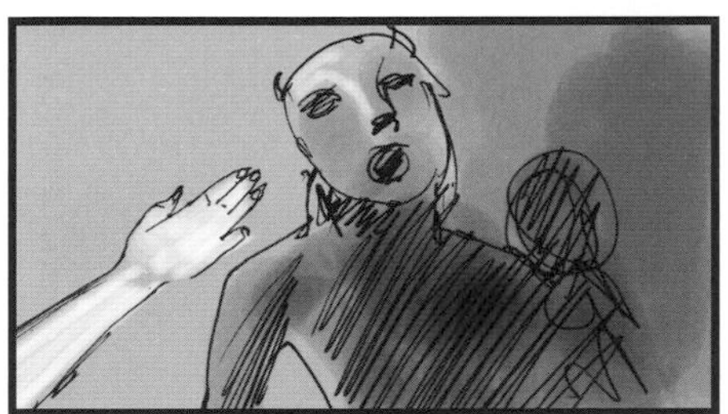

HELENA reaches out and touches him. His face – a mask – slides off, revealing blank blackness beneath. Then he crumbles into a pile of black ash.

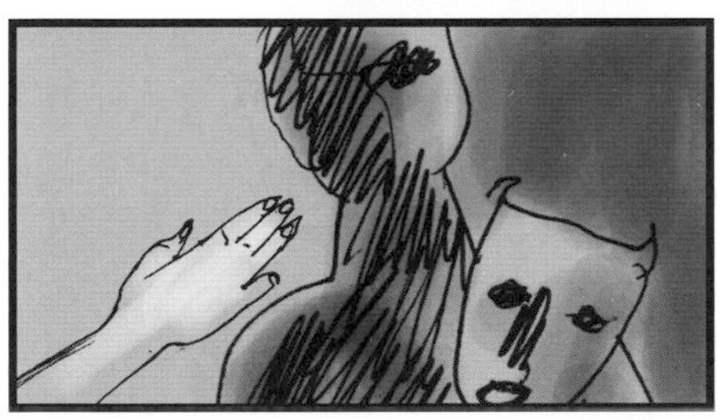

She stands there, gaping: upset, confused, suddenly scared. The shadow seems to hesitate, then it creeps towards her.

BING grabs her arm and pulls her away.

BING
Don't just stand there – you saw what it does . . .

HELENA
(thunderstruck)
But it's only a shadow.

VALENTINE, BING and HELENA run down a narrow street with the shadows coming after them.

BING
There's a door! Quick!

BING throws one of the light-balls back at the shadows, but the lights only delay the shadows, they don't stop them. VALENTINE reaches a small door at the end of the alley. He fumbles with the catch. HELENA is behind him.

BING brings up the rear, throwing his last light-ball.

BING (CONT'D)
Come on! That was my last light-ball!

VALENTINE
Hang on. . . . There. Got it.

The door opens – VALENTINE tumbles and wriggles inside.

BING
(to Helena)
You next. Move it!

HELENA slides through the door as the shadows reach BING. He turns to black. Then he crumbles.

The shadows ripple across the walls encircling the door, rising in, burning and blistering the white concrete.

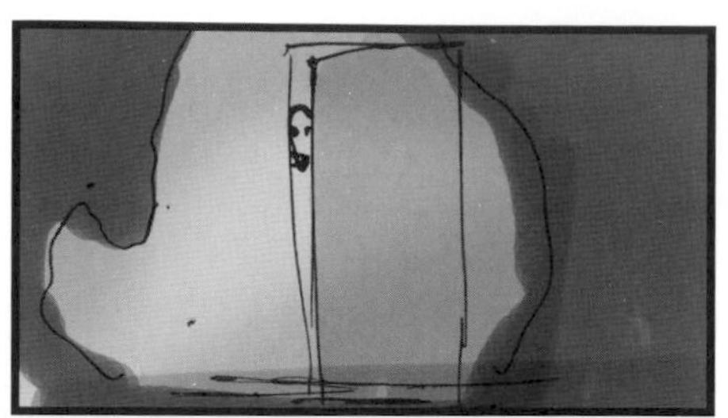

Just as the shadows reach the doorway, VALENTINE slams the door shut.

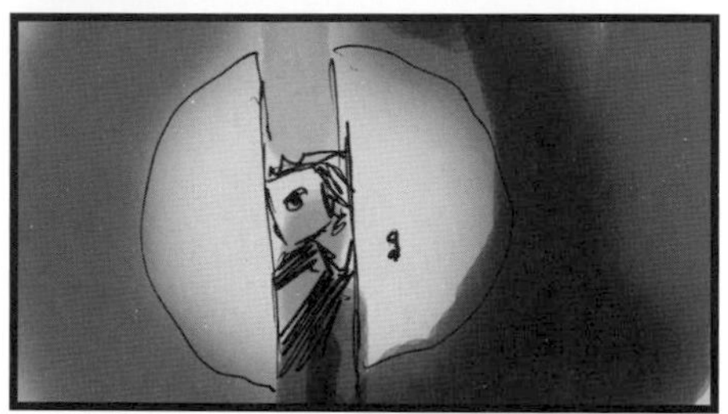

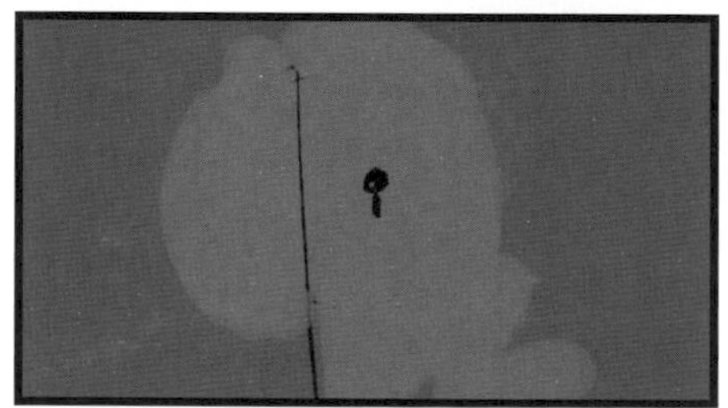

INT. WHITE CITY. ABANDONED HALL – DAY.

HELENA
What was that thing?

VALENTINE is trying to undo the door on the other side of the room. It doesn't open.

Meanwhile, the door blackens, as if it's been burnt, and a pool of shadow puddles under the door. Out of the puddle comes a small SPIDER creature, part of a human face mounted on eight legs.

With one eye, it looks around the room until it catches sight of HELENA.

VALENTINE
(distractedly talking while working out what to do and where to go next)
One of the many things to avoid in life. Like losing a comrade, a lifelong companion, a business partner and soul mate while attempting to rescue little girls . . . what the hell have you got on your feet?

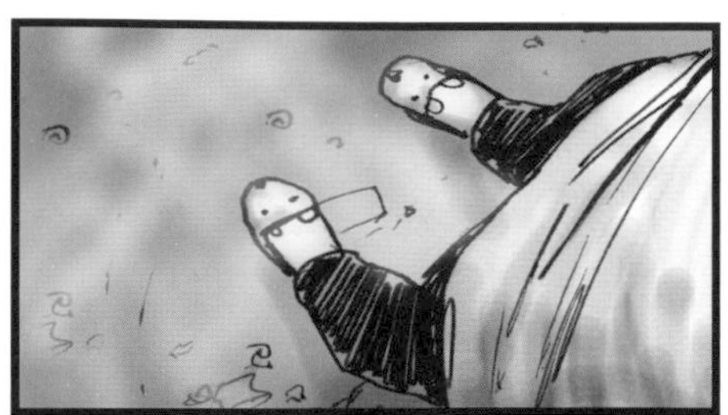

She has slippers with little rabbit faces on the toes.

HELENA
What?

VALENTINE
Is that some kind of sick joke?
Treading on little rabbity-type animals with every step, that's just . . . nasty.

HELENA
They're not real. And . . . I'm sorry about your friends, I thought the violinist was Eric . . . He's a friend of mine . . . but it wasn't . . .

VALENTINE is looking at the various doors and holes in the wall, trying to find a way out.

HELENA (CONT'D)
I don't really know where I am.

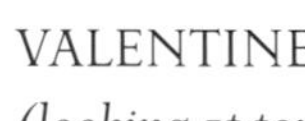

VALENTINE
(looking at torn and chewed pages from books on the floor)
You're in one of the other things in life to avoid.

HELENA finds a high shelf with a few worn hardback books.

HELENA
What, a junk room?

VALENTINE
No . . . trouble.

We hear a rustle. VALENTINE starts.

VALENTINE (CONT'D)
There!

HELENA gets her torch out again and shines it towards the noise. A creature is digging with its paws in the corner of the room; it looks like a large dog or cat. It's nearer her than VALENTINE.

VALENTINE (CONT'D)
Don't irritate it!

HELENA
What is it?

The SPHINX looks up suddenly; it has small wings and a woman's head. It growls and frowns and starts to pad over to VALENTINE and HELENA.

VALENTINE
Just a sphinx. Okay, throw it a book . . .

HELENA
What?

VALENTINE
Throw it a book, it likes books . . .

HELENA
Uhh, okay . . .

(looks at the books on the shelf)

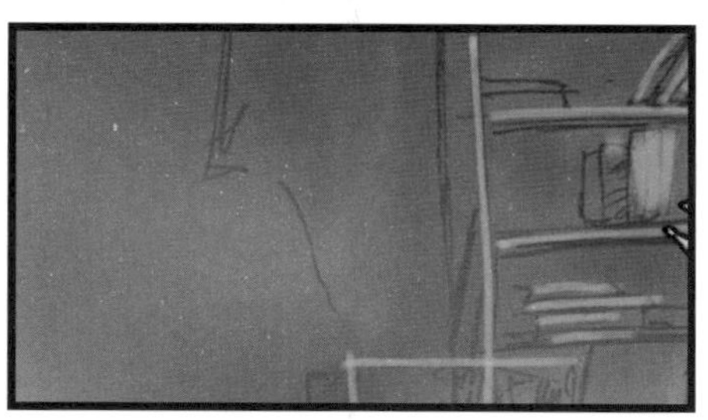

Finders Keepers, by Joe Grey; *A Short History of Future Fruit,* by Douglas Prawnhead; *Smoke and Mirrors,* by . . .

VALENTINE
Anything, anything, it's not going to read it!

HELENA picks a book and throws it towards the SPHINX, which immediately pounces on it and starts to eat it.

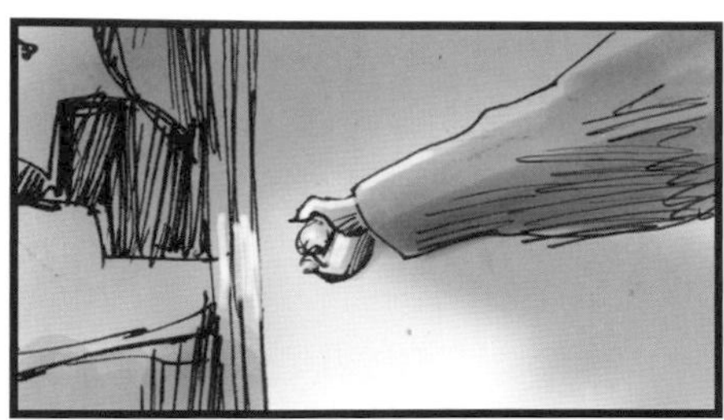

And VALENTINE successfully opens a door!

But the door that finally opens reveals that there's a deep trench – a thirty-foot drop on the other side of the door. There's no way to get out.

VALENTINE (CONT'D)
Right. Not a disaster. Right. Just grab a couple of really big books . . .

HELENA grabs two more books. The SPHINX is eyeing them suspiciously. VALENTINE takes one of the books off HELENA.

The SPIDER is above the door.

VALENTINE (CONT'D)
Okay, throw the book on the floor.

HELENA
Why? I like books.

VALENTINE
Please, please, come on . . .

HELEN drops it gently on the floor.

VALENTINE (CONT'D)
No, no, useless . . .

He picks it up and gives it back to her.

. . . it's really got to feel like it's being rejected . . . grrrrh, horrible, offensive, badly constructed book . . .

He throws it to the floor. Its covers open as it falls and it hovers off the ground, almost immediately orients itself, and floats off.

He jumps onto the book.
It goes through the door, and floats across the deep canyon, with VALENTINE on it.

HELENA
Oh.

(she lifts the book above her head)

Erm . . . nasty poorly paced book with a soppy ending that I didn't believe in for one minute . . .

She throws the book to the ground.

HELENA's book hovers and floats off in the same direction.

She hesitates, and realises if she doesn't hurry up, the book will get away. She runs and jumps onto it.

The SPIDER falls off the ledge, onto the ground.

HELENA drifts out of the open door, across the deep, impassable gully, and, meeting VALENTINE, into the city streets.

HELENA
How does this work?

VALENTINE
So long as they think you don't like them, they migrate back to the city library . . . and we get a free ride out of this hole.

In the foreground by the outside door, we see the little SPIDER creature watching them leave. It scuttles away in the opposite direction.

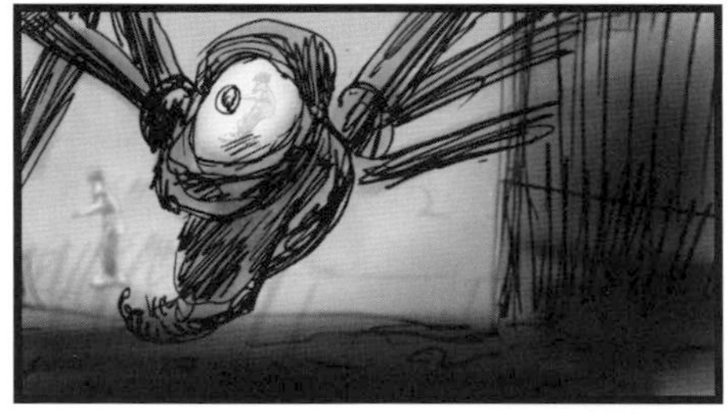

EXT. STREET IN WHITE CITY – DAY (ALL CGI).

In a series of jump cuts, we travel with the SPIDER to the end of the street,

– to the edge of the city,

– into the dark lands,

– finally into the Dark Palace.

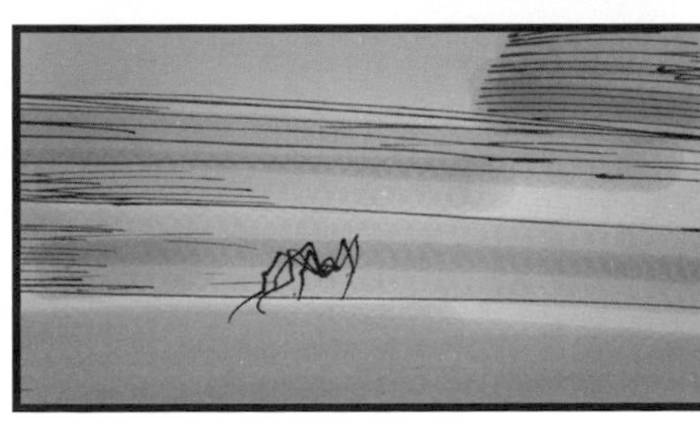

INT. DARK PALACE – NIGHT.

The SPIDER enters the Dark Palace, going up an endless set of steps, and heads into the Great Hall, where the DARK QUEEN (played by the same actor as JOANNE) sits on her outrageously high throne. She is very beautiful and pale, and wears a magnificent black dress. There are no windows in the Dark Palace.

The SPIDER thing scuttle-jumps onto her shoulder.

She turns to look at it, and it plasters itself on her face.

Perhaps she sees, very briefly, what the SPIDER thing saw in the Hall: a blurred vision of HELENA looking down at us, with VALENTINE behind her.

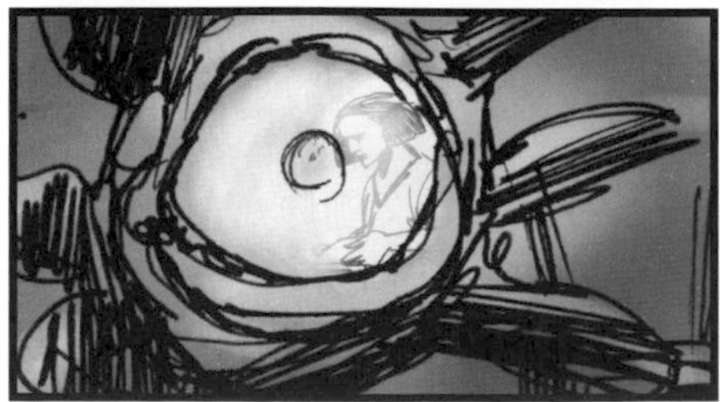

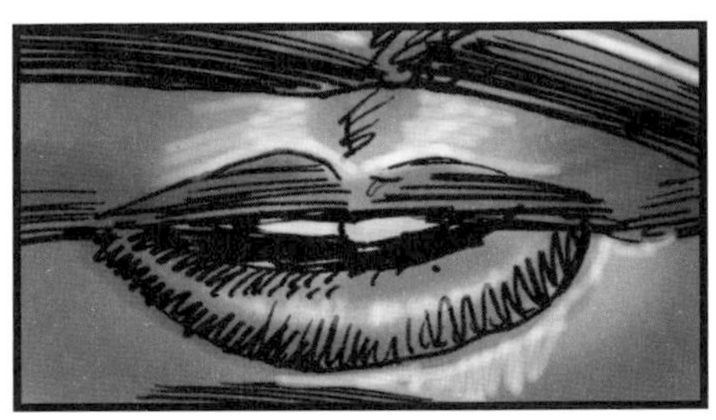

DARK QUEEN
I think . . . I think we may have found her.

EXT. WHITE CITY – DAY.

An odd-looking creature comes down the lane with its arms full of possessions.
Behind it comes another, bent over, with a huge pack of stuff piled up high on its back, much higher than it is.
Brightly coloured FISH swim past in the air.
Now we hear a creaking, and several creatures come down the lane pushing a cart with all their possessions – forks, pillows, plastic fruit and so on, all piled high in a teetering mass and tied with string.

VALENTINE sits, depressed, on a wall, watching them go. He has a handful of pebbles, which he drops from one hand into the other. HELENA's standing.

VALENTINE
What did you say your name was?

HELENA
Helena.

VALENTINE
Ye-es. It's a bit drab, isn't it? You know, you should think about changing that. Go for something with dignity and style, mixed with a bit of romance. Something like . . . "Valentine".

HELENA
Why? What's your name?

VALENTINE
Valentine.

HELENA
Hmph.

VALENTINE
We were going to leave the city today for good. As soon as we'd rehearsed.

HELENA
I'm so sorry.

VALENTINE
Musicians. I can find another fiddle player. They're a dime a dozen. It's Bing. You can't replace a juggler. Nobody round here can juggle.

HELENA
I can.

VALENTINE
Of course you can. Where am I going to find someone who can juggle like that?

HELENA
I already said . . .

VALENTINE
Hopeless. It's a complete disaster. Poor Bing. He was one in a million. My best mate. I'll never ever forget him. Never replace him.

One gloomy moment. Then he smiles, brightly, claps his hands together.

VALENTINE (CONT'D)
Ah well, onward and upward!

HELENA
Had you known him long?

VALENTINE
Who?

He starts to juggle with the pebbles. He's forgotten Bing already. HELENA puts her hand out and intercepts each falling pebble, tosses it to her other hand and then back to VALENTINE. A rhythm is established immediately. They keep talking while they juggle.

VALENTINE (CONT'D)
You can juggle.

HELENA
I said I could.

VALENTINE
Well. You don't have a mask. And you're very dull. But you're certainly better than nothing, now that whatsis-name's . . .
He waves his arms around instead of saying "gone" or "dead" or "gone on holiday".

HELENA
Does everyone here have a mask?

VALENTINE
Of course. How do you know if you're happy or sad without a mask? Or angry? Or ready for dessert?

HELENA
I've got a face.

VALENTINE
Ye-ess. So. Let's get out of town. Follow the rest of these oddments.

HELENA
Where are they all going?

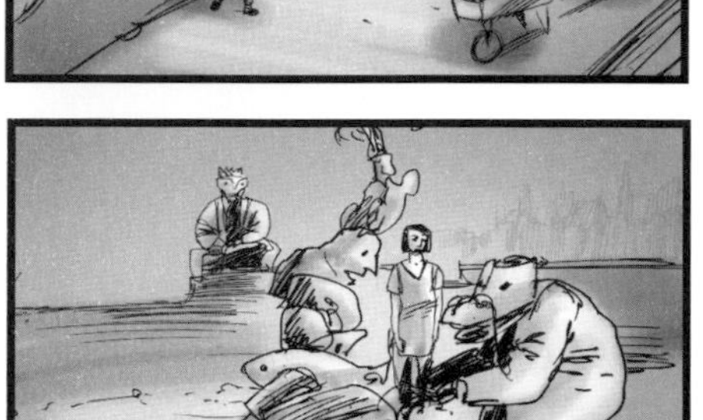

VALENTINE
I've no idea.

HELENA gets off the wall, stops a passing creature trundling a wheelbarrow filled with shoes.

HELENA
Excuse me?

SHOE-THING
Yes?

HELENA
Where are you going?

SHOE-THING
We're leaving the city. Heading for the hills. It's not safe here any longer. Shadows completely ate my house yesterday.

HELENA
Isn't anybody doing anything about it?

SHOE-THING
Since the queen fell asleep, there's not a lot they can do. They're looking for the charm, to sort it all out, but we're off out of it.

MRS SHOE-THING puts her head out of a shoe as they trundle off.

MRS SHOE-THING
Over the hills and far away, Bernard.

HELENA walks back to VALENTINE.

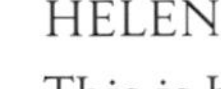

HELENA
This is bizarre.
Where do the shadows come from?

The SPIDER thing we saw earlier (or one just like it) peers out from the edge of an alleyway. It watches them.

VALENTINE
The Dark Lands. Over the border, there. This used to be a nice city, lots of opportunity to do a deal here and there. I mean, you wouldn't think it to look at me, but I'm a very important man. I've got a tower.

HELENA
The shadows? Where do they – ?

VALENTINE
I told you. They come from the dark.

There is a clattering noise. And the six members of the White City police force appear: they are to all intents and purposes stilt walkers; they skitter along in a line, looking like individual sections of a tall centipede.

COP 1
There she is, Sergeant!

COP 2
If you don't mind.

COP 1
Could we have a word with you?

And with a couple of steps they've encircled HELENA – which has the effect of imprisoning her in a cage. They lean down to look at her.

COP 4
Careful, lads. She's dangerous all right. Look at that changeable expression.

COP 2
And what I say is, it's the dangerous ones you have to watch out for.

HELENA
I'm not dangerous.

They pull back, suddenly terrified – she spoke!

Down at ground level, the SPIDER thing scuttles up a wall to get a better view of what's going on.

COP 2
No. Of course not. That was what we meant. Dangerous. Not dangerous. Same thing.

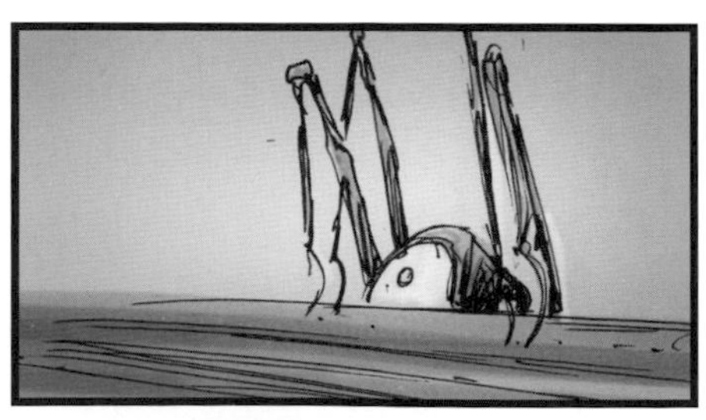

HELENA
Am I under arrest?

COP 2
Not exactly, miss. Or should I say . . .
(and then, triumphantly)
Princess!

HELENA
This is ridiculous.

COP 4
We're just making sure you get safely to the palace.

HELENA
But I don't want to go to the palace. And I'm certainly no princess.

VALENTINE
Excuse me. Officers. This young lady happens to be my business partner, juggling associate, and close personal friend. I think there's been some mistake.

The policemen start to move away, taking HELENA with them.

VALENTINE runs along beside them, arguing with them ad lib

– he's just a poor boy who needs a juggling partner – but is rapidly left way behind.

HELENA is really upset. Then they pass a window, and she looks into it and sees . . .

INT. TOWER BLOCK. AUNT NAN'S FLAT. HELENA'S BEDROOM – DAY.

Through the window, in her bedroom, HELENA is asleep in her bed, dreaming peacefully.

EXT. WHITE CITY – DAY.

Our HELENA is yanked past the window. She thinks about this for a moment, then smiles.

HELENA
I'm asleep. That's all. This is only a dream.

And she and the COPS move through the city to . . .

EXT. WHITE CITY. WHITE PALACE – DAY.

Once, obviously, really impressive, but like everything in the city it's crumbling at the edges.

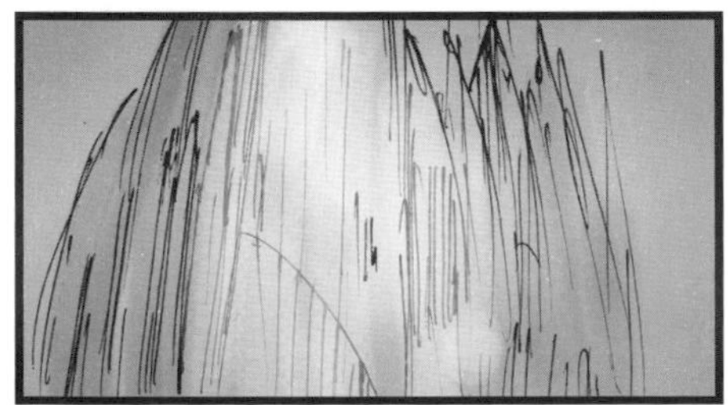

There's a line of ODD CREATURES going down the steps that lead to the palace. Some of them watch HELENA, in her cage, going past.

ODD CREATURE 1
I would hazard that they've caught a dangerous crinimal.

ODD CREATURE 2
I'll say. Look at that face.

ODD CREATURE 3
And those slippers. Hardened criminal, if you ask me.
(to police)
Good job. Nice one, officers.

ODD CREATURE 2
Hang on. Does she remind you of anyone?

ODD CREATURE 1
Can't be . . .

But now we've reached the top of the steps and we enter . . .

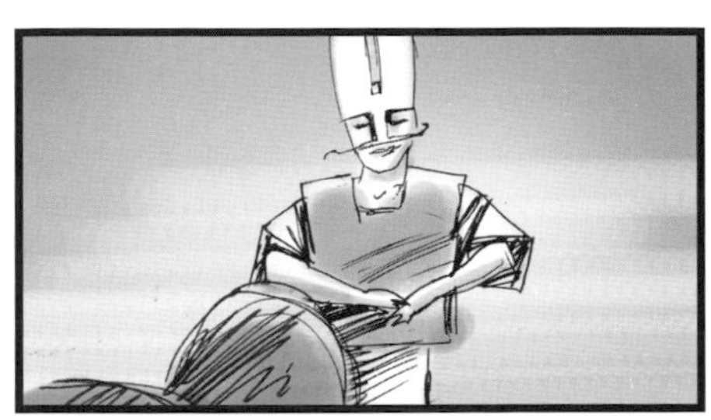

INT. WHITE CITY. WHITE PALACE – DAY.

Inside the palace. The PRIME MINISTER and his assistant, SPINY WILSON, who is sort of like a hedgehog, sit at a small table. The line of people goes up to the table. The PRIME MINISTER is interviewing the people as they arrive.

A GNOME puts half a brick on the table.

PRIME MINISTER
So, you reckon that's the charm, do you?

GNOME
Yes.

PRIME MINISTER
Well, I have to say, it looks – to me – like, uh, half a brick.

GNOME
Not really. Well. A bit. Maybe.

PRIME MINISTER
It is half a brick, isn't it?

GNOME
Er . . .

PRIME MINISTER
Well, good try. Thank you for coming. Next.

The GNOME pockets the half brick and leaves.

A TROLL puts a CHICKEN on the table. The TROLL grunts out the only two words it knows:

TROLL
The charm.

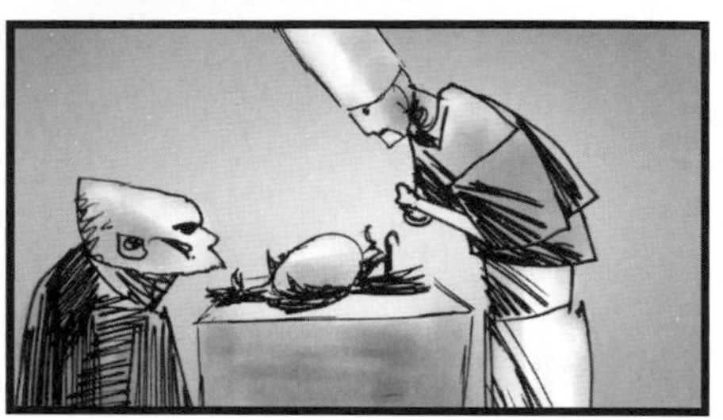

PRIME MINISTER
No. That's actually a chicken.

TROLL
(threateningly)
The charm!

PRIME MINISTER
I know this must be very painful for you, but –
(he shakes his head)
chicken.

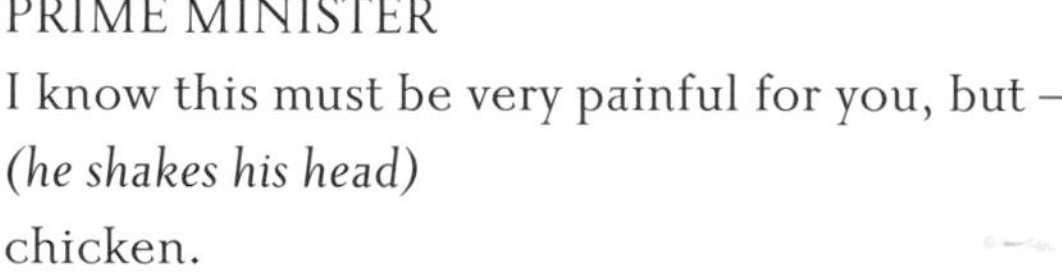

CHICKEN
I've been trying to tell him. He just doesn't listen!

The police have dropped HELENA nearby. COP 1 stays with her.

COP 1
Excuse me, Prime Minister. We caught the princess.

PRIME MINISTER
Good gracious! You caught her! How absolutely splen-did!

COP 1
Very kind of you to say so.

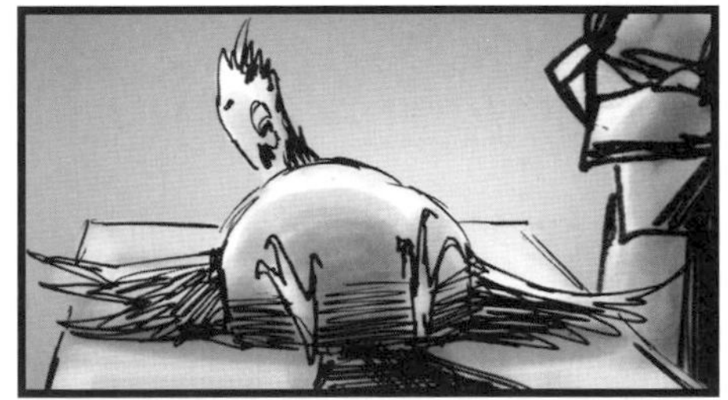

CHICKEN
Ooh! Look at her face! Gives you the willies!

PRIME MINISTER
Right. Well, well young lady. Either you return what you stole, or I'm afraid we'll have to stake you out for the shadows.

HELENA
I haven't stolen anything. I only got here just now. This is all just a stupid dream.

PRIME MINISTER
Lying won't help you. Tell us what you did to the charm –

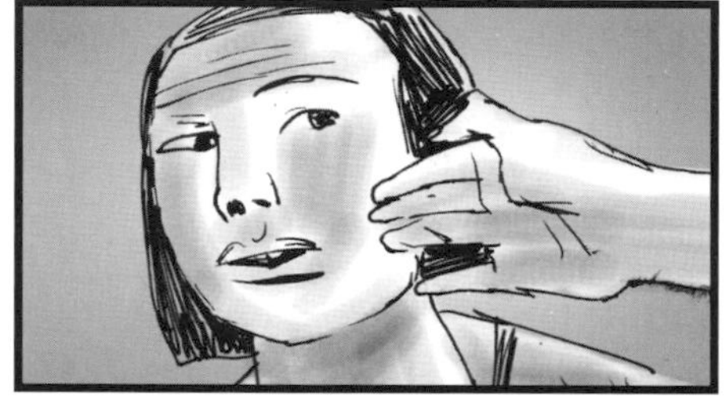

He prods at HELENA's face with his finger.

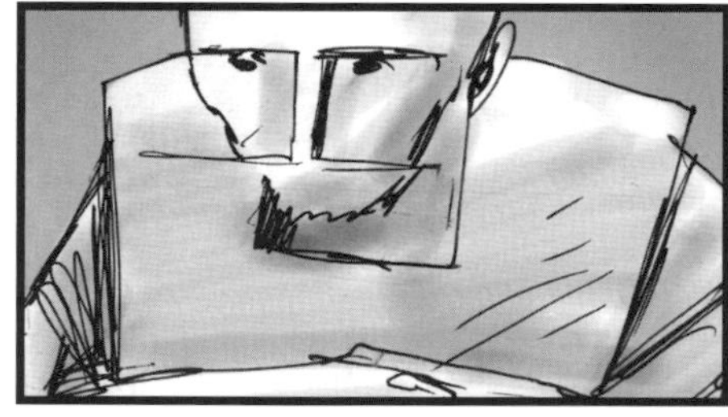

Then he looks at her eyes . . .

and down to her bunny slippers, and he knows.

PRIME MINISTER (CONT'D)
You look so much like her, but . . . you aren't her, are you? She said she was a princess – are you a princess?

HELENA
I'm not anything. I'm just me. I'm Helena Campbell.

PRIME MINISTER
Explain yourself. Why did you come here? What are you doing in the city?

HELENA
I don't know. You see, I'm not from here.

COP 1
Shall we lock her up for you?

COP 2
We could torture her.

COP 3
Extort a confession. Execute her? Deny her ice-cream?

PRIME MINISTER
For heaven's sake. Look at her. Listen to her. She's not her. I mean, she's not *her*.

(he looks at her, pondering)

I wonder.

HELENA
Who am I meant to be?

PRIME MINISTER
(he makes up his mind)
Right. Follow me. Take over, Spiny. You're in charge.

He heads up the flight of steps, and HELENA follows.

She asks again –

HELENA
Who did they think I was?

PRIME MINISTER
A princess. Not a very nice one. The other kind.

INT. WHITE CITY. WHITE PALACE.
WHITE QUEEN'S BEDROOM – DAY.

The WHITE QUEEN is asleep in a glass casket. HELENA walks around the glass casket, staring at the WHITE QUEEN – very pale and beautiful (and played by the same actress who plays JOANNE and the DARK QUEEN). On the casket is a stylised sun, an image that we will see repeated around the bedroom and around the White Palace.
On the WHITE QUEEN's breast, held in her sleeping hands, is a large white rosebud.

HELENA
Is she dead?

PRIME MINISTER
Just asleep. This room was her favourite – she could see the sun from here. We used to have a lovely sun, you know. Shone like anything, all over the place.

HELENA
She's beautiful.

PRIME MINISTER
We loved her. And she loved us. She ruled wisely and well.

HELENA
What happened?

PRIME MINISTER
Everything's out of balance.
Once we had days and nights, with suns and moons and those little twinkly things and everything.

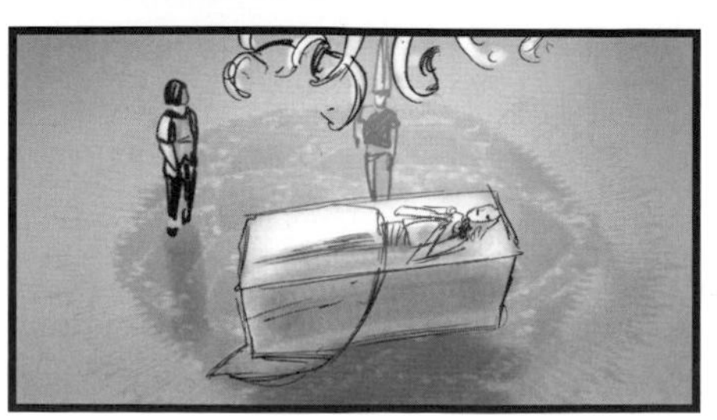

The city was filled with joy, and we entertained each other with our astonishing skills.
(he clears his throat, and, out of the blue, like a stand-up comic, shouts)
Are you in show business, sir? No? Then kindly get your feet off the stage.
(sighs)
Those were the days.

HELENA
What happened?

The PRIME MINISTER reaches his hand into the front of his hat, and pulls out a little box.

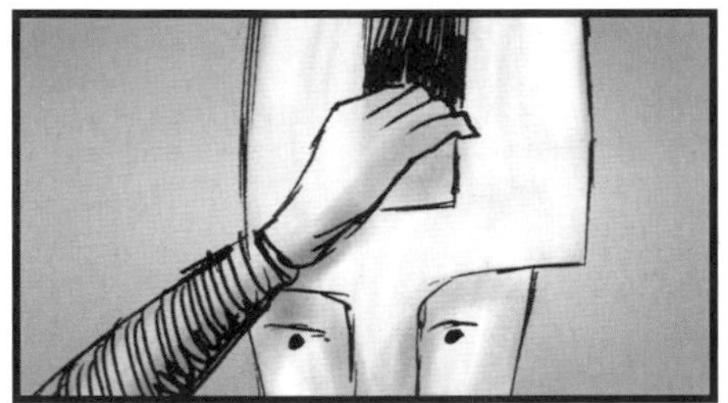

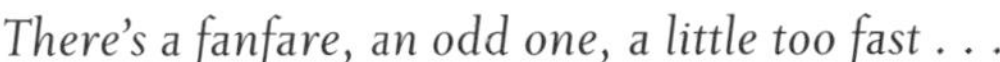

There's a fanfare, an odd one, a little too fast . . .

And then the box opens to reveal a little rabbit puppet. The rabbit opens its own box, and a little puppet play proceeds to illustrate what we're seeing.

The animated images hang in the air, translucent, illustrating everything he tells us.

PRIME MINISTER
The balance was broken. This was the city of light.

Across the border was the city of shadows.

We had our queen, they had theirs.

Then, one day, a girl like you came to our city, from the darkness. She said she was a princess.

Our queen took her in;

we had a party.

The next day, the princess had vanished, and without the charm we couldn't wake the queen.

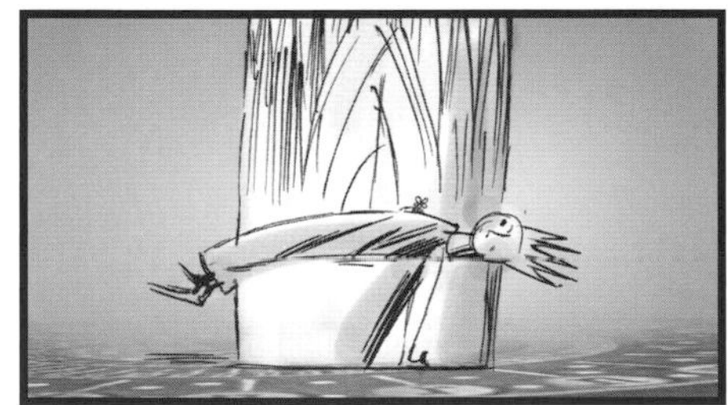

After that, well, everything went wrong.

The darkness has been leaking into our city, shadows eating away at our buildings, spiders spying on us, black birds flapping around our houses, searching through our rooms and dustbins.

Our queen was sanity and wisdom, the Dark Queen was beauty and madness. Ever since she fell asleep we've been searching for the charm, to see if it will wake her. No luck. Soon, there will be no one left in the city.

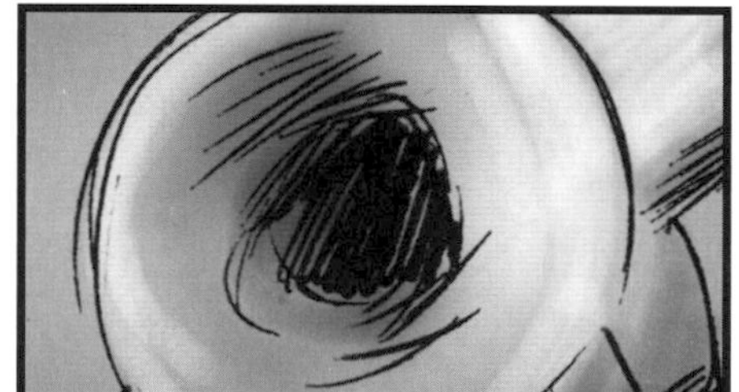

There's a final fanfare and the puppets collapse into their box.

HELENA
You keep talking about a charm. What kind of a charm?

PRIME MINISTER
It's a gateway. It is the scales upon which the whole world balances. The other girl – the one who said she was a princess – she was looking for it, too.

HELENA
I see. What does it look like?

PRIME MINISTER
Don't know.

HELENA
How big is it?

PRIME MINISTER
Nope.
He picks up the little box and puts it back in his hat.

HELENA
What kind of places could it be?

PRIME MINISTER
I wish we knew.

HELENA
Well, what do you know?

PRIME MINISTER
You know, I've always fancied that I'd know it if I saw it.

HELENA
Would you?

PRIME MINISTER
I don't know. What if someone's found it and I didn't see it? What if it was that chicken?

HELENA
I don't think it was the chicken.

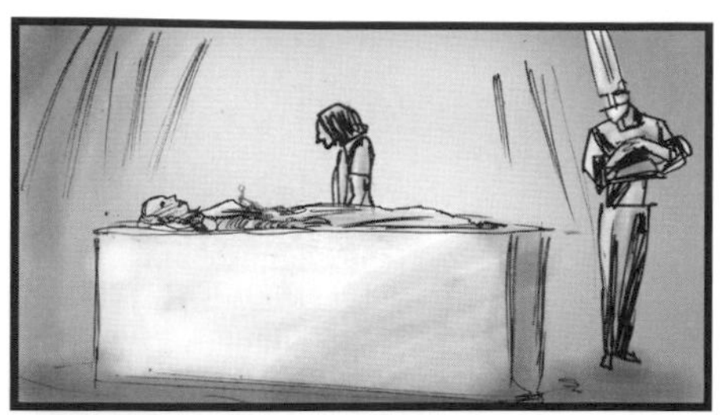

She walks up to the WHITE QUEEN and sits on the bed beside her, mirroring the scene in the hospital.

She touches her hand. A sudden flashback,

her mother opens her eyes.

JOANNE
Helena . . . ?

HELENA
Mum?

Back in the palace, the WHITE QUEEN remains motionless, asleep.

HELENA (CONT'D)
I wish I could do something.

(she remembers those words from the conversation with her dad)

Well, this is my dream.

(she addresses the PRIME MINISTER:)

I must be able to find it for you. I'll wake her up.

PRIME MINISTER
That's very kind of you, young lady. Very kind. But I'm afraid it's too late for that. Soon, our city will fall completely into shadow and the palace and the queen will be gone.

HELENA
Then you don't have anything to lose.

The PRIME MINISTER shakes his head.

PRIME MINISTER
Leave the city. It's too dangerous.

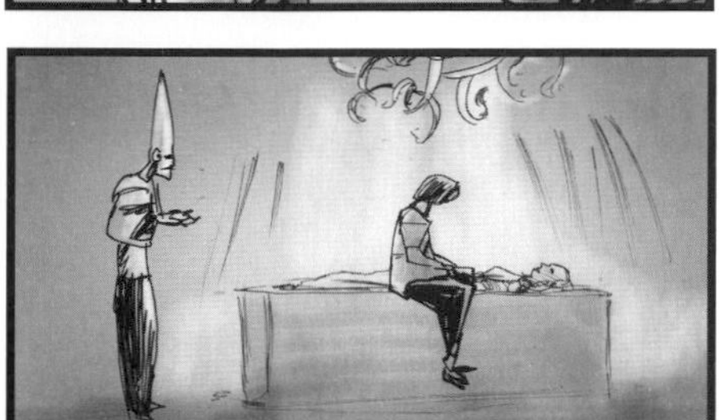

HELENA
Please let me try.

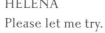

PRIME MINISTER
It would be like looking for a something, not a needle, something really even smaller than a needle that you don't know what it is, in a haystack, when you're not even sure that you've got the right field. I mean, as propositions go, it's completely, utterly, unarguably, quintessentially hopeless.

And HELENA is about to tell him why she won't do that, but instead she says:

HELENA
Look!

And the white rosebud on the WHITE QUEEN's chest is starting to open into a flower.

HELENA (CONT'D)
What does it mean?

PRIME MINISTER
Well, possibly . . . I suppose it may not be *quintessentially* hopeless.

INT. WHITE CITY. WHITE PALACE – DAY.

The PRIME MINISTER comes out into the hall, and announces . . .

PRIME MINISTER
If I can have a little quiet. This young lady. What is your name, my dear?

HELENA
Helena.

PRIME MINISTER
Helena. Rather a common name, isn't it? Yes. Well, she is going on a quest, to find the charm!

The few CREATURES in the line cheer halfheartedly.

VALENTINE, who has just wandered up the stairs into the palace, makes it over to them.

VALENTINE
(to Helena)
You are?

PRIME MINISTER
She is!

VALENTINE
Is there a reward?

PRIME MINISTER
Of course. Who finds the charm will wake the queen from her sleep, restore the city, save us all from the shadows and make the world right again . . . what finer reward could anyone wish for?

VALENTINE
(doubtfully)
Yessss . . . I was thinking more along the lines of a hill of treasure? Half a kingdom?

HELENA
Quiet, Valentine. Look. You said they thought I was that princess –

PRIME MINISTER
(then to Valentine)
We hadn't really thought about the details.

VALENTINE
Don't you worry. It's small print. As long as we're all clear on the main thrust of the thing – kingdom, treasure, and as her manager,everything comes to me to divvy up. Cleaner that way.

HELENA
Where's the best place to start looking?

They look at each other, puzzled. Honestly, this lot are quite hopeless, HELENA thinks.

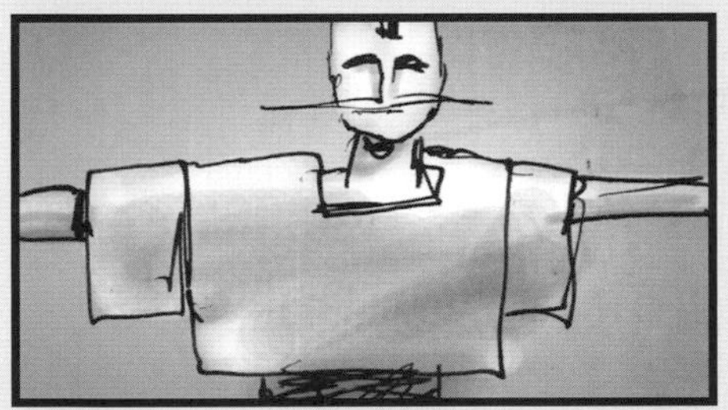

HELENA (CONT'D)
Those books we got here on. They were going back to the library, you said, Valentine. So there's a library, right?

PRIME MINISTER
Yes! Yes, there is! Jolly good place, filled with books and things. Information all over the place! Brilliant place to start. Brilliant!

EXT. WHITE CITY. LIBRARY – DAY.

The PRIME MINISTER's face turns into the cover of a book, which glides away from us, revealing the library. Books float inside. The library is a head on its side, and we enter through the eyes.
Over this, in voice-over:

VALENTINE
So. We're on a quest. Right. *(Beat.)*
How big's the reward?

HELENA
The reward is, we wake the queen and save the world.

VALENTINE
No treasure? As your manager I would have made sure that –

HELENA
You're not my manager.

VALENTINE
We can sort out the contractual details after we . . . what are we doing now?

HELENA
We're going to the library. For information.

VALENTINE
Right. Good idea. They've got books and . . . well, predominantly books.

INT. WHITE CITY. LIBRARY – DAY.

A sign that says "Library". Books in impossibly high teetering piles, with a LIBRARIAN at a desk, writing a list of books in a ledger. HELENA and VALENTINE walk up to the desk.

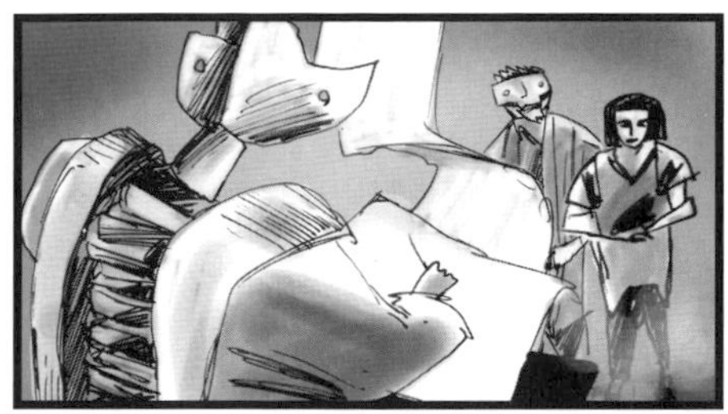

HELENA
Excuse me . . .

LIBRARIAN
Shhh.

HELENA
But, excuse me, we need a really useful –

LIBRARIAN
Shhh.

Points to a "Silence" sign.

VALENTINE bounces over the desk, and says –

VALENTINE
Charm. Information. We're saving the world. Help us, or I start singing. Loudly. A-one, a-two, a-one-two-three-you-put-your-right-arm-in –

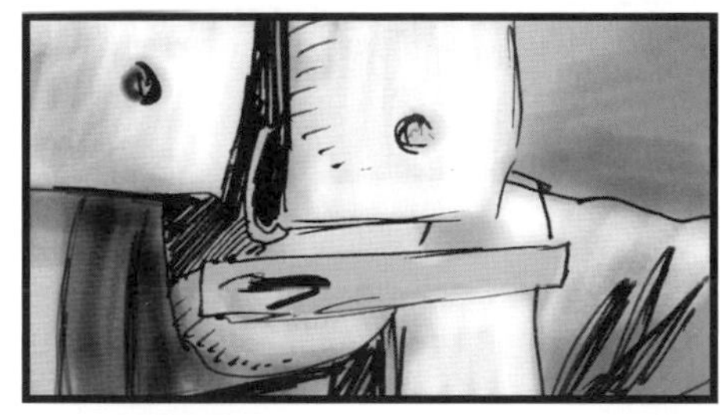

The LIBRARIAN makes a snatching gesture, and VALENTINE's voice is almost silent, muffled, as if held in the LIBRARIAN's hand.

LIBRARIAN
(whispers)
Information? Paperbacks. Top floor. You'll need a net.

The LIBRARIAN eats whatever's in his hand. VALENTINE looks suspicious.

The LIBRARIAN hands them a huge butterfly net each, then, with one final "Sshhh", returns to his work.

INT. WHITE CITY. LIBRARY – DAY.

VALENTINE and HELENA walk up the stairs, carrying their nets. They are puzzled about the nets.

HELENA
The princess they were talking about. Did you ever meet her?

VALENTINE
To be honest, all you people look alike to me. Without proper faces you could be anybody.

HELENA
I've got a proper face.

VALENTINE
Can you do this?

He peels off his mask-face, revealing a new mask-face underneath, with a different expression.

HELENA
No.
Can you do this?

She crosses her eyes.

VALENTINE
Eugh. That's disgusting.

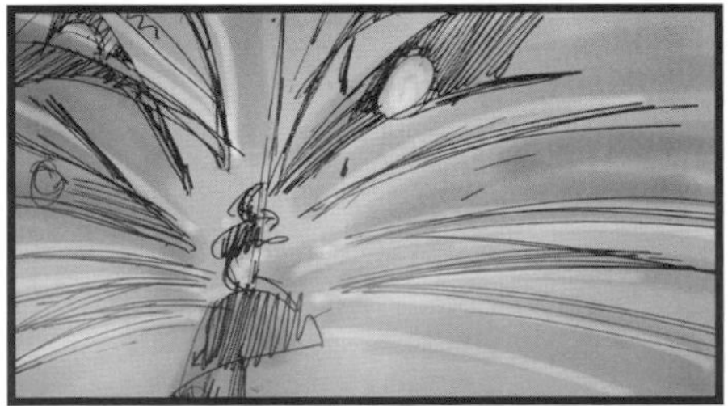

They come out into the:

INT. WHITE CITY. LIBRARY. UPSTAIRS – DAY.

A high room, which reminds us a little of an aviary. There are faint noises and rustlings, as in a dovecote.
All the books in the upstairs shelves are thin and paperback-ish.

HELENA looks along a row of books.

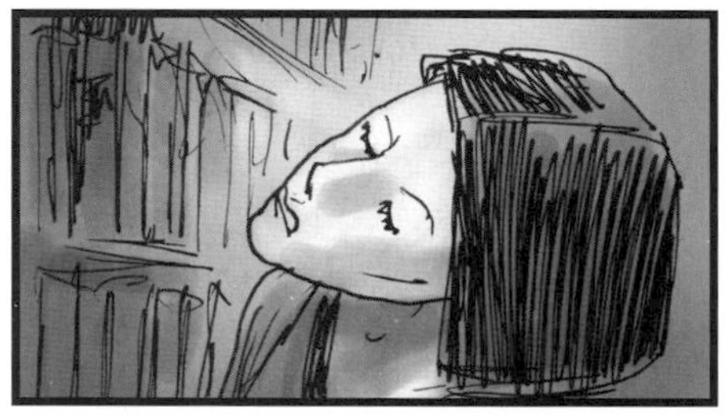

Halfway down the shelf we see a black book with "The History of Everything" on its spine.

But before she can pull "The History of Everything" off the shelves, the whole shelf of books takes off, fluttering madly into the air, like pigeons.

HELENA
Oh no!

They swoop and fly, while HELENA and VALENTINE madly try to catch them in their nets. The books are fluttering away out of reach.

HELENA (CONT'D)
I can't reach. You know, I had no idea books had such different personalities.

Valentine . . . hold very still.

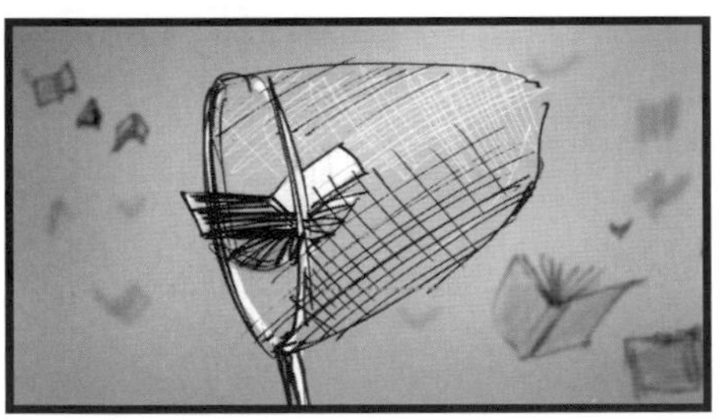

HELENA catches a book in the net.

It's "The History of Everything".

She takes it out of the net. Then she lets go of it, and in a moment it's off again.

A hand snaps out and grabs it from the air.

It's the grumpy LIBRARIAN from downstairs. The other books land back on their shelves . . .

Except for one, a small, red-covered book, which is fluttering about. HELENA looks at it and smiles.

It looks down at her, then perches, delicately, on top of her head.

The LIBRARIAN opens "The History of Everything" to the first page.

As he talks, we see a montage of what he's talking about: and strangely enough, the first image is of HELENA, sitting in her caravan, drawing cities and buildings.

LIBRARIAN
Arrrhhhm. In the beginning, she found herself in a new and empty space. And all was white, and the corners were a bit flaky, and the carpet was a bit manky, but it was a good space.

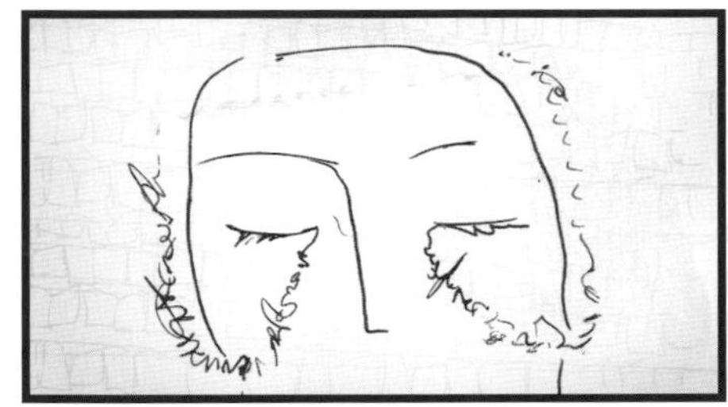

And she sat in the centre of it all and beheld a clean white sheet of void.

She held her charm to her face.

And reflected in the charm was a city of lost horizons and tall and towering stories.

And just as it had been reflected in the charm, so it appeared in the void.

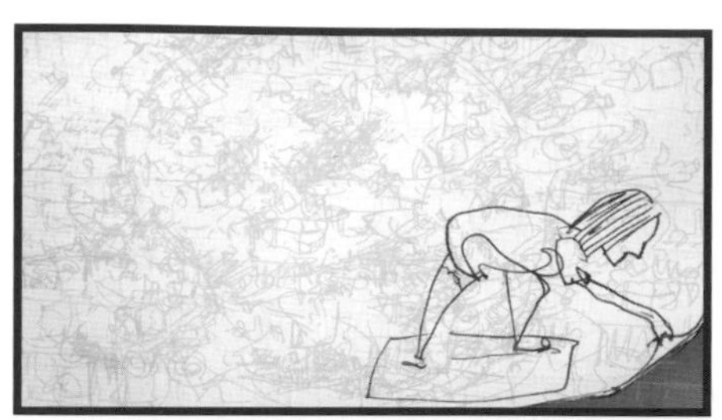

And when there was no more room in the void, she turned it over and continued on the other side.

And so the void was filled from corner to corner on both sides, a city of front and back, a city of light and shadow.

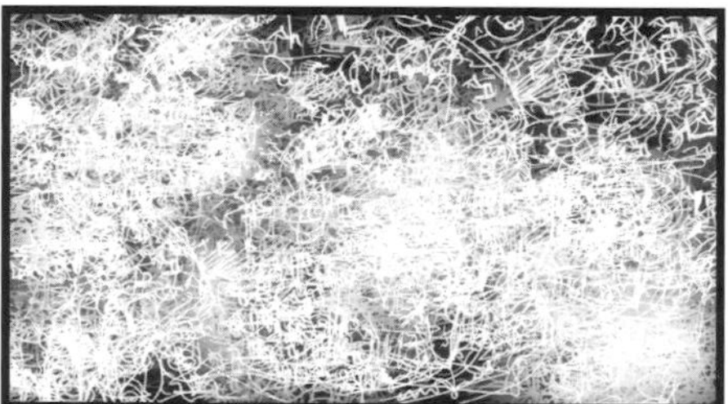

Then she rested on her bed and dreamed of her creation, and the lives that inhabited it.

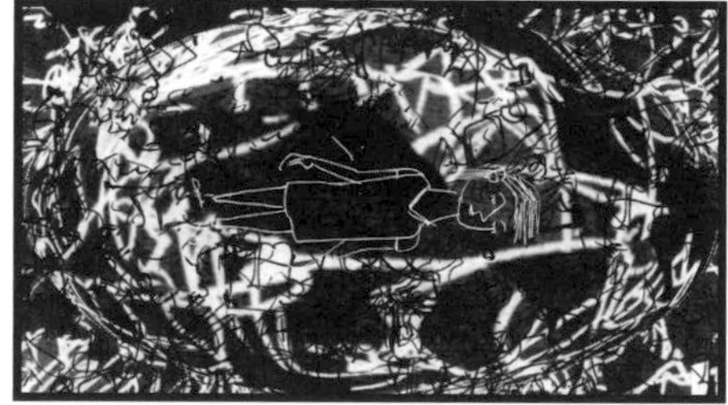

And in the days that followed, there were other voids and other lights and other shadows.

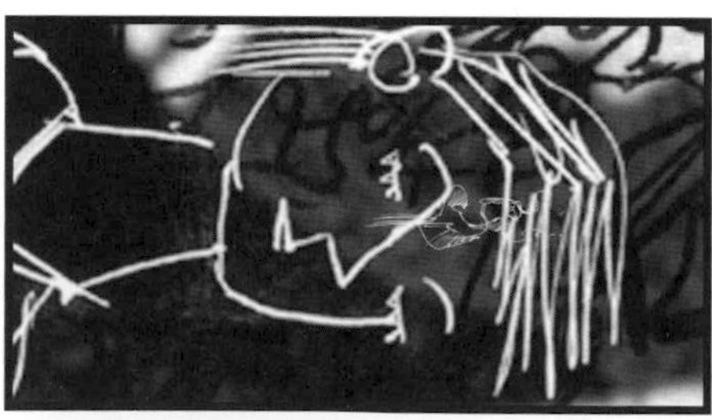

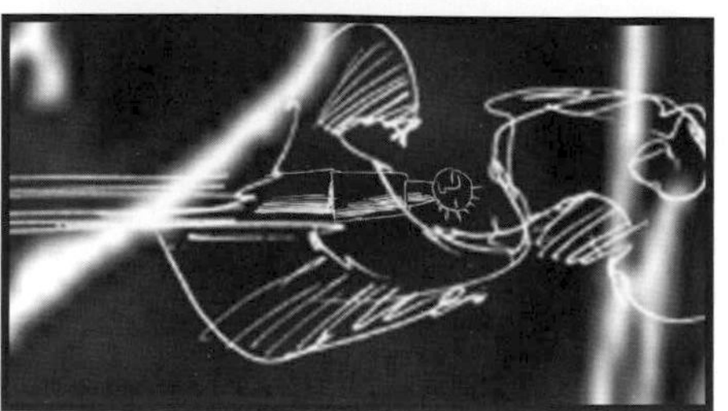

Preproduction logo and cover sheet.

Shooting Helena in her caravan bedroom.

Pickup shot a year later from the same scene, shot at Pinewood Studios.

Shooting the final circus scene on the beachfront in Brighton.

Shooting the ticket booth scenes.

Gina McKee at the circus as Joanne Campbell.

Rob Brydon as Morris Campbell.

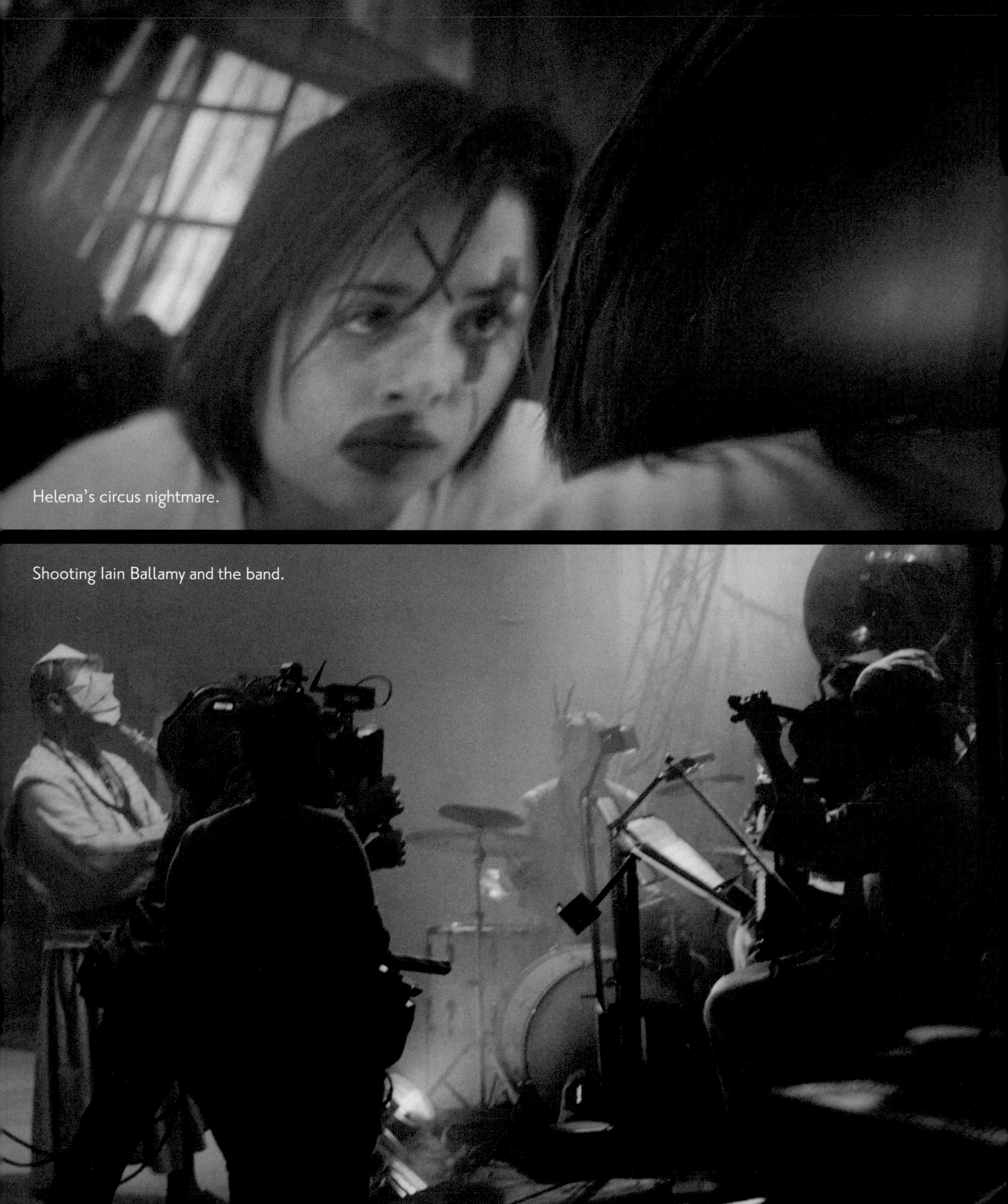

Helena's circus nightmare.

Shooting Iain Ballamy and the band.

Stephanie Leonidas as Helena.

Periscope lens needed to shoot the long tracking shot as Helena draws her "get well soon" card on the bed.

Rob and Stephanie on the roof of Embassy Court in Brighton.

One of the many city drawings decorating Helena's wall.

Outside Mrs Bagwell's mask shop.

Surrounded by sphinxes.

Jason Barry as Valentine.

Monkeybirds, and some preliminary visuals.

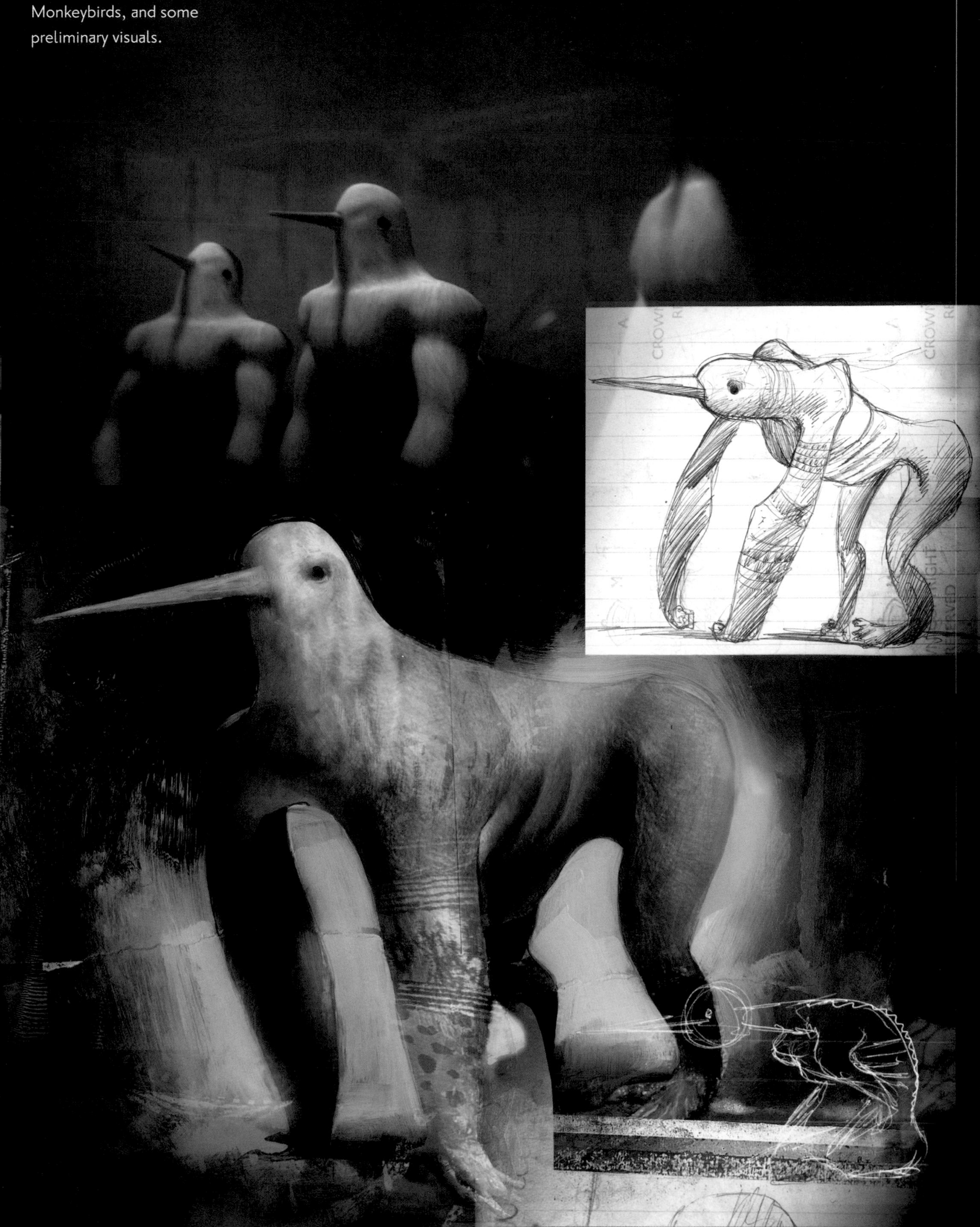

The Prime Minister's story.

Rob Brydon again,
this time as the Prime Minister.

The orbiting giants.

Ginger the sphinx,
with the face of Simon Harvey.

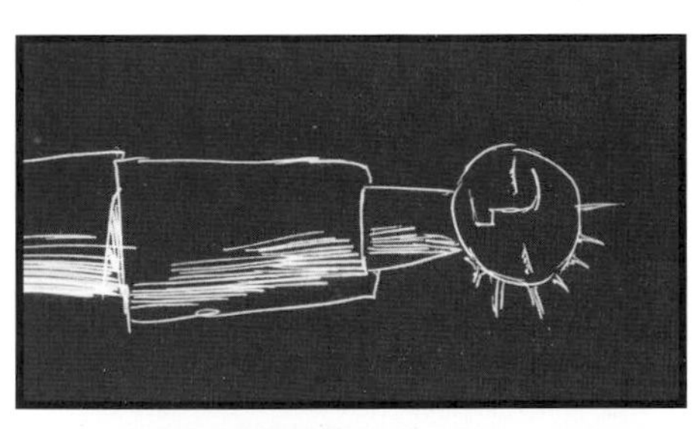

The charm she placed beneath the sign of the queen, to show the city that she knew it would never be finished, because the city was her life and her dream, and it would live forever.

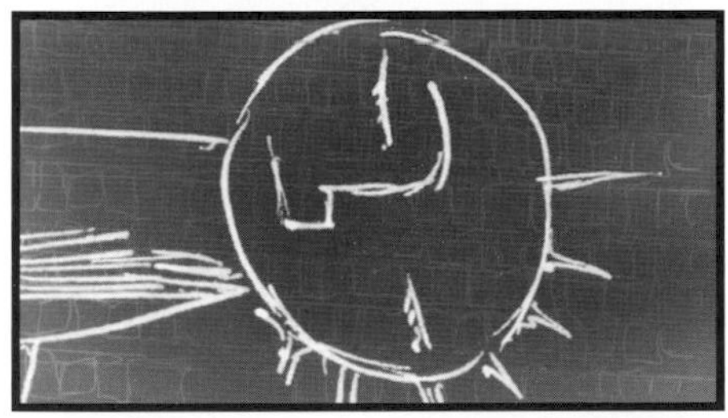

Then he closes the book and lets it go. It flaps back up to the shelf and settles there, the other books nudging over to make room for it.

HELENA
Thank you. I think. I'm not sure I understood it all.

LIBRARIAN
Who does? I certainly don't. Hullo . . . I think you've made a friend.

The little red book is still perched on HELENA's shoulder.

HELENA reaches up and takes it down. The cover says "A Really Useful Book".

HELENA
It's a really useful book.

(she flips it open, reads)
"Remember what your mother told you."
(flips again to another page, reads)
"Why don't you look out of the window?"

On each page is one neatly handwritten sentence.

VALENTINE
Really useful? Utter piffle. Sounds perfectly useless to me.

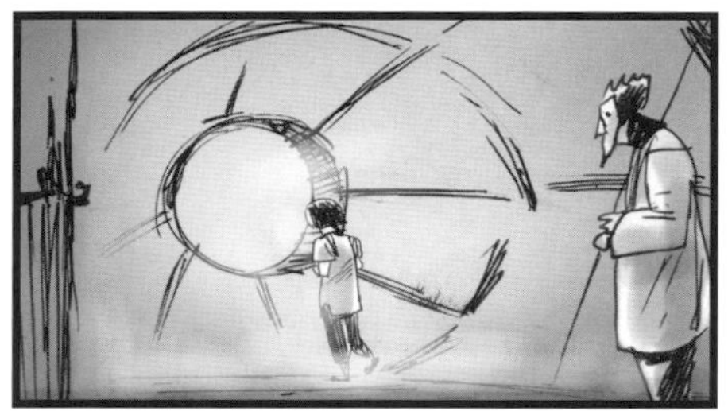

But HELENA has looked out of the window.

She sees a long, straight avenue leading to an open space, on the edge of town, which, as she moves, glints and glows in the shape of a sun.

HELENA
"Placed it beneath the sign of the queen."

VALENTINE
It's all rubbish, isn't it? Doesn't mean anything. "Why don't you look out of the window?"

HELENA
The queen's sign is the sun. It was all over her bedroom.

HELENA (CONT'D)
And look, Valentine . . .
(she points to the sun)
We have to go there.

This is a really useful book, isn't it?

The book rustles its pages happily. She makes to put it back on the shelf, but the LIBRARIAN stops her.

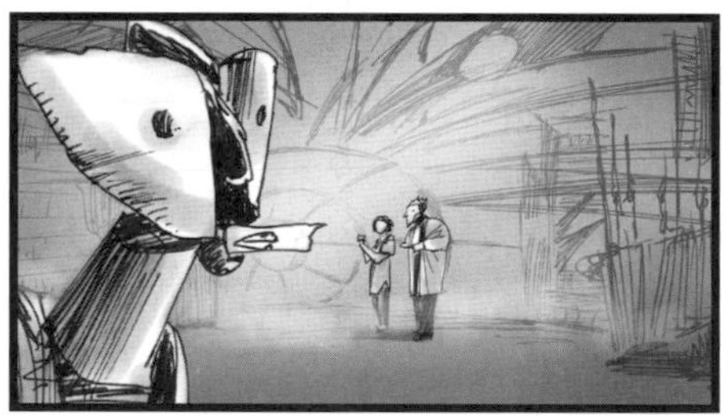

LIBRARIAN
You'd better take the book with you. If you leave it behind it'll just depress the rest of them, and before you know it they'll start moulting. Pages everywhere.

HELENA
That's very kind of you!

LIBRARIAN
(blushing)
Sshhh. Stop it.

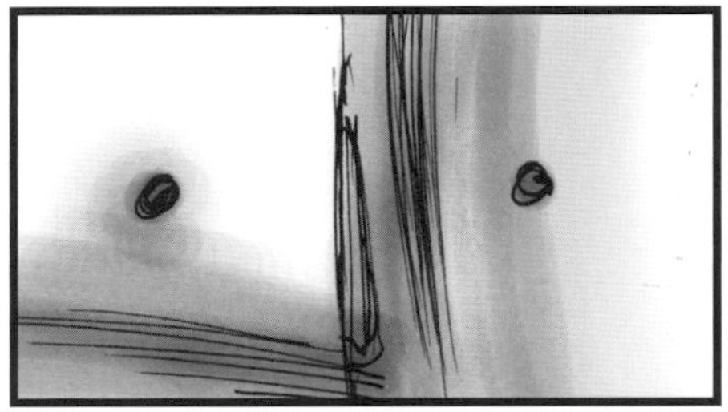

EXT. WHITE CITY. LIBRARY – DAY.

HELENA and VALENTINE are walking through the city.

VALENTINE
So we find this thing quickly, save the world, they give us the contents of the treasury, we can be out of the city by tomorrow. I knew you needed a manager – stick with me kiddo, you'll have a tower of your own, almost as nice as mine.

That's just for starters. Forget juggling, we'll do what the rich people do. Bathe in fish. Eat our own weight in chocolate buttons. Learn to play the concertina.

HELENA
I definitely don't need a manager. I'm not actually sure I need you.

VALENTINE
Do you think I'd look good in a crown? I've always thought I was more of a hat person.

They are walking past a house. HELENA looks at it.

HELENA
You know. I knew there was something really familiar about the houses, here. They all look like things I drew.

VALENTINE
So I'll be rich, important, famous . . . um. What are we looking for again? And how do we know when we've found it?

HELENA
Shh. I wonder.

HELENA looks through the window.

INT. TOWER BLOCK. AUNT NAN'S FLAT. HELENA'S BEDROOM – DAY.

We see HELENA's bedroom again . . . but now the bed is empty and unmade. It's daylight.

EXT. WHITE CITY. LIBRARY – DAY.

HELENA
That's odd. I should be in there, shouldn't I? If I'm asleep.

VALENTINE
You're asleep?

HELENA
Well, yes. I think we've rather definitely established that. This whole thing is just a dream. But look at it.

VALENTINE shakes his head, apologetically.

VALENTINE
I can't see anything. It's just a window.

VALENTINE's POV through the window. Just another room in the city.

HELENA
It's my bedroom!

VALENTINE
It's not, it's somebody's junk room.

HELENA
You can't see my bedroom in there?
My wardrobe?
My moon mask?
My cuddly sea anemone?

VALENTINE looks at her as if she's mad.

**INT. TOWER BLOCK. AUNT NAN'S FLAT.
HELENA'S BEDROOM – DAY.**

HELENA looks into her bedroom through the window.

She notices that the mirrored doors of her wardrobe are ajar. She can see the wall of drawings describing the city reflected in them. Half the wall is in sunlight, the other half is in shadow.

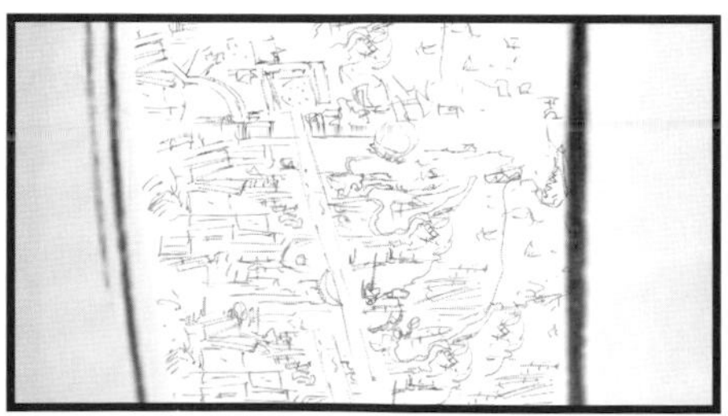

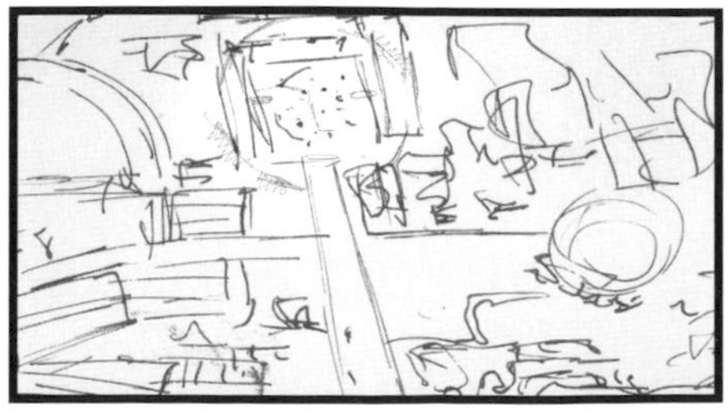

We see, from her POV, the drawing of the White Palace and the library, then the line of drawings describing the long avenue she saw from the library window, and the park at the end, a large sun-face in the middle of it.

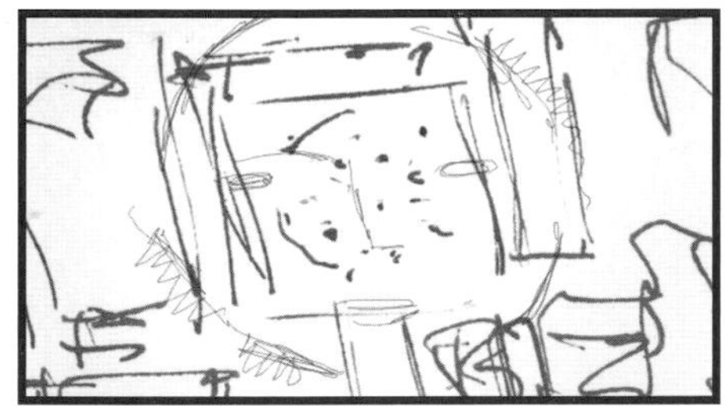

EXT. WHITE CITY. LIBRARY – DAY.

HELENA

That's strange . . . I knew there was something familiar about this place.

Well, dream or not, we're definitely heading the right way.

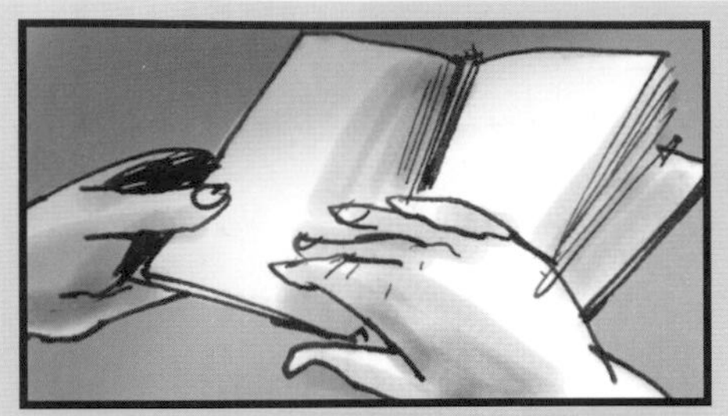

VALENTINE
Right. Well, this is where I stop.

HELENA
What?

VALENTINE points to the sign at the entrance to the park – "Giants Orbiting: Enter at your own risk."

HELENA (CONT'D)
Giants orbiting?

VALENTINE
Sounds a bit iffy, doesn't it? Good luck. I'll be here when you come back. If you come back.

He sits down and starts juggling with pebbles.

HELENA walks through the gate.

EXT. WHITE CITY. GIANTS-ORBITING PARK – DAY.

HELENA walks into the park. It's peaceful and beautiful, yet odd.

A GRYPHON steps out into her path. It is the size of a lion, and it is fulfilling its mythological imperatives.

GRYPHON
Halt! You shall not pass.

HELENA
I bet I shall.

GRYPHON
Riddle.

HELENA
Riddle?

GRYPHON
Answer my riddle, and only then you can pass. Fail, and I devour you, bones and all! What walks on four legs in the morning, two legs in the afternoon, and three legs in the evening?

HELENA
(thinks for a second, then says)
William. He's a performing dog.

GRYPHON
No. The answer is – Man!

HELENA
I think you'll find it's William, actually. I saw him.

He walked on four legs in the morning, on two legs during the afternoon show, and he was limping on three legs at night, because he hurt his paw. And he can skateboard. My go. What's green, hangs on the wall, and whistles?

GRYPHON
Um . . .

HELENA
Give in?

GRYPHON
No. Let me think about it.

HELENA
You have a good think. I'll be back in a bit.

She leaves the GRYPHON scratching its head and muttering to itself.

HELENA approaches an open square. There are seemingly random towers dotted around the square. Each has a spiral staircase around a central pillar. They are made of rough metal plate, except the odd step of section of column which is made of glass. There is a small convex mirror on the top of each tower, surrounded by an orrery of shapes and suns.
HELENA looks around, puzzled and amazed.

EXT. WHITE CITY. GIANTS-ORBITING PARK – DAY.

VALENTINE is leaning against a wall, juggling pebbles.

He looks up. Slowly drifting towards us, like an enormous jellyfish in the sky, we can see a black tendril.

VALENTINE
Oh no.

EXT. WHITE CITY. GIANTS-ORBITING PARK – DAY.

VALENTINE comes running in through the park entrance.

The GRYPHON steps out in front of it.

GRYPHON
You shall not pass!

VALENTINE
Right. Riddle. If you've got it you want to share it. If you share it you haven't got it?

GRYPHON
Um.

VALENTINE
Look, haven't got all day. Give in?

GRYPHON
(sighs, disappointed)
All right. What is it?

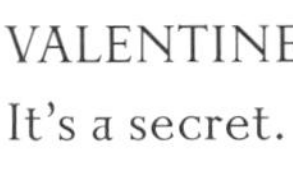

VALENTINE
It's a secret.

GRYPHON
Well, what is it?

VALENTINE
It's a secret!

GRYPHON
Please. Just tell me.

VALENTINE
Look. An idiot.

GRYPHON
Where?

EXT. WHITE CITY. GIANTS-ORBITING PARK – DAY.

HELENA
(to herself)
I hope I'm not expected to look in every one of these tower things, I'll be here all . . .

And as she says this she steps into a space at the dead centre of the square,

where all the glass gaps in the tower structures line up to form unbroken lines, making a perfectly drawn sun mask.

HELENA (CONT'D)
This must be the place.

We see a floating mass, like a lumpy statue, in the sky, drifting towards us.

HELENA walks toward the thing that looks like a floating statue. As she approaches it looms over her.
It is two figures balancing against each other, each the size of a spaceship: a male figure gravitationally attracted downward, the other female figure attracted upwards. So long as they push against one another, they hover perfectly in space, about twenty feet off the ground. They have small rocky round heads, huge arms and bodies, legs that are ground down to stumps through lack of use, yet they have an almost zenlike poise as they drift slowly around their territory, making tiny adjustments to the mirrors on top of the towers.

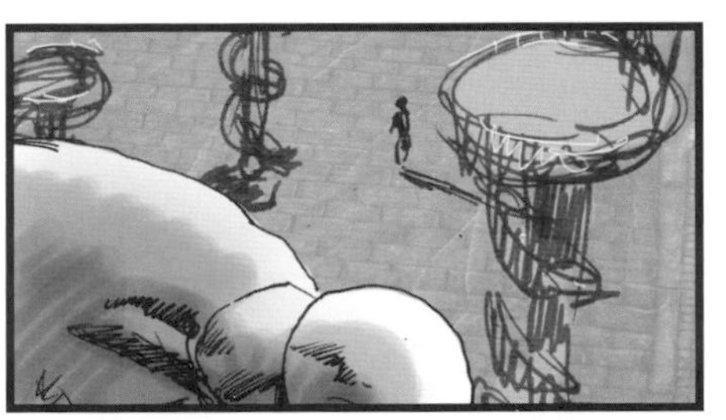

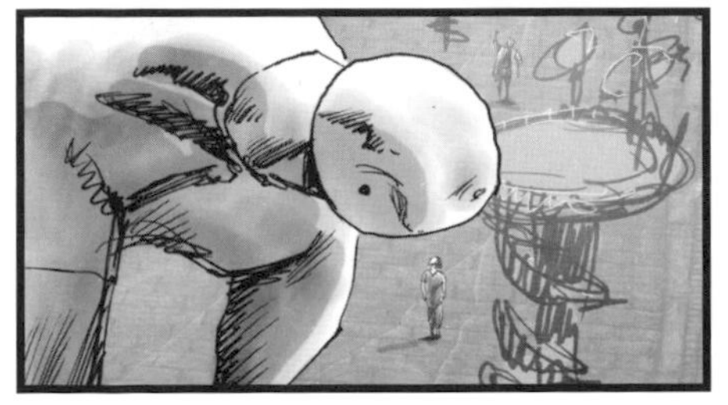

We hear running footsteps.

VALENTINE (O.S.)
Hey! Hold up! Big change of plans!

HELENA
You weren't coming. Remember?

He's out of breath . . .

HELENA (CONT'D)
I think those giants may be able to help us.

VALENTINE
Mm. Possibly. But there's no time for that now.

There's a shadow coming,
and it won't be a quick hullo-how's-your-father? job with those giants. They aren't succinct, like me.

Nope. You've got to come in low, share an observation about life or two, a bit of banter about erosion or grit, open them up a bit, and then you're in, the charges are laid, the fuse is lit, the conversational excavation under way . . .

HELENA
(already climbing one of the towers)
Hello, can you help us?

VALENTINE
. . . and I'm talking to myself again.

HELENA
We are looking for the charm, to wake the queen. Can you help us?

The giants seem to become aware of HELENA. They re-orient their orbit so they are revolving around her tower.

GIANT FEMALE
Many . . .

HELENA
many, yes . . .

GIANT FEMALE

. . . have . . . asked . . .

HELENA
Many have asked . . .

By this time VALENTINE is running up the tower. He's reached HELENA.

GIANT FEMALE
. . . where . . .

VALENTINE
Many have asked where the charm is, yes?

GIANT FEMALE
. . . the . . .

VALENTINE
. . . the charm is . . . ?

GIANT FEMALE
Charrrrrrrmmmm . . .

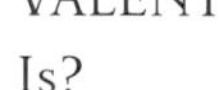

VALENTINE
Is?

GIANT FEMALE
Is.

VALENTINE
Helena. We have to get out of here.

HELENA
Not now. I think we're on to something.

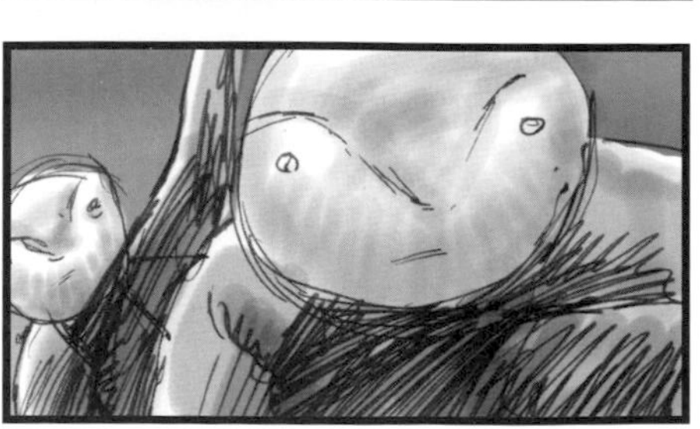

GIANT FEMALE
But . . . we . . .

VALENTINE
Know?

GIANT FEMALE
Sadly . . .

VALENTINE
No sadly, happily . . . I know where it is and I will tell you really quickly . . .

GIANT FEMALE
Solemnly . . .

VALENTINE
No adjectives please.
We don't have time. Can't you just blurt it out?

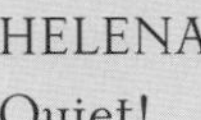

HELENA
Quiet!

GIANT FEMALE
We . . . guard . . . the . . .

VALENTINE
Charm?

GIANT FEMALE
Box.

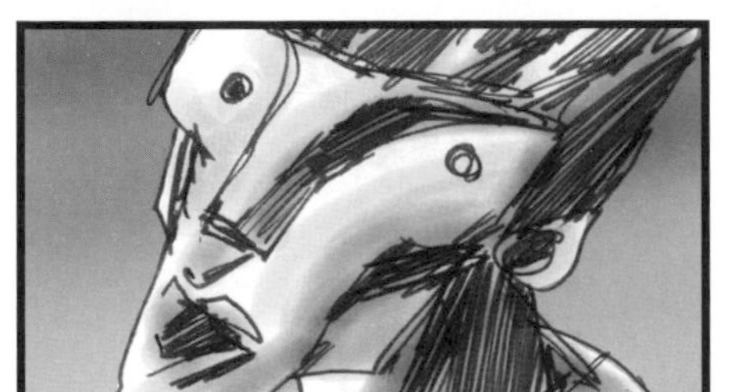

VALENTINE
What?

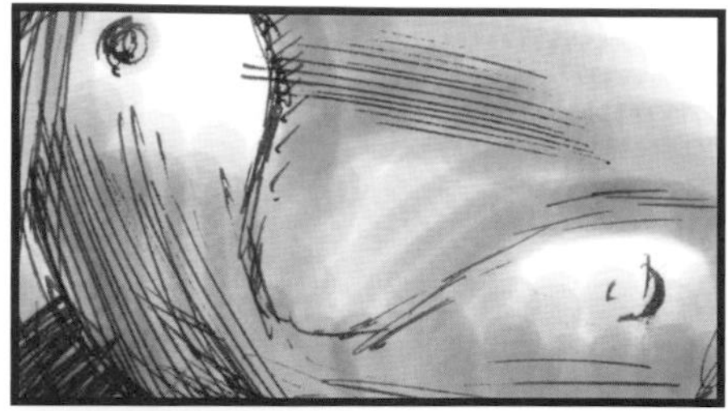

HELENA
Look, up there in her hand, a little silvery box.

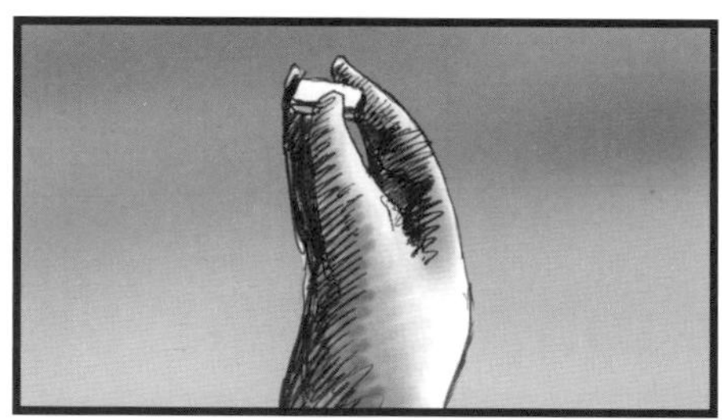

And the GIANT FEMALE does have a box in her hand. The dark tendrils have now drifted into the square.

GIANT MALE
Shadows come.

VALENTINE
That was what I was trying to tell you! If she doesn't get to the end of this sentence in the near future we are dead.

HELENA
Is the charm in your box?

GIANT FEMALE
For . . .

VALENTINE
Oh no, not for, just yes or no.

GIANT FEMALE
. . . the queen.

HELENA
"We guard the box for the queen." Listen! We're here for the queen. She's asleep forever unless we can find the charm for her! We don't even know what it is!

Shadow tendrils are wrapping around the GIANT MALE's stumpy leg.

He slowly reaches down, shifting his weight against the GIANT FEMALE, takes a black tendril delicately between huge fingers and snaps it off.

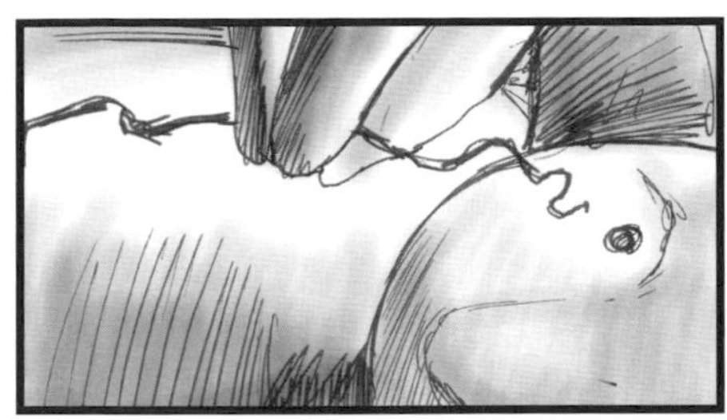

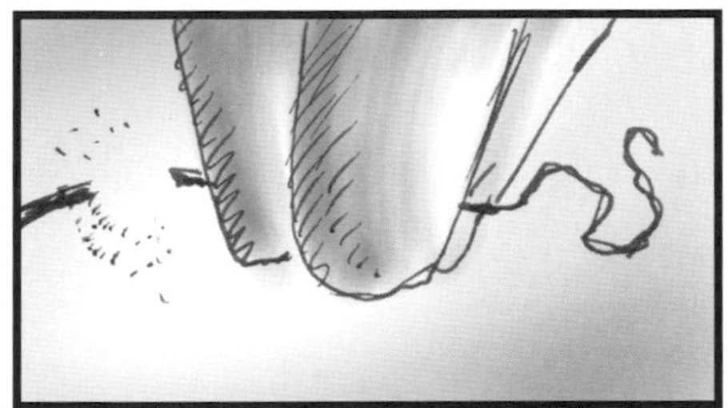

He drops the piece of shadow to the ground. It re-forms into a misshapen SPIDER that limps/scuttles away.

VALENTINE
(running on overdrive)
Come on, forget it, time's up, come on, run. It's polite conversation or death, polite conversation or death.

The shadows are continuing to wrap around the GIANT MALE. Too many for him to fight easily.

HELENA
Please! You must believe me!

GIANT MALE
Charm is . . . the Mirror . . . Mask . . .

GIANT FEMALE
(to him)
Yes?

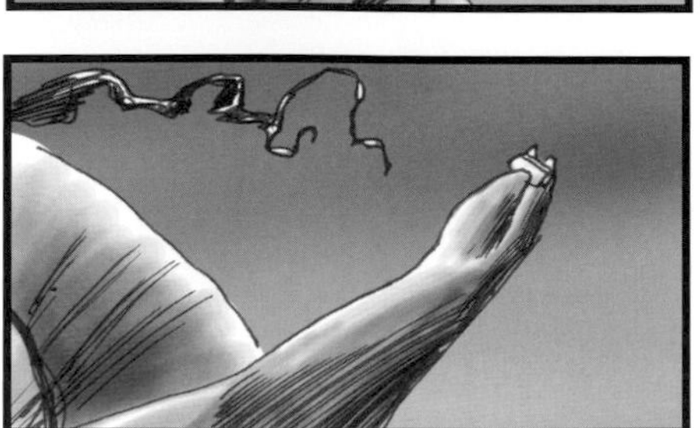

The male convulses with pain, the rocks grind, the shadow starts to carbonise the stone.

HELENA
Now!

VALENTINE is tugging on her clothes from below. Slowly the giants shift their weight, trying to keep the GIANT FEMALE and the box as far away from the shadows as possible.

HELENA reaches out her hand.
As the shadows engulf the body of the GIANT MALE, their point of balance becomes more and more tenuous; finally the GIANT FEMALE lowers the box to HELENA.

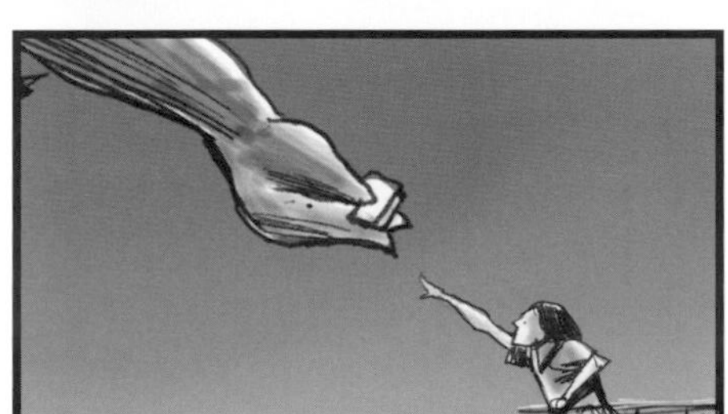

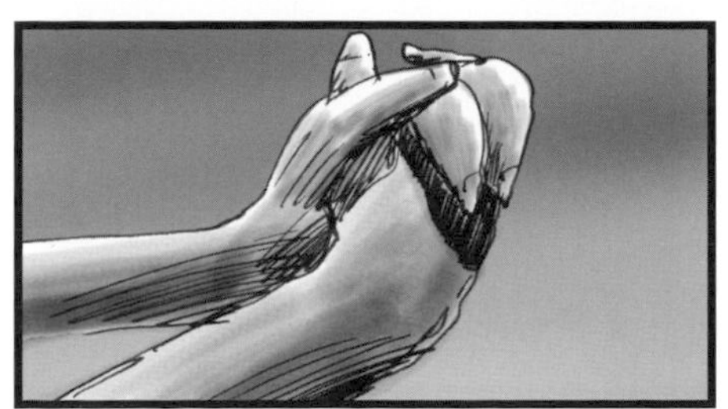

GIANT FEMALE
Get . . .

HELENA
The box?

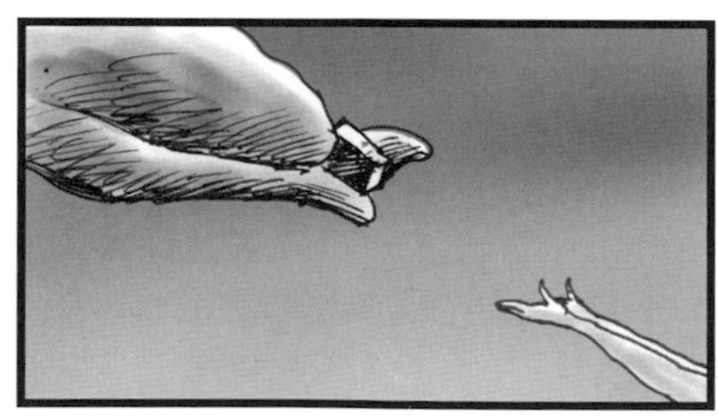

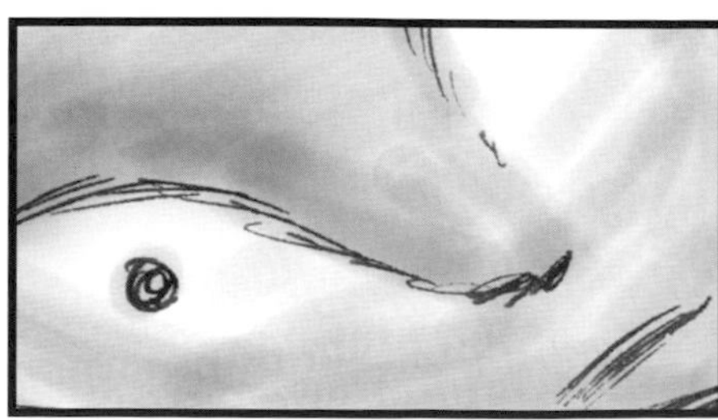

GIANT FEMALE
. . .higher.

As the box drops into HELENA's hands, the gravitational attraction between the two giants fails.

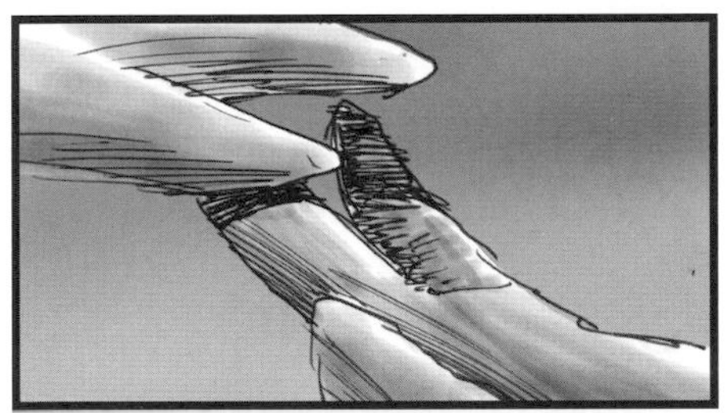

The GIANT FEMALE lurches into the air, and drifts into the sky –

The GIANT MALE, now three-quarters covered in shadow tendrils, crashes slowly to the ground, the stone merging into the pavement, the rock returning to its source, as if falling into water. An outstretched hand is the last piece to melt into the rocky floor.

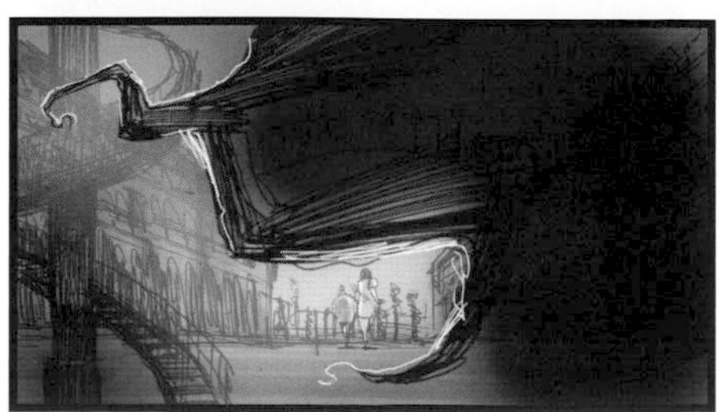

The shadows melt into the ground, and are gone.

HELENA
Poor things.

HELENA and VALENTINE run.

EXT. WHITE CITY. GIANTS-ORBITING PARK – DAY.

VALENTINE and HELENA are slowing up as they come towards the exit.

VALENTINE
Okay. Let's see the charm then.

HELENA
I don't think that's what it is. He said the charm was a MirrorMask.

She opens the silvery box to reveal . . .

VALENTINE
(disappointed)
Oh.

It's an ornate key.

As HELENA takes the key out of the box, the box folds into itself and vanishes.

HELENA
A key. It's a start.

VALENTINE
Absolutely. We just have to try the key in every single lock we pass, and when we find the one that key opens, we'll know that ten thousand bloody years have gone by.

HELENA
Come on. Think positive. Think of treasure and all that stuff you like.

Something shoves HELENA out of frame.

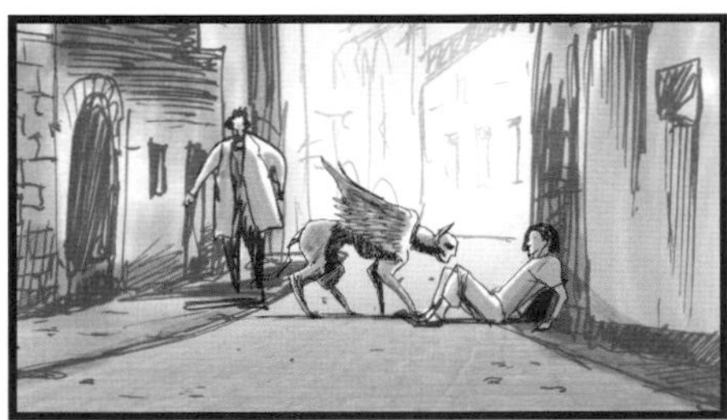

The big GRYPHON they passed on the way in bounds over. It pushes HELENA over so she's pressed up against a wall and says:

GRYPHON
You shall not pass. Unless you tell me, um, the answer to the riddle you asked me before.

HELENA
Riddle?

GRYPHON
What's green, hangs on a wall and whistles, remember?

HELENA
Oh. Right. Yes, that one. So you give up?

GRYPHON
Kind of. Not really. I mean, I'm sure I'll know it when you say what it is.

HELENA
Okay. It's a herring.

GRYPHON
But a herring isn't green!

HELENA
You can paint it green.

GRYPHON
But a herring doesn't hang on a wall!

HELENA
You can nail it to a wall.

GRYPHON
But a herring doesn't whistle!

HELENA
Oh, come on. I just put that in to stop it from being too obvious.

The GRYPHON looks miserable.

VALENTINE
And the answer to my one is still "a secret".

And they pass on.

EXT. WHITE CITY. MASK HOUSE – DAY.

HELENA and VALENTINE are now on the edge of the city. Everything is completely decayed.

HELENA
So. We've got a key. Just nothing to put it in. Get higher. What did she mean by that? Think.

VALENTINE
Just the interminable ravings of an unsound and enormous mind, I expect. Very big. Not very bright.

HELENA
MirrorMask. What kind of a thing is a MirrorMask?

VALENTINE
Well. It's a. It's an. It's the. I've got it!

HELENA
Tell me.

VALENTINE
Yes. We should ask an expert.

HELENA
Like who?

VALENTINE
Like whoever owns that place.

They are passing a huge old manor, with a sign over the door saying "Mask Shop".

INT. WHITE CITY. MASK SHOP – DAY.

HELENA pushes the door open.

The bell over the door rings. It's a grimy mask shop, hung with cobwebs and old – very old – masks.

A little sphinx, the size of a largish cat, yawns on the dusty counter.

HELENA leans over to look at the masks.

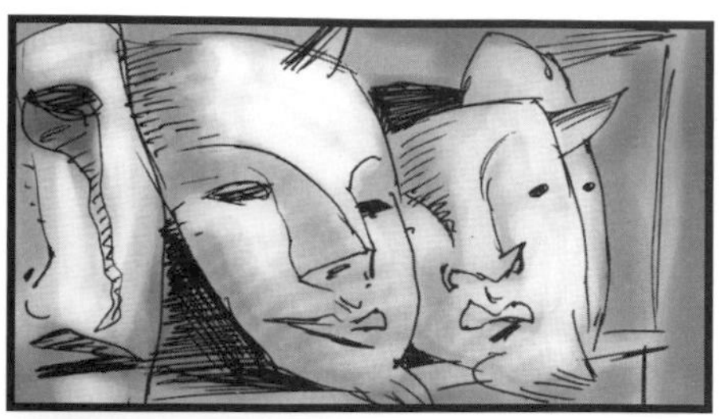

They make faces at her.

A nervous old lady, MRS BAGWELL, comes out.

MRS BAGWELL
Can I help you, dear?

HELENA
I saw the sign. We're looking for a mask. We wondered if you could help us.

MRS BAGWELL
Well, come in dears, both of you. I was just about to have tea. Do you like cakes? Oh, you young people, it's all tea and muffins and excitement in your world, I expect.

She pats the sphinx as she passes.

VALENTINE reaches out to stroke it, but it gapes open a vicious mouth at him, and he doesn't.

INT. WHITE CITY. MASK SHOP – DAY.

MRS BAGWELL is very vague – dressed in once rather nice clothes that have grown extremely tattered over the years, with a layer of grime on her clothes and skin.

The house has completely been taken over by feral cat-sized sphinxes.

MRS BAGWELL
Well, just sit anywhere and I'll go and get the tea.

They look around for somewhere to sit. The chairs are mostly firewood.

HELENA makes for one chair that's still standing, and a little sphinx walking past sharpens its claws on it. The arm of the chair collapses. VALENTINE's chair has a sleeping sphinx in it.

He picks up the poker from the fireplace and reaches it towards the sphinx to wake it.

It opens one eye, yawns, and bites the end off the metal poker with its sharp teeth.

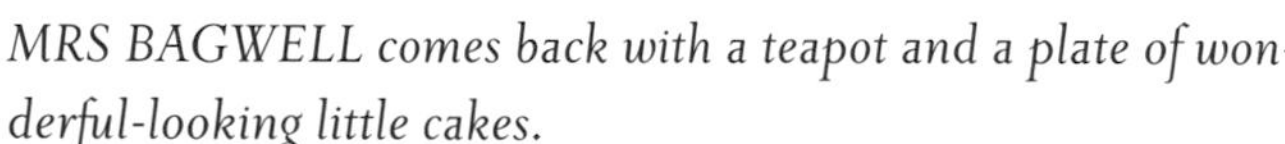

MRS BAGWELL comes back with a teapot and a plate of wonderful-looking little cakes.

MRS BAGWELL (CONT'D)
Oh, is Ginger sitting on the chair again? Just push him off, the daft ha'p'orth.

VALENTINE
It's fine, I'll stand.

MRS BAGWELL
Tch. Oh, Ginger won't bite, he's just a big old silly.

She smacks the sphinx sharply on its rump.

It gives her a filthy look and slowly climbs down.

HELENA
How many do you have?

MRS BAGWELL
I don't really have them, dear. I could have sworn that when I first started feeding them there were only two or three.

There must be thirty of them right now. Let's see . . . Snowdrop, Stripes, Fluffy, you've met Ginger, there's Spot, Whiskers, Blackie . . .

They are all identical.

HELENA reaches for the cup of tea,

but MRS BAGWELL strikes her hand sharply.

MRS BAGWELL (CONT'D)
I don't think so. What do we do before we eat? We wash our hands, young lady. Hygiene, hygiene, hygiene.

**INT. WHITE CITY. MASK SHOP.
BATHROOM – DAY.**

HELENA walks into the bathroom, a little nervously. Like every other room in the house, this is trashed. A sphinx in the bath gets up and stretches like a cat, then pads away.

HELENA turns the faucet. A thin trickle of cold water, no soap, and she rubs her hands together then looks to her left.

Next to the sink is a window.

And through the window she can see her bedroom.

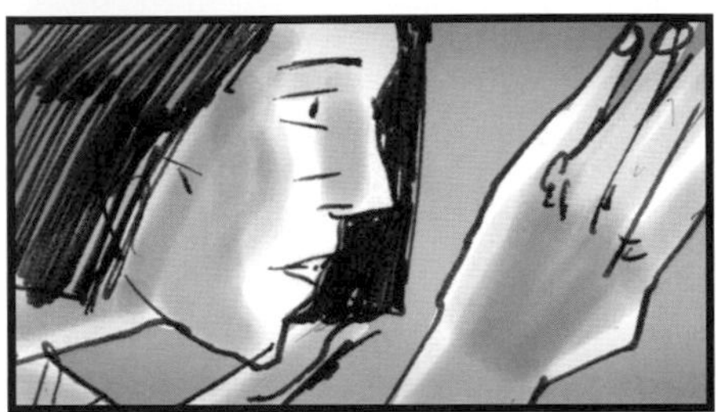

INT. TOWER BLOCK. AUNT NAN'S FLAT.
HELENA'S BEDROOM – DAY.

The door is pushed open suddenly and HELENA storms in. She looks a little different – she's wearing obvious make-up, and her clothes are new. Louder. Older.

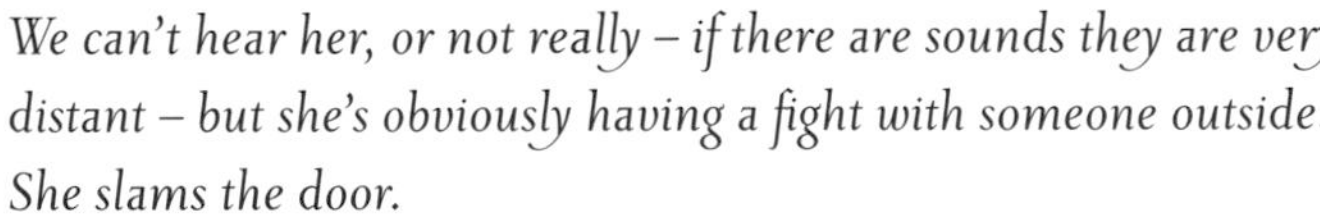

We can't hear her, or not really – if there are sounds they are very distant – but she's obviously having a fight with someone outside.
She slams the door.
Then she runs her hands through her hair and looks furious.
This isn't HELENA. Not even faintly, although it's played by the same actress. We'll call her ANTI-HELENA.
Now the father, MORRIS, follows her in, and is shouting at her.
She's giving as good as she gets.

Then she looks up and glances directly at us. We're not sure if she sees us or not.

**INT. WHITE CITY. MASK SHOP.
BATHROOM – DAY.**

And we're back in the bathroom. HELENA looks disturbed by what she's seen.

A sphinx in the toilet bowl smiles at her.

INT. WHITE CITY. MASK SHOP – DAY.

A passing sphinx sharpens its claws on a velvet curtain, shredding it further.
HELENA comes back, a bit shaken, to see VALENTINE take the last little cake.

MRS BAGWELL
. . .the kittens do the funniest things. My husband, the late Mr Bagwell, thought they were a nuisance. He called them moggies. They loved him, though. They were so upset after he disappeared that they wouldn't touch their food for a week.
More cake, dear?

HELENA
I haven't had any yet.

MRS BAGWELL
You must force yourself. Now, what can I do for you, dears?

HELENA
There's something we're looking for, and we think it's a MirrorMask.

MRS BAGWELL
That's nice, dear.

MRS BAGWELL
Well . . . Fluffy, don't do that!

Let me see. . . There was a girl about your age over here, not long ago. She was asking about it. I'll tell you what I told her. Now let me see. . .

He used to talk about it, of course. Mr Bagwell used to say the MirrorMask concentrated your desires.

Your wishes.

It would give you what you needed. I remember I said to him, "Mr Bagwell, how can a mask know what you need?" And he said, "Cynthia, remember, I don't know what I'm talking about."

VALENTINE
Excuse me. I just wondered if there were any more of those amazing cakes?

MRS BAGWELL

I'll go and see, dear.

She gets up and totters out. HELENA looks at VALENTINE angrily.

HELENA
Why did you have to interrupt her?

VALENTINE
Because she's barking mad.

HELENA takes her really useful book out. Every sphinx in the room looks up expectantly and stares at her.

HELENA
(disappointed)
Oh.

VALENTINE
What does it say?

HELENA
"Don't let them see you're afraid."

VALENTINE
Don't let who see – ?

A sphinx blinks at them. It shows its sharp, sharp teeth.

MRS BAGWELL
Are you sure you don't want to stay, dear? I can freshen up the spare bedroom, throw Sooty and her kittens out, and your jester can sleep in the attic.

VALENTINE
I'm not a jester. I'm a very important man. I've got a tower.

MRS BAGWELL
Have you, dear? That's nice.

HELENA
I don't think we have any time, I'm afraid. But thank you.

MRS BAGWELL
Well, here are cakes for the road, dear. You never know when you'll need them.

She hands over a big paper bag of small cakes.

MRS BAGWELL (CONT'D)
And, dear? Don't let them see you're afraid.

EXT. WHITE CITY. ROAD FROM MASK SHOP – DAY.

A black SPIDER crawls up a lamp post. It carries a piece of paper. It uses one leg to jab the paper to the post.

It's a wanted poster with a picture of HELENA in a pretty dress on it. "Reward paid," it says, "All the jewels you can carry. Enquire: the Dark Palace."

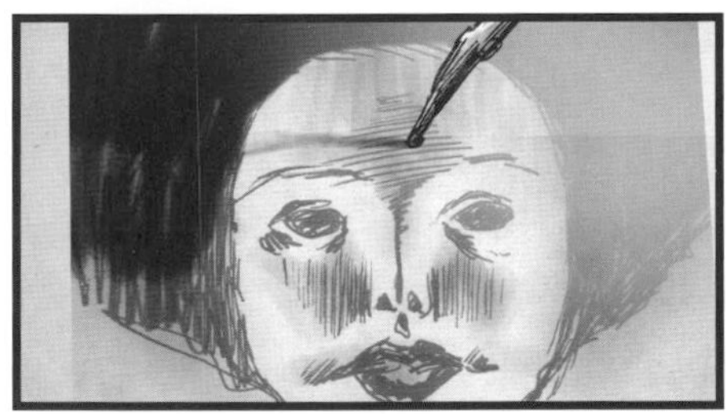

HELENA and VALENTINE are walking towards us down a winding cobbled alley.

Derelict buildings on either side of them. A pantherlike shadow slips along the edge of the road as they walk, keeping pace with them. HELENA is finally eating a cake.

HELENA
Why do you keep saying you've got a tower?

VALENTINE
Because I have.

HELENA
Well, where is it?

VALENTINE
Well . . .

HELENA
Do you live in it?

VALENTINE
Well . . .

HELENA
Is it a big tower?

VALENTINE
Huge. Enormous. Hundreds of rooms. Stairs. Doorknobs. A scullery. . . possibly more than one scullery, actually.

HELENA
And I can't see it because . . . ?

VALENTINE
(says "we're not talking" inaudibly)

HELENA
What?

VALENTINE
We aren't talking. The tower and I had a . . . minor disagreement. And it left without me. I said something stupid and it flew off without me.

HELENA
Why don't you find it, and say you're sorry?

VALENTINE
I wouldn't give it the satisfaction. Heap of rubble. Anyway, I don't know where it is. Up there somewhere. Anyway. Valentines Never Apologise. Stupid building.

HELENA
Buildings never leave without you where I come from.

She stops, pulls down a wanted poster.

HELENA (CONT'D)
Valentine! Look at this! It's . . . she looks like me. But I've never worn that dress . . .

VALENTINE
Helena?

HELENA
What?

VALENTINE
Look.

There's a noise behind them.

It's a sphinx – GINGER – from the house. Just one, cat-sized sphinx. It's stepped out into the road in front of them.

They look back down the road the way they have come. Now three more sphinxes are padding towards them, eyes bright.

One of the sphinxes bares its very, very sharp teeth. GINGER, who is sitting in the front of the rest of the sphinxes, looks up at us. It says, in a feline voice:

GINGER
Hungry.

HELENA
Is this a riddle thing?

GINGER
(shaking its head solemnly)
Hungry.

HELENA throws it the rest of her cake. It swallows it without chewing, and says:

GINGER (CONT'D)
Still hungry.

VALENTINE
(to Helena)
I've got a plan. Leave this completely to me.

VALENTINE (CONT'D)
(his voice cracks in terror)
Er. Hullo, puss. I'm out of riddles. But how about a knock-knock joke? I know the best one in the world.

The sphinxes look at each other, then, uncertainly, GINGER says:

GINGER
The best?

VALENTINE
Absolutely. You start.

GINGER
Knock knock.

VALENTINE
Who's there?
(whispers to Helena)
Keep walking.

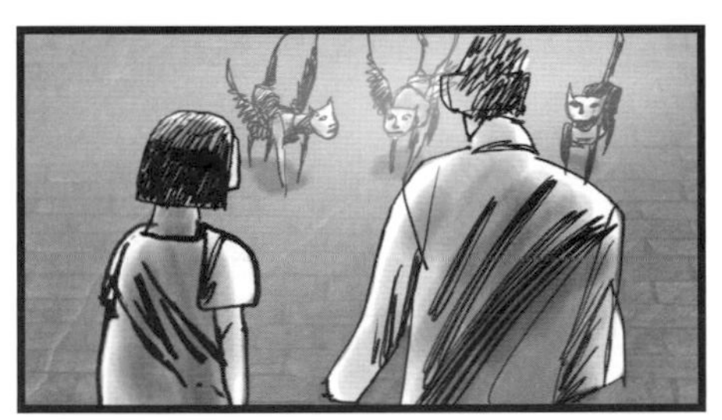

GINGER tries to work out who's there.

VALENTINE grabs HELENA's arm and begins to walk. There's a long, long pause. GINGER looks around desperately. The rest of the sphinxes stare, puzzled, at GINGER.
VALENTINE and HELENA think they may be able to get away. Then they look ahead of them to see all the rest of the sphinxes – twenty or thirty of them – have stepped out, barring the way. There's no way ahead.

They are surrounded by sphinxes who growl and bare their teeth.

HELENA
What do we do now?

VALENTINE
That was as far as my plan went.

HELENA
Right.

She takes out the really useful book. All the sphinxes are immediately at attention.

HELENA (CONT'D)
(upset)
Oh.

VALENTINE
What does it say?

HELENA
"My pages taste excellent, but are stickier than toffee and very difficult to chew."

VALENTINE
What an appalling book. That's the most useless thing it's told us so far.

HELENA
No. It's a very brave thing to say.

And HELENA rips a page out of the book, crumples it, and throws it down to the sphinxes. Several of them leap for it, one gets it and starts chewing.
HELENA throws more pages. As soon as they begin to chew, the sphinxes' jaws are stuck – the pages are like thick, gluey toffee.

She throws down the rest of the pages, leaving only one page remaining in the book, between the covers. The sphinxes chew enthusiastically . . .

And HELENA and VALENTINE run for it.
A black SPIDER sits on top of a post, looking down at them. We crash into its black eyes, and see in them . . .

EXT. DARK TOWER – NIGHT (ALL CGI).

The wind whistles about the dark tower.

INT. DARK PALACE. THRONE ROOM – NIGHT.

The DARK QUEEN in her throne room. We see a portrait of her – the queen – on one wall. On the opposite wall is a portrait that looks like HELENA in a posh frock.

When the queen opens her eyes, they are jet black.

Then she opens her mouth.

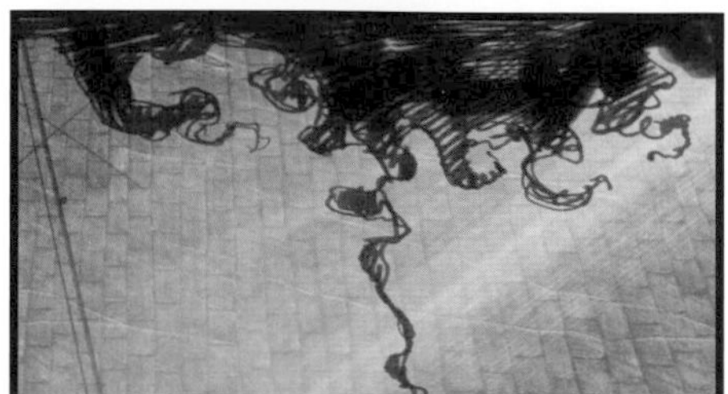

Shadow tendrils come out, first a few, like smoke, then as if a giant octopus is somehow flowing out from her mouth.

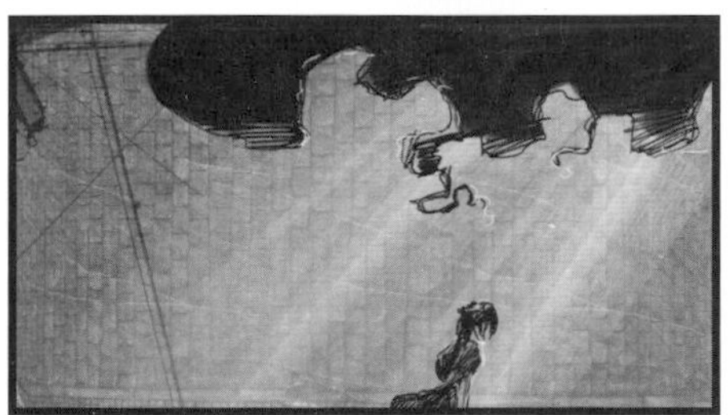

The darkness hangs in the air, as if awaiting a command.

DARK QUEEN
This nonsense has gone on quite long enough. She needs to grow up, and come home.

(beat)

Well, what are you waiting for? Go and get her!

EXT. WHITE CITY. STREET NEAR CATHEDRAL – DAY.

The sphinxes have gone. Out of breath, HELENA and VALENTINE stop running.

HELENA
If I tell you something weird, will you think I'm crazy?

VALENTINE
Yes. I expect so.

HELENA
Because when I look through windows – not all of them – I see somebody who isn't me.

VALENTINE
How odd. I do the same thing: Me. Window. Look through it. Not me. The ones I see me in are called "mirrors".

HELENA
No. I mean, she looks like me. But she's not me. She was fighting with Dad.

HELENA and VALENTINE have reached the bottom of a rubbly set of steps that curl around the base of an enormous cathedral.

Almost skeletal now, it has been eaten away by successive encroachments of shadows. The main pillars and crossbeams are still intact, but many of the walls have collapsed. The tower reaches into the clouds, weather-worn edges, gnarled gargoyles. The whole edifice is supported by a single spiralling stone staircase. It couldn't possibly balance, but yet it still stands.

HELENA (CONT'D)
"Get . . . higher."

VALENTINE
What?

HELENA
The giant statue said "get higher". Do you see anything higher than that place?

VALENTINE
Long way up.

HELENA
And look –

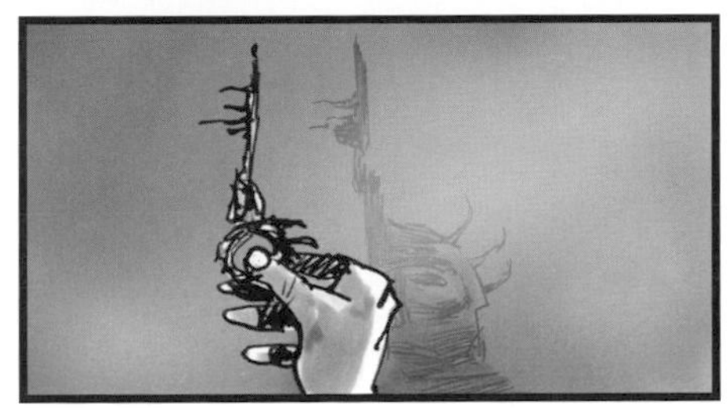

She holds up the key. The key and the building look astonishingly similar.

They start to climb. Giant rubble heads from fallen gargoyles have to be avoided. There are cracks and boulders everywhere. Two tiny figures dwarfed by the scale of everything.

They reach the top of the stairs, and head into the main hall.

INT. WHITE CITY. CATHEDRAL – DAY.

VALENTINE
There's nothing here.

This place is just waiting to collapse into rubble.

And it can't be safe.

HELENA
You are such a coward. It's perfectly –

She tumbles through the rotted floor, a cloud of dust behind her.

INT. WHITE CITY. CATHEDRAL BASEMENT – DAY.

From far above, VALENTINE's voice calls:

VALENTINE
Coward, eh? I prefer to think of myself as prudent. Cautious. And, unlike some people I could name, still up here.

He looks down at us.

HELENA opens her eyes. We pull back to reveal a dark cellar room.

One side is completely eaten away revealing the sky and cityscape.

HELENA sits up and we see that she is surrounded by a perfect circle of monkeybird creatures. They crouch on their knuckles, long pointy beaks wavering slightly, little black eyes fixed on her.

HELENA
Hello?

VALENTINE
Hey! I'm not coming down there after you, you know. It's not safe.

HELENA
No I'm not hurt, thanks for asking.

All the monkeybirds look up towards VALENTINE in one synchronised movement.
HELENA stands; twenty beaks stay pointed at her.

HELENA (CONT'D)
Hello?

All the monkeybirds make a chirruping "tick" sound that rapidly runs, bird by bird around the circle, until it reaches MALCOLM, the monkeybird odd-man-out. He tries to remember the only word of English he knows and says:

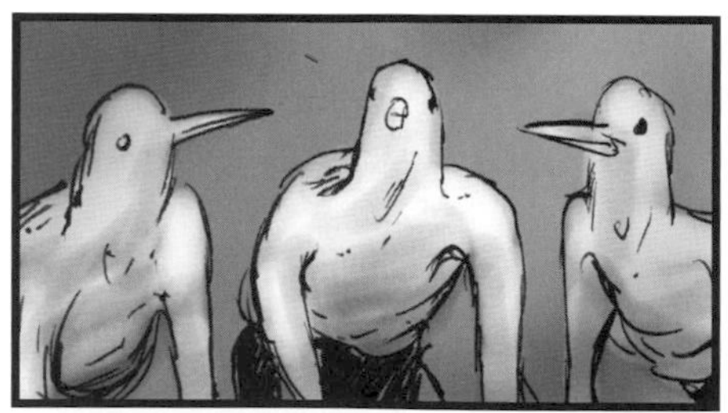

MALCOLM
Nicely.

And all the other birds stare at him.

HELENA
Umm . . . my name is Helena.

MONKEYBIRDS
Bob, Bob, Bob, Bob, Bob, Bob, Bob, Bob, Bob, Bob –

MALCOLM
Malcolm.

MONKEYBIRDS
Bob, Bob, Bob.

They all stare at MALCOLM. The MONKEYBIRD next to him gives him an offended thump on the back of the head.

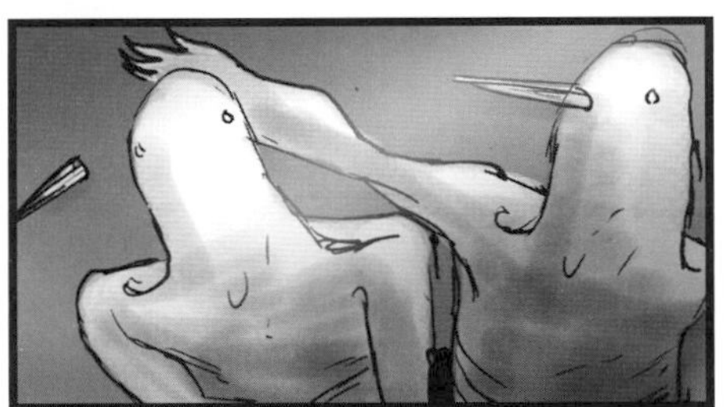

MALCOLM's beak falls off. He sheepishly reaches down and re-affixes the beak to his face.

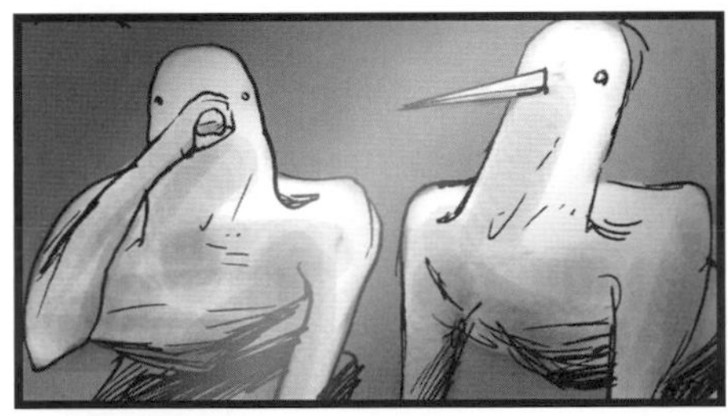

HELENA
Well, nice to meet you, Bob, all the Bobs. Malcolm. Bobs. I'm, ahmm . . . I'm looking for something. The charm. Something like a mask, no?

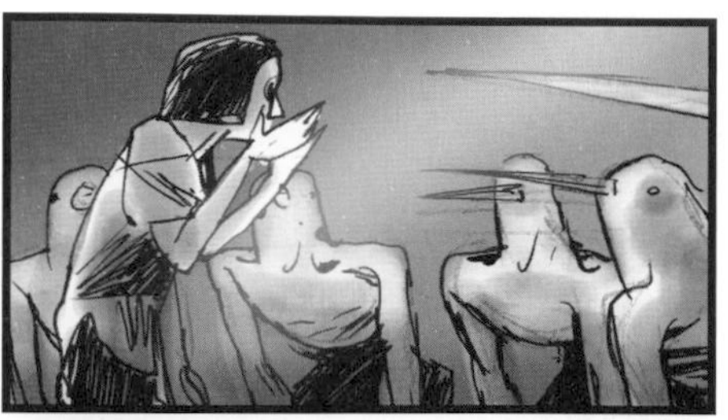

HELENA
Like a face? Yes? Face?

VALENTINE
Are you having a party down there or something?

HELENA
Valentine, you should come down. I've made some friends.

MALCOLM
Nicely.

Again all the monkeybirds look disapprovingly at Malcolm for breaking ranks.

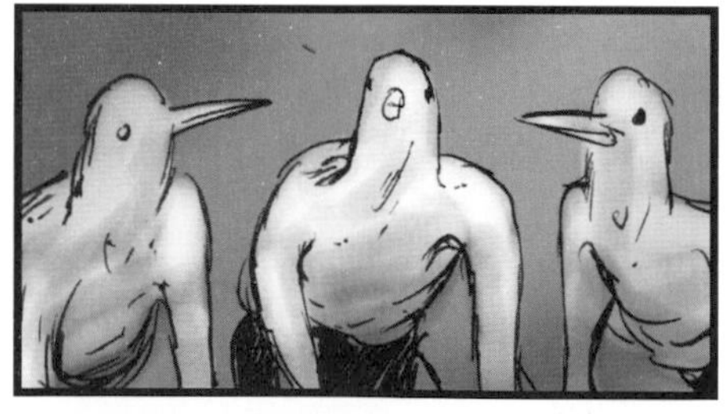

He dodges another sideswipe from a neighbour, but bumps into his neighbour on the other side, whose beak falls off.

That monkeybird bumps another neighbour . . . four or five of the monkeybirds lose their beaks. They all have to re-attach them, and look, disgruntled, at MALCOLM.

HELENA
It's a MirrorMask. I've got a key already.

All the monkeybirds seem both excited and concerned about this news.

MALCOLM
Mask?

HELENA
Yes, is it here?

One of the monkeybirds looks up, catches sight of something, nudges its neighbour.

MONKEYBIRD
Blak.

MONKEYBIRDS
Blak-blak-blak-blak –

MALCOLM hangs on to his beak with both hands and looks around at the others nervously. HELENA looks at him hopefully, since he's the only one that seems to make sense.

Then they look up: black shapes, like crows, are visible, high above us.

MALCOLM
Uh-oh. Regrettable.

Without warning a black flying shape zooms directly at MALCOLM's neighbour and splashes in his face. His beak goes flying, leaving a roughly round head with a dried black splat forming a mask. The splattered monkeybird staggers. It's under the DARK QUEEN's control.

All hell breaks loose:

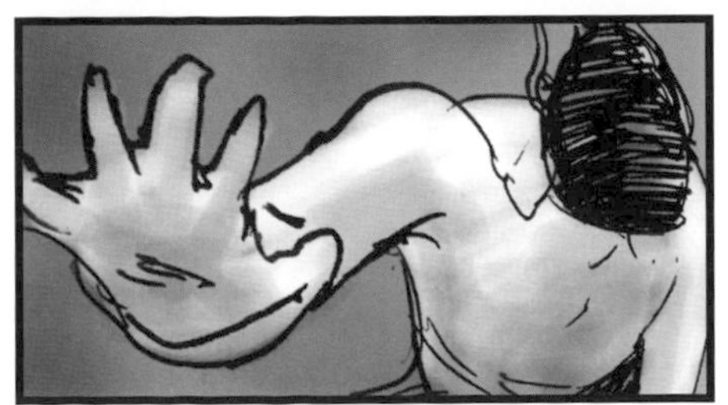

The splattered monkeybird grabs HELENA by her shoulders in his back claws as he leaps into the air.

Then many more black shapes, flapping like birds, splash into the faces of a few of the monkeybirds.

The monkeybirds try to dodge the shadow birds. When the shadows miss they splash on the floor or the walls, hardening instantly and then re-forming as SPIDER shapes and scuttling off.

The first black monkeybird has jumped out of the cellar and is swinging up from strut to strut towards the stairs still carrying a terrified HELENA.

We can now see that the stairs are swamped with shadow tendrils, some of which break off and immediately start flapping as more and more shadow birds are created.

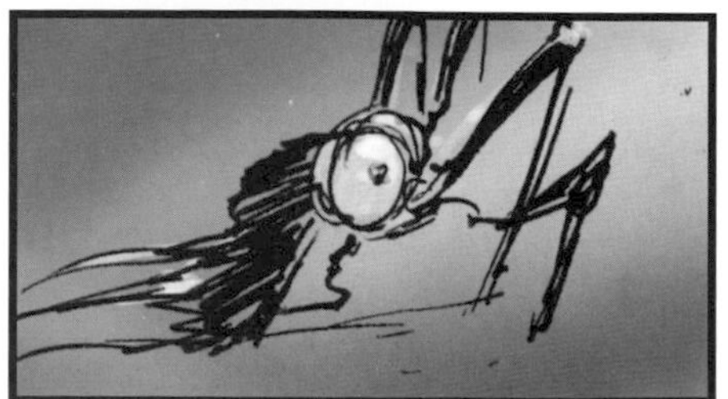

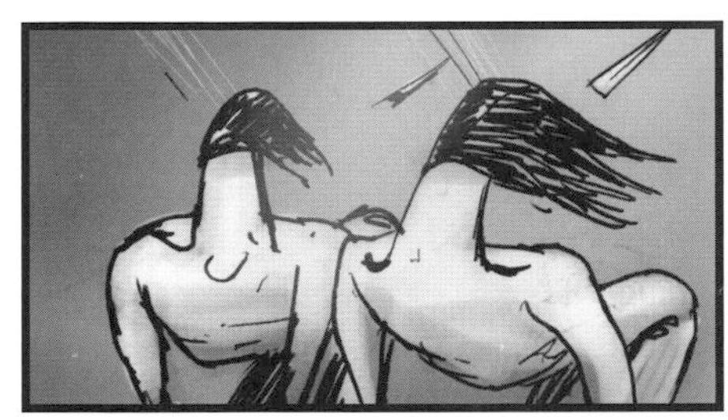

A chase ensues, black-masked monkeybirds chasing the others, some of the others fighting back with smacks to the head as they pass.

They swing from rafters and girders like monkeys but then reach into the air where membrane skin billows out between their arms allowing them to glide for great distances before needing another swing.

VALENTINE makes himself useful by hiding under a rock.

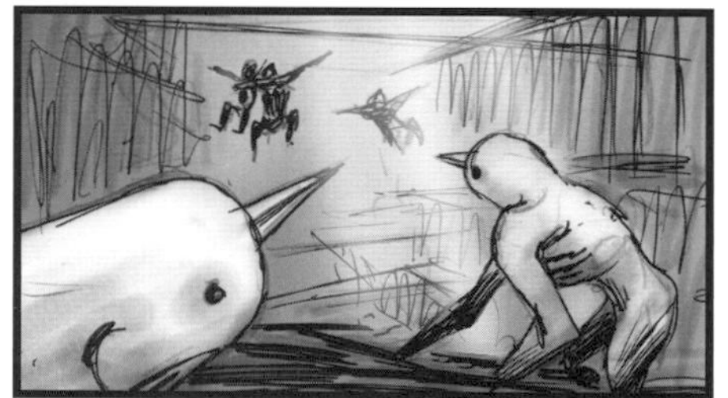

Two of the good monkeybirds – one of whom is MALCOLM – chase after HELENA.

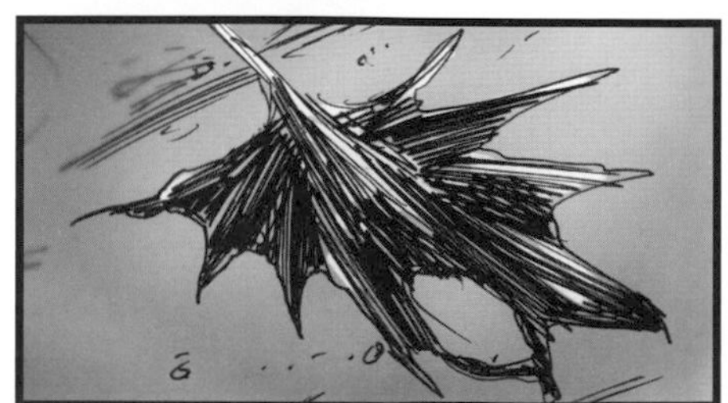

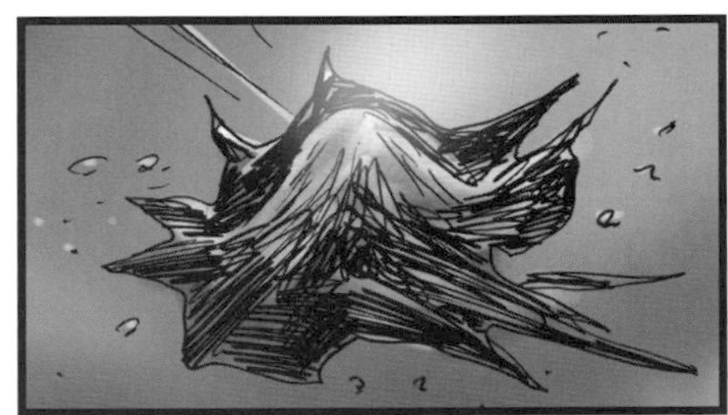

They hit the masked monkeybird from both sides and catch HELENA as she falls.

The good monkeybirds pull the black masks from the black monkeybirds as they catch them – the black shadows tumble away.

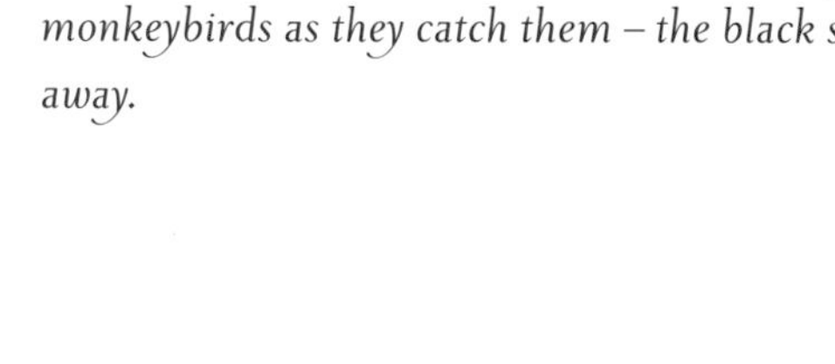

The chase continues up the tower.

The last of the shadow things chase after HELENA, up through the rafters of the tower, shadow birds following her and her two monkeybirds escorts to the roof and the spire.

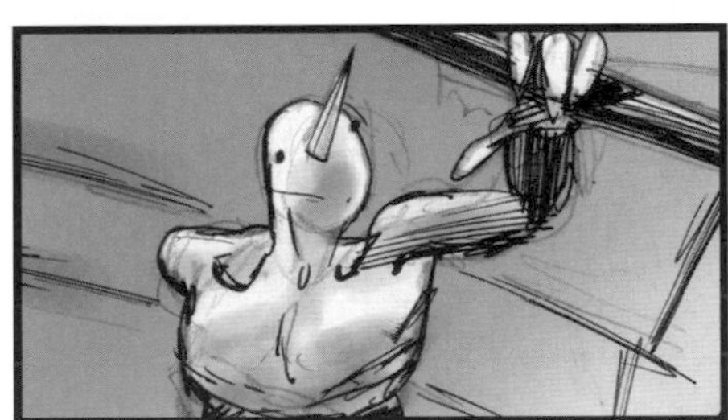

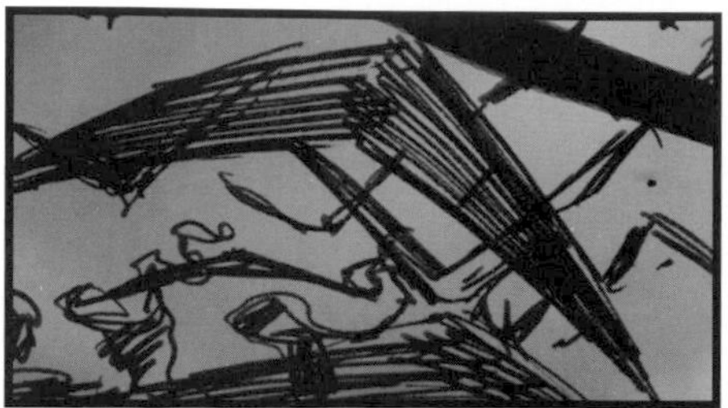

VALENTINE
I can go.

I know I'm not supposed to be here. I can go.

The monkeybird swoops down and picks VALENTINE up.

Nooooo!

HELENA
Get higher!

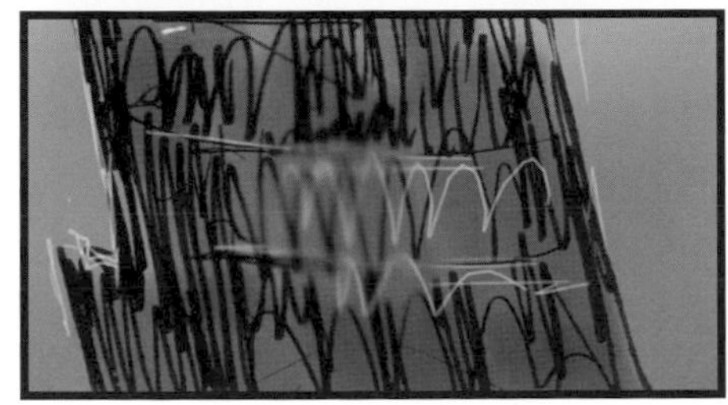

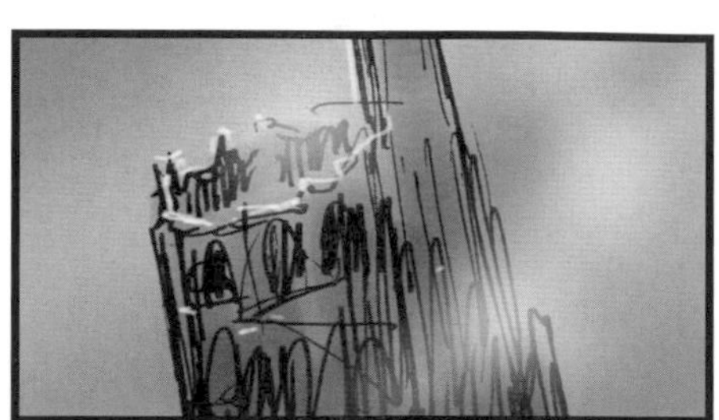

The monkeybirds swing around the spire and sling themselves into the air, leaving stranded tentacles behind them.
The black birds frizzle and vanish in the full burning sunlight.

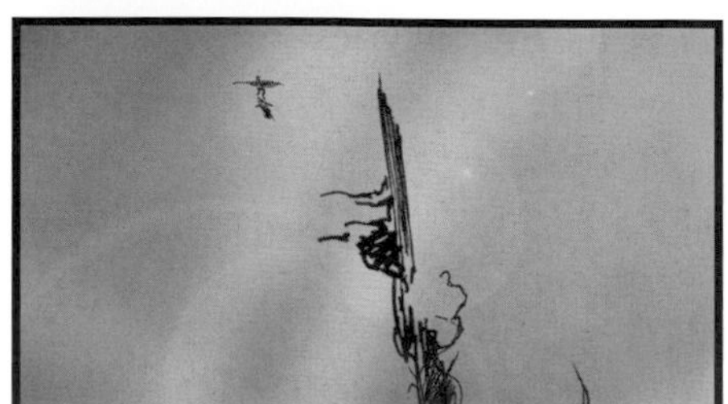

HELENA starts to laugh as they fly. She looks around as they glide away from the cathedral.

She can see the whole city. This is higher than she's ever been. In the distance we can see the shadow lands, leaking tendrils of darkness into the light city.

As she looks down, she can see the shape of everything – and she can see that there is a border between light and darkness. And she can see that the shapes of rivers, of walls, of buildings, mean that, at the border, we get, on the light side, A SUN-FACE, and on the dark side, A CRESCENT MOON-FACE, which meet, forming one face, with the border line down the middle.

And between the two eyes, something catches the light and burns like a diamond.

HELENA (CONT'D)
Did you see that?

A few more monkeybirds have escaped; two of them carry VALENTINE upside down by the ankles.
They glide over the city.

HELENA (CONT'D)
Can we go over there, please? Toward the border.

The monkeybirds seem scared by this idea.
They drift down to the ground, well on the way towards the dome.

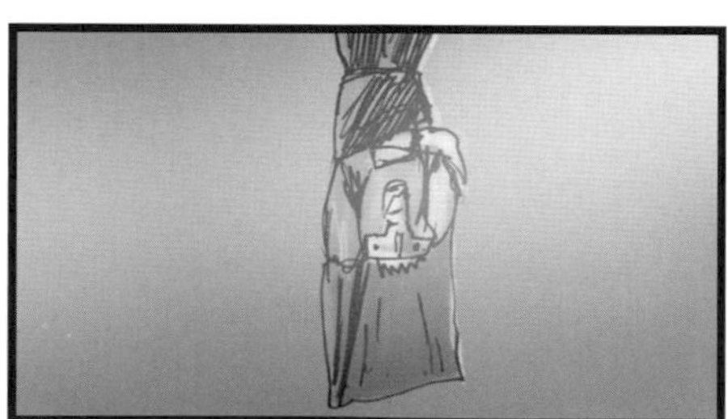

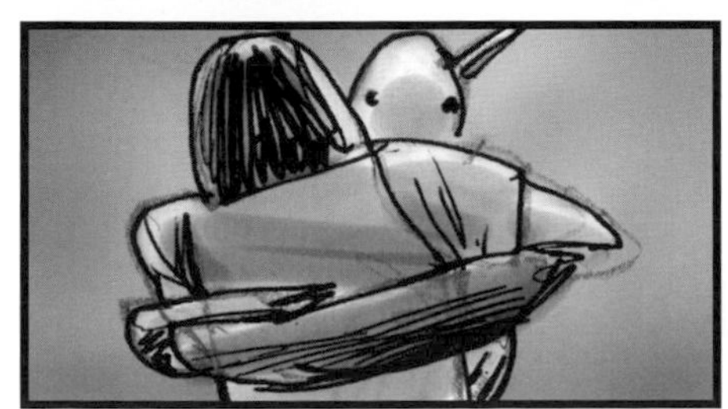

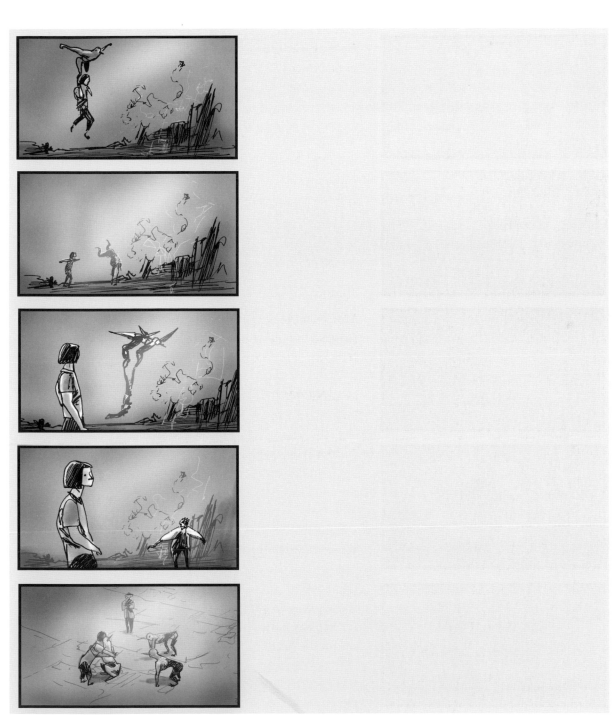

She hugs MALCOLM.

HELENA (CONT'D)
Thank you. Bobs. Malcolm.

His beak falls off and, embarrassed, he puts it on.

MALCOLM
(wistfully)
Nicely.

VALENTINE
What are we doing here?

HELENA
We're going to get the MirrorMask. I know where it is. It's halfway between the night lands and the day lands. It's on the border.

VALENTINE
Oh.

HELENA
I saw it. I know I did.

VALENTINE
Ah.

HELENA
I knew it. I knew I could do something to help. I hate feeling so helpless.

Then she turns, excited, and points –

HELENA (CONT'D)
Valentine! Look!

It's a window, on the side of a ruined building.

VALENTINE
We call them windows. They aren't unusual.

But HELENA has approached it and is looking through –

INT. TOWER BLOCK. AUNT NAN'S FLAT. HELENA'S BEDROOM – DAY.

WINDOW: To her bedroom at home.
The ANTI-HELENA (made up, looking older than HELENA) is sitting on the bed. She looks up, sullenly: a TEENAGE BOY, who looks faintly thuggish, comes across the room. He sits down on the bed next to her. He's eating chips from a newspaper. He gives the ANTI-HELENA a chip, and she eats it.

Then, without putting down the chips, he pulls the ANTI-HELENA over and starts to kiss her.

HELENA
Stop that! Don't do that! He's horrible. You're horrible!

HELENA starts to bang on the window.

VALENTINE
Hey. Hey, calm down. There's nothing there.

And from his POV we can see there's nothing through the window.

EXT. WHITE CITY. STREETS – DAY.

One of the wanted posters with the face of HELENA in the black posh frock. It gets pulled off the wall and scrunched up.

Pull back to see that HELENA herself pulled it from the wall.

She rips it in half and drops it.
The fragments blow away. She and VALENTINE keep walking.

A SPIDER watches them go and scuttles after them.

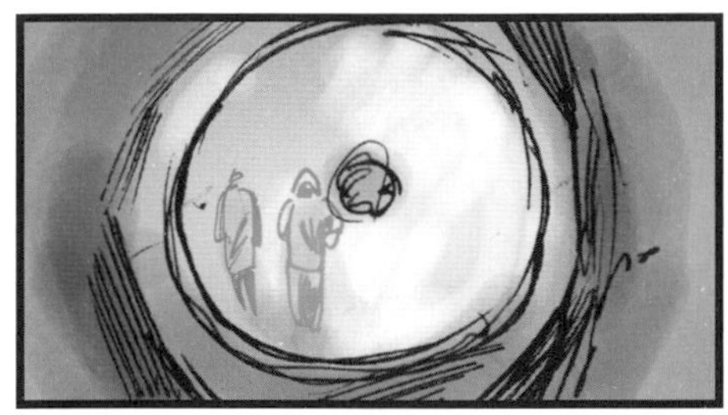

EXT. BORDERLANDS. PARK – DAY.

HELENA and VALENTINE are walking towards the border – toward the night side.

We pull up into the air to see HELENA and VALENTINE passing a lake, which forms the sun's eye on the light side of the border. They are almost at the place that HELENA saw.

Then we crash down to move beside them.

There are shapes suggesting trees, but the whole place feels more like a painting, semi-abstract shapes, partly formed ideas, lines and colours hang in space.

They reach a small pond in the centre. But there is only a small flame in the centre, reflected in the water.

VALENTINE
So, what are we meant to be seeing? Is this like the windows again?

HELENA
I know it's here. It was so obvious when I saw it.

VALENTINE
We often confuse what we wish for with what is. Well, I know I do . . .
(for a moment he loses his thread)
. . . that was weird. I had a case of déjà nu.

HELENA
What's that?

VALENTINE
It's when you feel – you've been here before, – you did the same things, and said the same – only this time you've all got your clothes on. Talk about embarrassing. These are the dream-lands, on the border. They aren't proper places.

HELENA
Maybe it's under the water?

VALENTINE steps into the water. It barely covers his toes.

VALENTINE
I don't think so. We're on the border, Helena. Come back tomorrow, this could all be a spaghetti orchard.

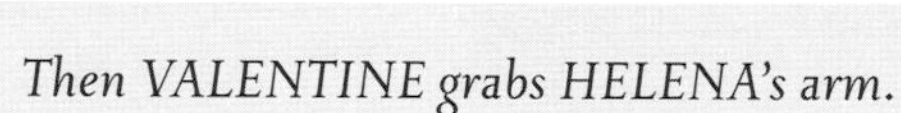

It's all wishes and hopes and memories.

Then VALENTINE grabs HELENA's arm.

VALENTINE (CONT'D)
Did you see that?

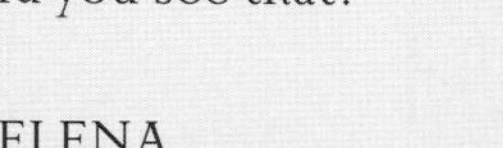

HELENA
What?

VALENTINE
My tower! It was up in the clouds. Up there!

HELENA
I didn't see anything.

Frustrated, VALENTINE skips a stone across the water. It hops many times right up to the flame.

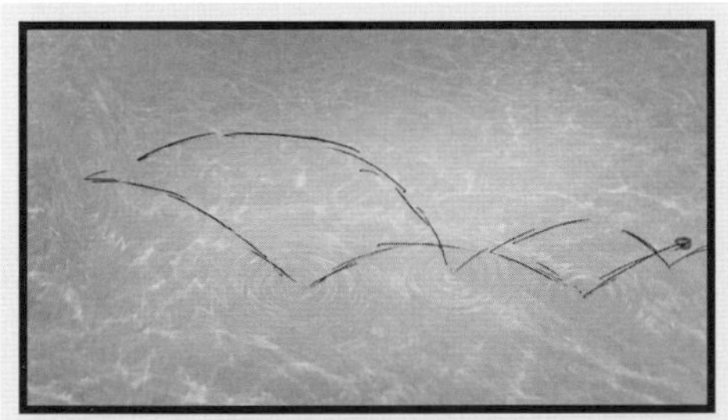

Then, suddenly, it comes skipping back across the pond towards him.

It comes to rest about twelve inches in front of him in the shallow water.

VALENTINE
You don't see that every day.

He tries again.

HELENA walks around the pond, trying to figure it out.
She comes upon more specific frozen images, dreams captured.

An enormous sunflower losing its petals; a life-size female doll with no face suspended in midair, her hair drifting as if she is underwater; part of a door warps to form a face; a collection of geometric shapes form a small, brightly coloured topiary garden.

We intercut HELENA walking through the park with shots of her walking through her flat, then with shots we've already seen of her getting ready to leave for the hospital, running for the door.

We now see all the references in the park within these shots: flowers in a vase; a doll falls off a shelf; a drawing of a face on the back of a door; a drab but once brightly coloured carpet with geometric designs.

HELENA
It's all so familiar . . . I know all this.

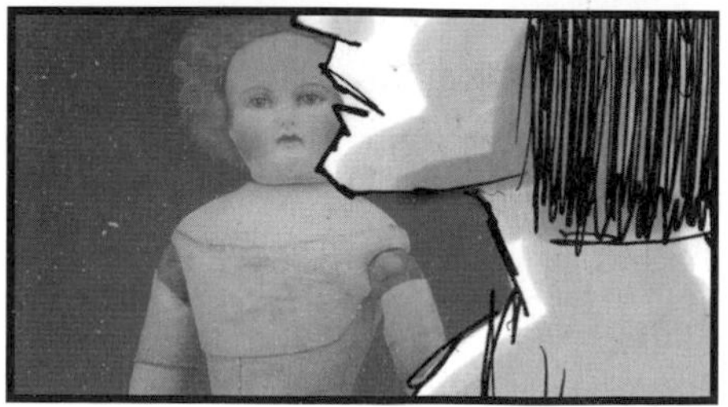

She walks behind a sculptural tree in the foreground and appears in her bedroom.

It is empty. Just like it was when they first moved in. She looks around the room, the cracks in the walls, the grimy window.

INT. HOSPITAL. JOANNA'S ROOM – DAY.

See below.

INT. CAMPBELL FAMILY CIRCUS – DAY.

See below.

INT. TOWER BLOCK. AUNT NAN'S FLAT. HELENA'S BEDROOM – DAY.

See below.

INT. BUS – DAY.

The scene that follows will be cut together from versions of the same scene shot in many different locations, sometimes shot with the WHITE QUEEN and sometimes with the mother, as storyboarded by Dave. We'll shoot the whole scene in the hospital, in the circus, in the flat, in the bus, then cut it together, so the conversation is the same, but the specifics of location, and whether HELENA is talking to her mother or to the WHITE QUEEN, are completely fluid.

WHITE QUEEN
Honestly, love. What have you lost now?

Mum, dressed as the WHITE QUEEN, is standing in one of the corners of the room, in shadow. She steps forward.

HELENA
Mum?

WHITE QUEEN
Come on, love. I'll give you a hand.

HELENA
I was looking for a MirrorMask, but I don't know what it looks like, or how big it is, or why it's missing, or anything, really.

WHITE QUEEN
Well, where did you last see it?

HELENA
I don't think I ever have.

HELENA has her back to us. We move slowly behind her. On the other side the WHITE QUEEN is now HELENA's mother, JOANNE.

JOANNE
Well, who had it last?

HELENA
I suppose you did. No, she did.

Or maybe the princess they were talking about. I don't know. I was sure it was here.

JOANNE
OK, then look again, you probably just missed it the first time.

HELENA
But I looked. It's all empty.

JOANNE
You give up too easily.

HELENA walks up to her mum, who puts a hand to HELENA's face.

HELENA
I'll never find it.

JOANNE
Mm. Never put off till tomorrow what you can put off till the day after. Eh?
You've got that from your dad, haven't you? He needs a kick up the pants sometimes.

HELENA
(she hugs her mum round the waist, closes her eyes.)

I want to come home now. I want you to be OK. I'm scared, Mum.

JOANNE
I'm scared, too, love. That's why I'm having this dream.

Do you think they've started to operate yet? Maybe everyone gets dreams like this, when they start poking around in your head.

HELENA
It's not your dream, Mum. It's mine.

JOANNE
That's the kind of thing people say in dreams. I wish your dad was here.

We can see VALENTINE skipping his stones.

JOANNE
Hullo. Did I dream you a boyfriend?

HELENA
You did not! He's a – he's just a – he's not –

JOANNE
I'm sorry I brought it up. Now, you're looking for something, you know it's here, you can't find it.

So look again.

I'll bet it's just like Aunt Nan's teeth. It's probably staring you in the face.

And then JOANNE is gone and HELENA's back in the park, on the far side of the pool.

HELENA
Mum . . .

For a moment she has to pull herself back together.

HELENA (CONT'D)
This is the centre, the centre of the centre.

It must be here, I'm just not looking hard enough.

EXT. BORDERLANDS. PARK – DAY.

VALENTINE is still skipping stones; HELENA squints and as the stone reaches the centre it bounces off something and starts to return to VALENTINE. HELENA sees a faint ripple from the impact start to describe a dome.

HELENA
It's not her dream. It's my dream.

And if it was me, I'd put a little building out there in the middle.

We start to see a slight mismatch between the background and the part of the background refracted through the building.

HELENA (CONT'D)
Its foundations would be right there.

We now see a plinth in the water.

HELENA (CONT'D)
A little building the right size . . . it's obvious.

We see the building more clearly.

HELENA (CONT'D)
And I'd put a small bridge across. . . Just like that one . . . I don't know why I didn't see it before.

Robert Llewellyn as the confused face of the gryphon.

Music box dolls.

Eryl Maynard as
Mrs Bagwell.

Shooting Mrs Bagwell's living room.

Anti-Helena.

6mm. extremely wide angle lens, shooting Anti-Helena's bedroom.

Valentine in the dome set.

The Dream Park.

Eve Pearce as the Future Fruit lady.

Shadow mum and daughter at home.

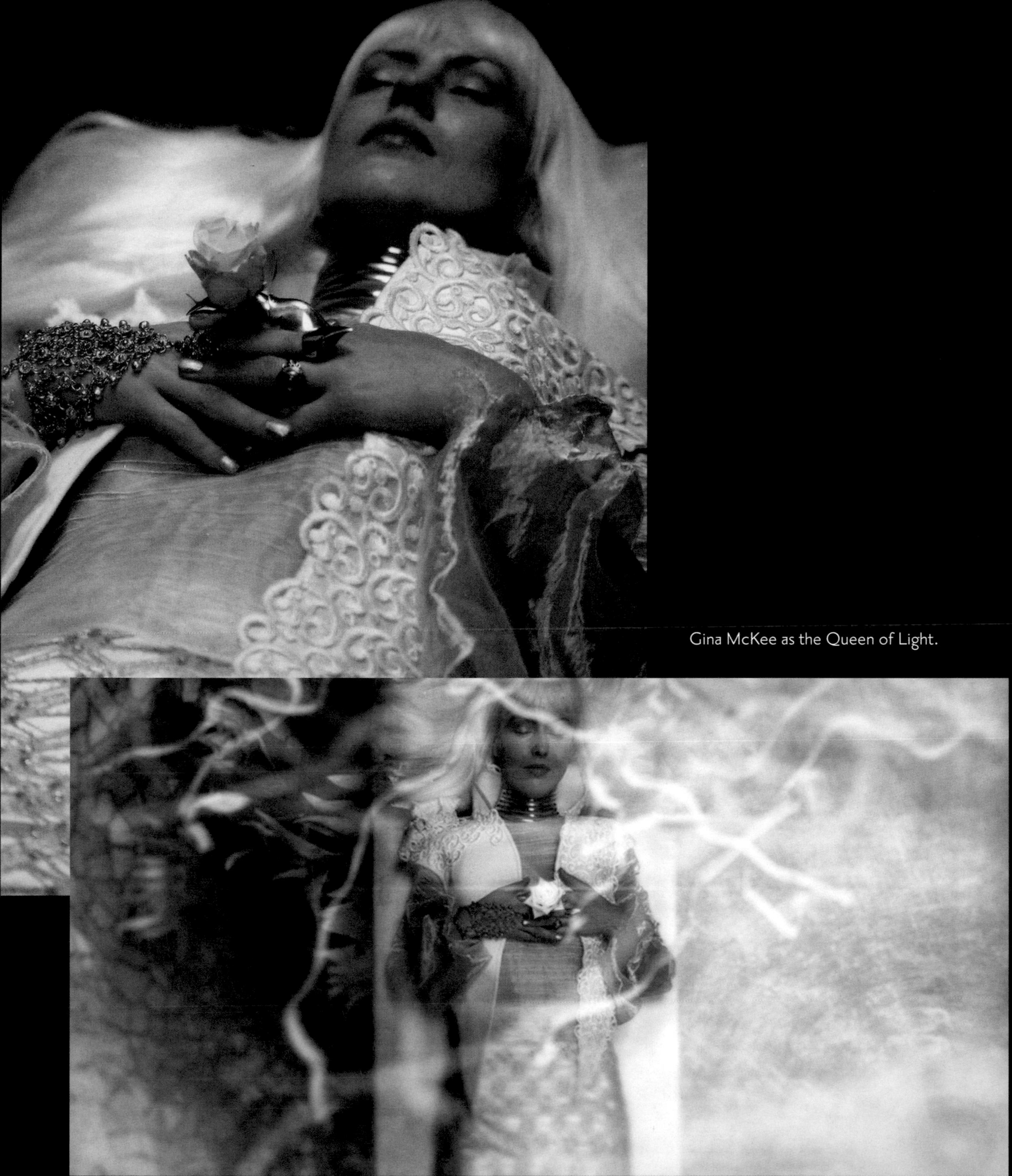

Gina McKee as the Queen of Light.

Shooting Anti-Helena destroying
the city of drawings.

Shooting Anti-Helena on the roof.

Helena asleep on the roof.

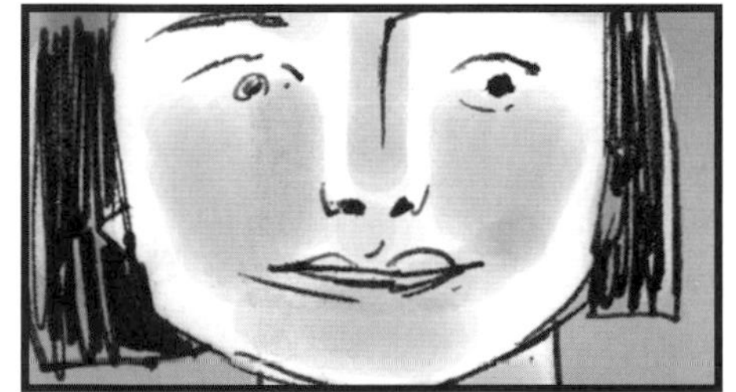

(to VALENTINE, who is open-mouthed at this)

Come on.

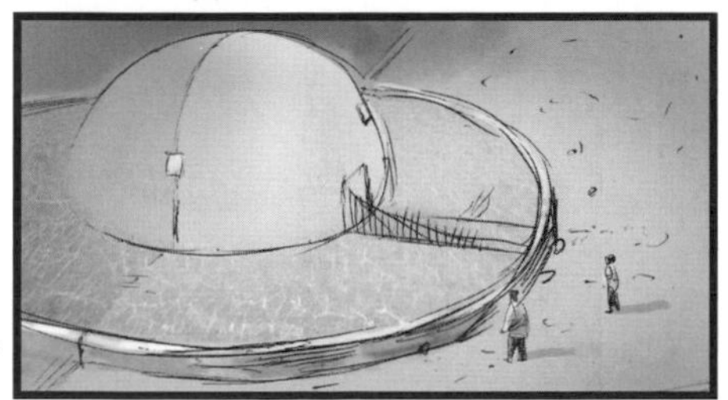

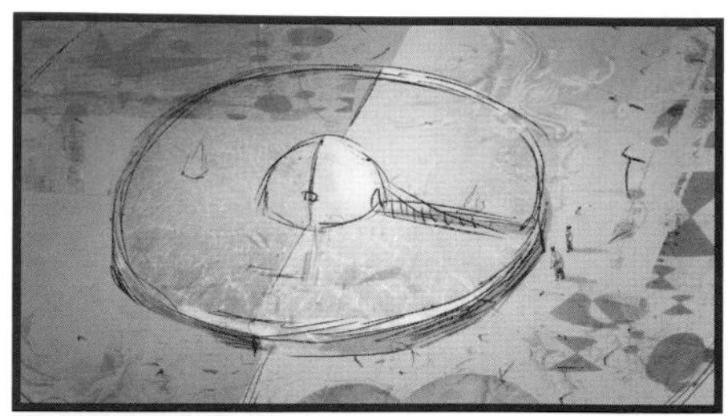

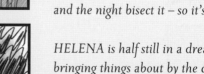

They walk across the bridge, a slightly raised walkway above the water; they still look like they are walking on water.

HELENA (CONT'D)
You aren't my boyfriend, you know. Even if this is my mum's dream.

VALENTINE opens and closes his mouth, unable to think of what to say.

The dome is featureless, except for two little windows. The day and the night bisect it – so it's half in light and half in shadow.

HELENA is half still in a dream, detached and concentrating, bringing things about by the certainty that they will happen.

HELENA (CONT'D)
There has to be a door right here, because that's where the door goes.

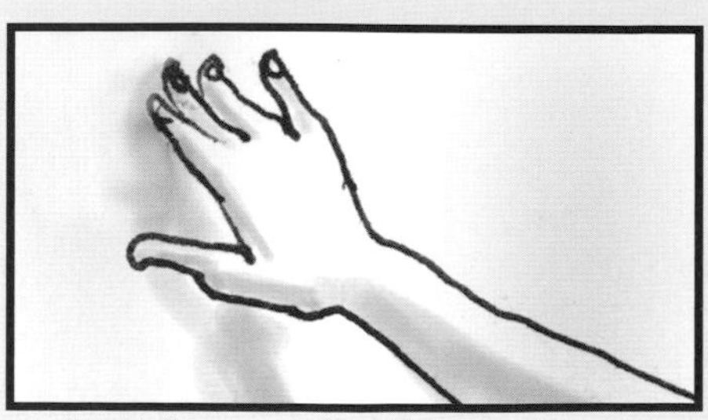

There is a tiny line indicating a doorway; the dome has gone from transparent to milky to white.

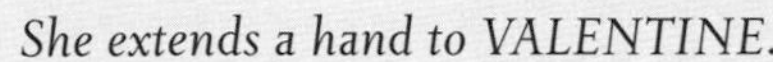

She extends a hand to VALENTINE.

HELENA (CONT'D)
Easy-peasy! Key.

VALENTINE
(turns to imaginary person next to him)
Key.

Then he takes the key and gives it to her.
But there's no keyhole. It doesn't seem to be that sort of a door.

VALENTINE (CONT'D)
Hah! Not so easy-peasy now, is it?

She looks at the key. It has a wedge design at the other end.

HELENA
Hmmm . . .

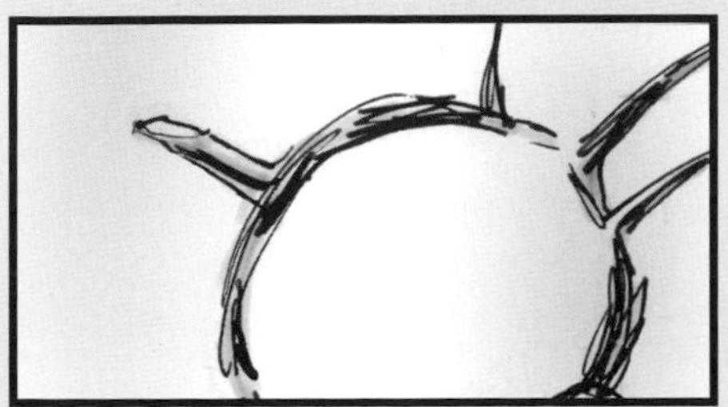

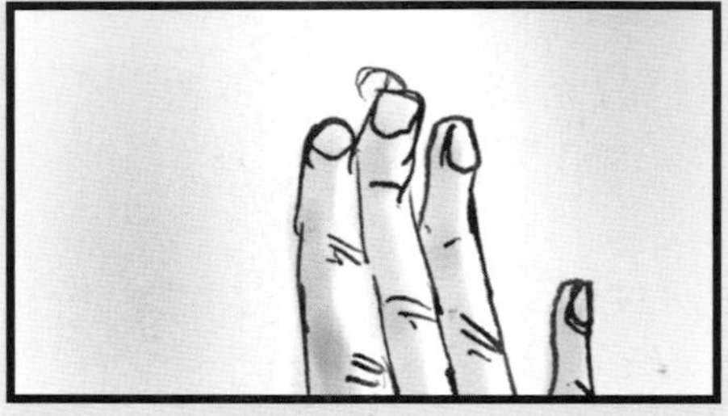

She runs her fingers over the edge of the door; we see two almost flush screw heads. She starts to unscrew the door with the key.

HELENA (CONT'D)
I think I'm getting the hang of this place now.

The screws easily fall onto the floor, freeing the door, which leans open slightly.

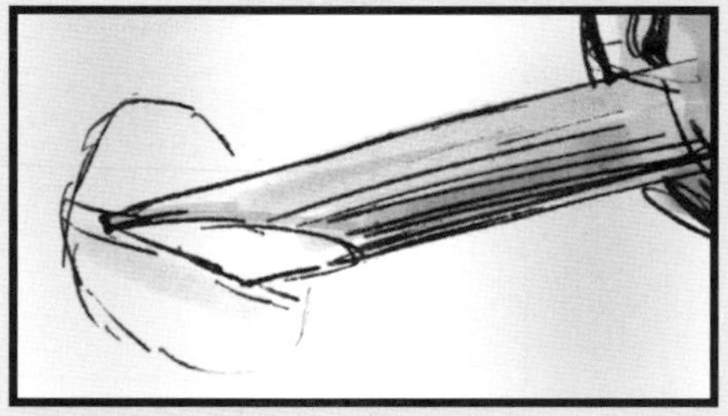

HELENA (CONT'D)
Got it.

INT. WHITE CITY. DOME – DAY.

VALENTINE
That was just . . . cheating.

Inside the room is a perfect dome, like an egg. White light creates an all-over glow. In the centre of the room is a flame-coloured cabinet.

They walk towards it.

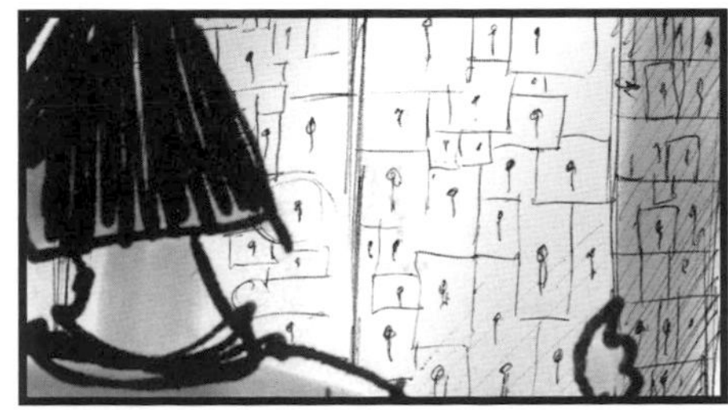

HELENA
The centre of the centre of the centre.

She opens the cabinet to reveal hundreds and hundreds of keyholes!

HELENA (CONT'D)
One of them must fit.

She tries one. It doesn't work.

There's a low, rumbling noise.

HELENA looks through one of the two windows in the dome.

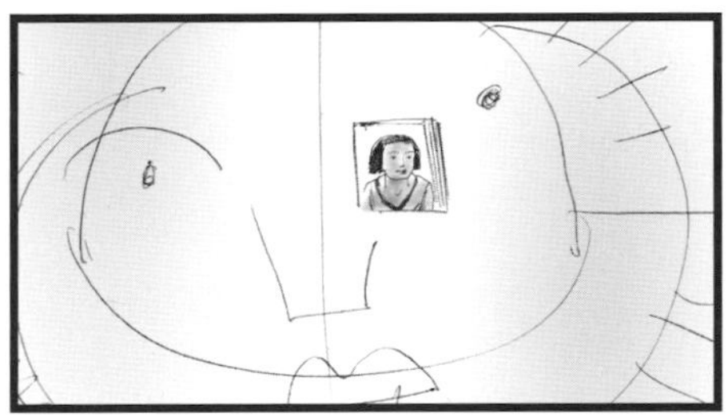

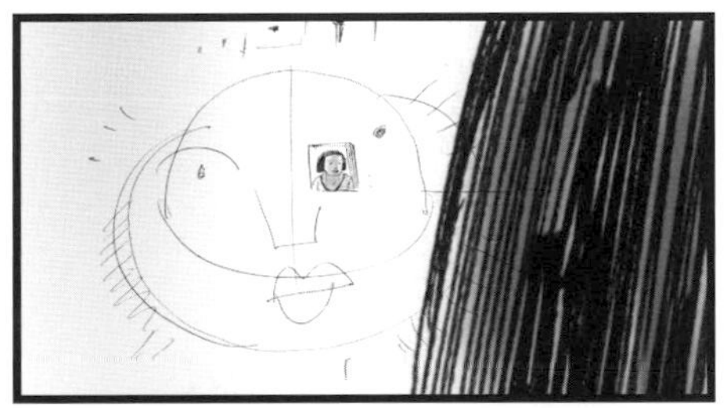

INT. TOWER BLOCK. AUNT NAN'S FLAT. HELENA'S BEDROOM – DAY.

Through the window she can see, huge, the ANTI-HELENA's face.
For a moment, from the ANTI-HELENA's point of view, we can see HELENA looking at us through a tiny window in the eye of a drawn face on the wall.
Then back to looking at the ANTI-HELENA staring at her, and the A-H's expression is not very nice.

INT. WHITE CITY. DOME – DAY

Suddenly HELENA and VALENTINE are thrown against the side of the room. An immense rumble/tearing sound.

HELENA
What's happening?

And she pulls herself back to the window and looks through . . .

INT. TOWER BLOCK. AUNT NAN'S FLAT. HELENA'S BEDROOM – DAY.

The window: We see the ANTI-HELENA tearing the picture of the dome out of the paper it's on. She carries it over to the other side of the room, and pins it to a paper in the darkness.

INT. BORDERLANDS. THE DOME – DAY.

HELENA and VALENTINE are being tossed from one side to the other.

VALENTINE grabs HELENA with one hand and the key cabinet with the other and holds on.

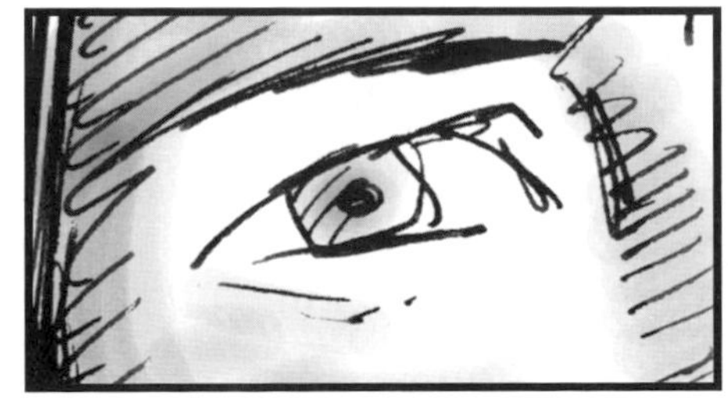

ANTI-HELENA looks down at them and then with an evil grin,

pins the paper dome onto the wall. It lands with a crash.

The room is tilted on its side.

HELENA
Oww. My arm.

INT. TOWER BLOCK. AUNT NAN'S FLAT. HELENA'S BEDROOM – DAY.

We see the drawing of the dome pinned onto a wall full of dark trees and shadow drawings.

INT. DARK CITY. DOME – NIGHT.

VALENTINE
You stay here. I'm going to fetch help.

HELENA
I'll come with you.

VALENTINE
You're hurt. Stay here. Don't move.

HELENA
But what about you?

VALENTINE
Oh, I'm a panther. I shall slip unnoticed through the darkness like a dark, unnoticeable slippy thing.

HELENA
Valentine. That's really nice of you. I know we haven't always got on, but I'm really grateful for all your help. I couldn't have done any of this without you.

She squeezes his hand. He looks uncomfortable.

VALENTINE
I do my best.

HELENA
Come back soon.

EXT. DARK CITY. DOME – NIGHT.

VALENTINE steps outside. He tosses the key into the air and catches it again.

INT. BORDERLANDS. THE DOME – NIGHT.

HELENA sits on the floor, rubbing her arm, which was hurt in the fall.

There are two windows in the dome. Through the round window something catches her attention. She looks through.

INT. TOWER BLOCK. AUNT NAN'S FLAT. HELENA'S BEDROOM – DAY.

She sees, reflected in the wardrobe mirror where the dome has landed, the middle of the dark forests.

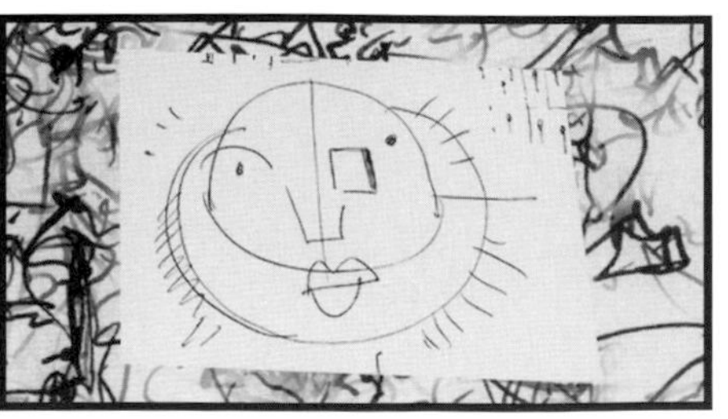

EXT. DARK PALACE – NIGHT.

It's night in the Dark Palace, as it always is. Enormous steps.

VALENTINE stands in front of the steps, staring up at the palace.

EXT. DARK FOREST – NIGHT.

INT. BORDERLANDS. THE DOME – NIGHT.

HELENA looks through . . .

INT. TOWER BLOCK. AUNT NAN'S FLAT.
HELENA'S BEDROOM – DAY.

WINDOW: Into her bedroom.

ANTI-HELENA is pulling all the pictures HELENA has drawn off the wall, thoughtfully. She puts up some teenage heart-throb posters in their place.

She sits on the edge of the bed, takes out a packet of cigarettes (a packet of ten), and a box of matches.

Then she takes a match and lights a cigarette for herself. Almost as an afterthought, she sets light to one of the sheets of paper.

EXT. BORDERLANDS. THE DOME – NIGHT.

Through the open window frame, we can see, on the horizon, a sudden column of flame.

INT. TOWER BLOCK. AUNT NAN'S FLAT.
HELENA'S BEDROOM – DAY.

HELENA's father comes in. He's upset that she's smoking – and likely to start a fire. ANTI-HELENA swears at him. He takes the cigarettes and matches from her. She shouts at him and –

INT. BORDERLANDS. THE DOME – NIGHT.

HELENA
Dad? She's not me . . . oh Dad . . .

There's a noise behind her, in the dome,

and HELENA looks up, horrified, to see –

EXT. DARK FOREST – NIGHT.

The DARK QUEEN's faceless servants.

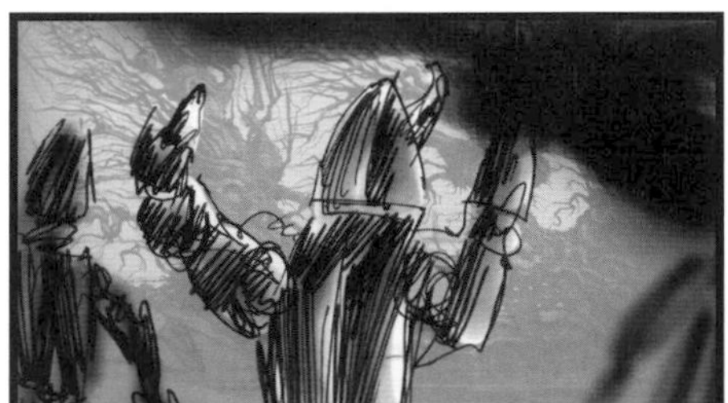

They throw a sheet of black fabric-matter over her, and bundle her up in it.

We hear HELENA'S screams fade as she is carried through the forest.

INT. DARK PALACE. THRONE ROOM – NIGHT.

The DARK QUEEN is up on her perilously high throne, pale and dangerous. There is a portrait of the queen on the wall. The package containing HELENA is hauled by the faceless BLACK GUARDS to a place on the floor in front of the throne. They open it, and HELENA looks up at the DARK QUEEN.

DARK QUEEN

(just like a mum, very normally)

So. I don't know what kind of time you call this. I've been worried sick about you.

HELENA just stares. The DARK QUEEN comes down the steps to her.

DARK QUEEN (CONT'D)

I just want to hear a little "sorry for putting you to all this trouble". Would it be too much to ask for an apology?

HELENA

Me? You're the one who's causing all the damage.

DARK QUEEN

Don't be ridiculous. Who do you think is destroying this world?

HELENA

You are. I've seen the black shadows.

DARK QUEEN
Well, what would any worried mother do? I was just trying to bring us back together.

HELENA
That's why you put up wanted posters?

DARK QUEEN
People do it for lost pets. And a daughter is a lot more important than a pet . . .

HELENA
I'm not your daughter.

The DARK QUEEN thinks about this for a moment. She realises that HELENA is telling the truth. She makes her choice –

DARK QUEEN
You'll do. We can fix your hair – those clothes will have to go. I'll get the servants to burn them.

HELENA
I don't know what you're trying to pull, but there are people who know where I am. Valentine will rescue me.

DARK QUEEN
Valentine. Yes, I'd nearly forgotten about him.

She snaps her fingers.

VALENTINE sidles in. He is wearing a magnificent black hat and an expensive suit.

HELENA
Valentine?

VALENTINE
Well, we were already here. She'd put up the posters. Reward paid. Nothing personal. It's just supply and demand.

HELENA
You pathetic creep.

VALENTINE
Rocks and logs can bite like dogs, but words will never hurt me.

HELENA
You useless, cake-hogging, cowardly, treacherous –

VALENTINE
I did not hog that cake!

DARK QUEEN
I'm sorry, Mr Valentine, but I have to hurry you along. I need to spend some serious quality time with my little girl. Thank you for popping by.

VALENTINE
Um. Right. I believe somebody said something about jewels, as many as I can carry . . . ?

DARK QUEEN
If you must –

She whistles, sharply.

Jewels – all of them black, except for a few very dark red and green and blue ones –

fly and roll out from holes,

and VALENTINE fills his pockets with them.

Then he fills his hat, like a bucket.

HELENA has turned her back on them both. Arms folded. Furious.

VALENTINE
So, um, no hard feelings?

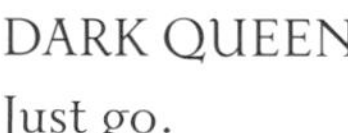

DARK QUEEN
Just go.

VALENTINE
Right. I'm on my way out. Nothing more to say. Off to get the, um. Right. Well. Have a nice.

The DARK QUEEN gestures, and several of the BLACK GUARDS step into the throne room.

DARK QUEEN
Throw him out. Hard. The princess will be going to her chambers.

VALENTINE backs hastily out, then starts to run. HELENA is choking back tears.

HELENA
Let me go. Please.

DARK QUEEN
Darling. You know what you need?

HELENA
I need to find the charm. I need to wake the White Queen. I need to –

DARK QUEEN
You need a pretty frock. And a happy smile.

HELENA
A smile?

DARK QUEEN
With a smile on your face, everything will seem brighter. Because from now on we're – what?

HELENA
I don't know.

The DARK QUEEN looks at a BLACK GUARD.

DARK QUEEN
Tell her.

BLACK GUARD
Not at home to Mr Grumpy, Your Majesty.

DARK QUEEN
Exactly.

She claps, and the remaining BLACK GUARD takes HELENA away. The QUEEN stands there and watches her go.

INT. DARK PALACE. PRINCESS HELENA'S BEDROOM/DRESSING ROOM – NIGHT.

HELENA is pushed into the dressing room by the BLACK GUARD. Bolts slam.

It's a big room, filled with things that look like bass drums flat on the ground – huge roundish objects. We will learn they are music boxes.
HELENA starts to push her way towards the centre of the room.

Music begins – music-box kind of music. She looks around, wondering where the music is coming from.

Slowly rotating human-size dolls, like the rotating ballerinas on music boxes, start to rise from the drumlike boxes. As they rise, they sing . . .

DOLLS
Why do birds suddenly appear every time you are near?
Just like me they long to be close to you.

They sing the Hal David lyrics a syllable at a time, doll-like and robotically. The effect is both haunting and disturbing.

DOLLS (CONT'D)
Why do stars fall down from the sky every time you walk by?
Just like me they long to be close to you.

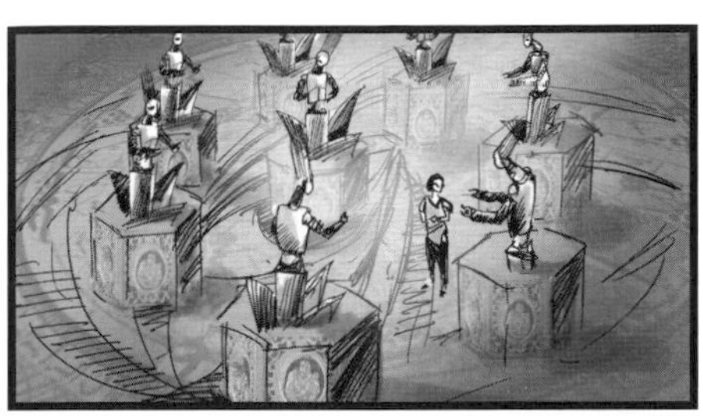

They are also reaching for HELENA.

DOLLS (CONT'D)
On the day that you were born the angels got together and decided to create a dream come true . . .

Now the most beautiful doll of all, from the central drum box, has begun to rise. She reminds us a little of HELENA herself. Her hands are filled with glowing dust, which she sprinkles on HELENA.

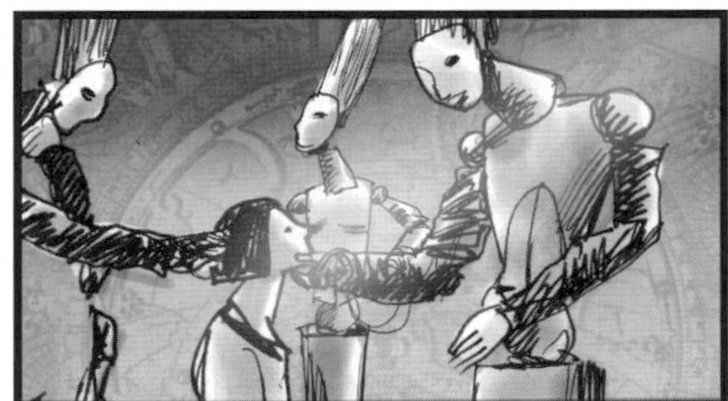

BEAUTIFUL DOLL
So they sprinkled moondust in your hair and golden starlight in your eyes of blue.

Angrily, HELENA brushes off the twinkling dust.
The rotating dolls reach their hands for her.
HELENA's changing, where the dust has touched her. Her hair is elaborately coiffed, her dress is black velvet, elegant, accented with pearls.

DOLLS
That is why all the boys in town follow you all around.
Just like me they long to be close to you.

Close to you.

She has been transformed into a princess of darkness. And we move from her eyes, still looking desperately around, to the faces of the dolls, each with its perfect smile and blind eyes, then back to HELENA.

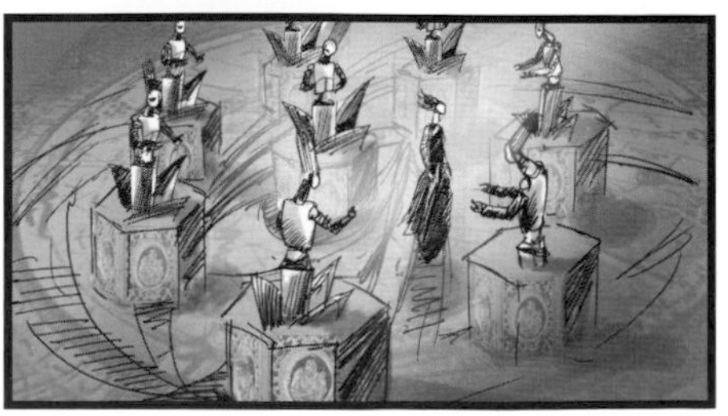

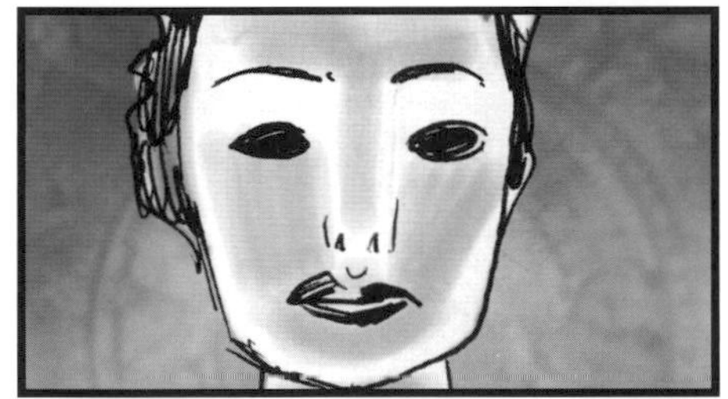

Her eyes now blank and passive and black. Her smile now perfect. She looks like a doll herself.

INT. DARK PALACE. THRONE ROOM – NIGHT.

The DARK QUEEN hears the distant music, and she looks satisfied.

INT. DARK PALACE. PRINCESS HELENA'S BEDROOM – NIGHT.

A song plays over this silent sequence . . . something haunting and slightly sad.

HELENA sits on the bed in her bedroom. It contains a four-poster bed, a mantelpiece, a tilted mirror above it. HELENA is staring at herself in the mirror.

We move in on the mirror, looking at the reflection of HELENA, looking brainwashed and doll-like – and then we realise there are two dark eyes staring at us through the mirror.

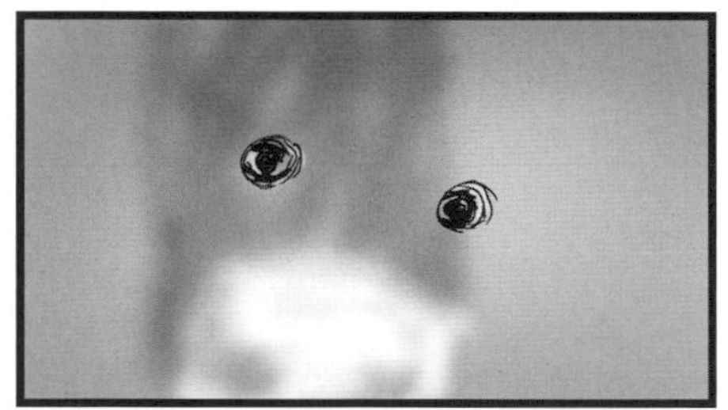

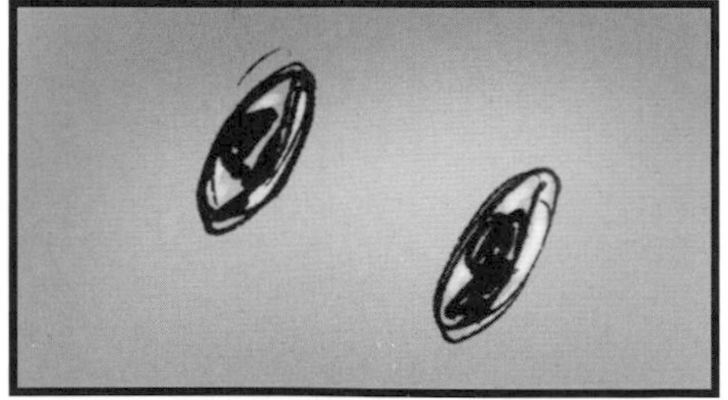

We revolve slowly to find ourselves in –

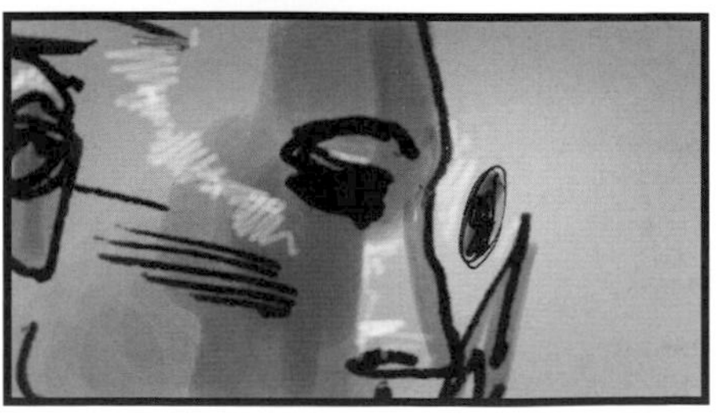

INT. DARK PALACE. THRONE ROOM – NIGHT.

The DARK QUEEN takes her face from the wall. She was looking through two eyeholes in a full-sized portrait of herself.

EXT. DARK LANDS – NIGHT.

VALENTINE walks along, carrying his hatful of jewels. He sees a poster on a wall of HELENA – a "missing, reward paid" poster – and he pulls it down.

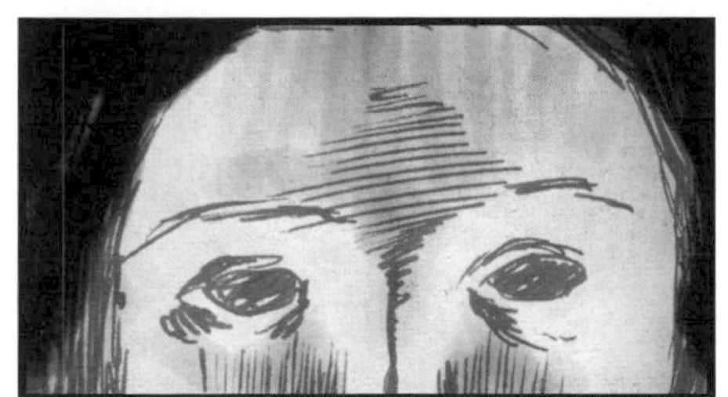

The wind nearly whips it from his hand, but he catches it. He thrusts his hat into his shirt.

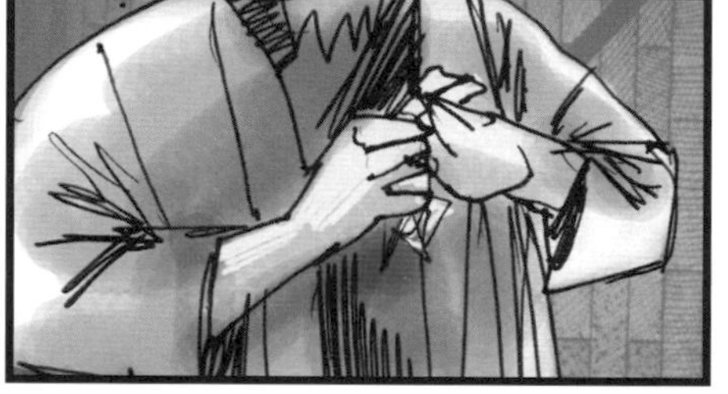

He walks and rips and tears the wanted poster as he walks, making it into a flower.

He drops the flower and the wind carries it away.

INT. WHITE CITY. WHITE QUEEN'S BEDROOM – DAY.

We look at the WHITE QUEEN in her glass casket. She's still asleep.

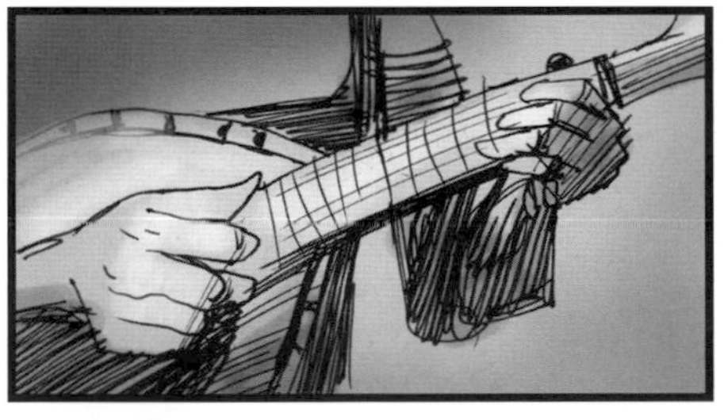

INT. DARK PALACE. THRONE ROOM – NIGHT.

Music. The DARK QUEEN is playing beautiful music on a lute-like instrument: it harmonises with the song in the background.

HELENA is sitting on the floor at the DARK QUEEN's feet. She's playing with dolls, which look exactly like the huge dolls we saw earlier, only much smaller.

The DARK QUEEN finishes playing.

HELENA looks up at her and puts her head on one side, smiles sweetly. The DARK QUEEN reaches out and strokes HELENA's hair, as one would stroke a pet.

HELENA strokes her own doll in the same way. Her doll doesn't smile.

EXT. BORDERLANDS. THE DOME – NIGHT.

VALENTINE reaches the dome. He whistles. His whistling ties in to the song.

INT. BORDERLANDS. THE DOME – NIGHT.

He walks inside. Looks up and down.

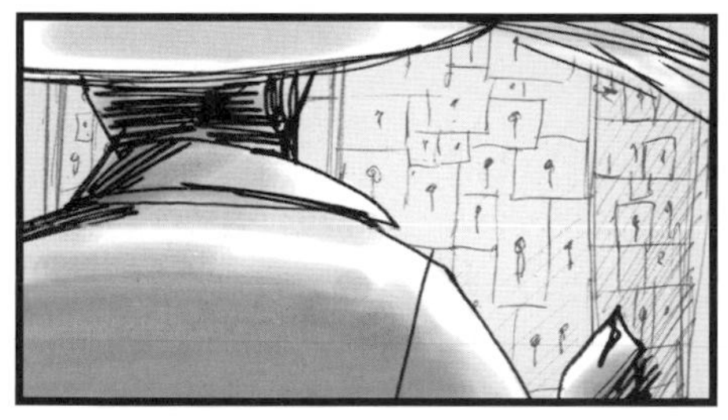

There are hundreds of keyholes.

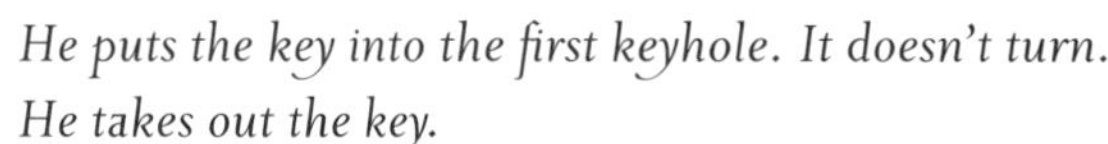

He puts the key into the first keyhole. It doesn't turn.
He takes out the key.

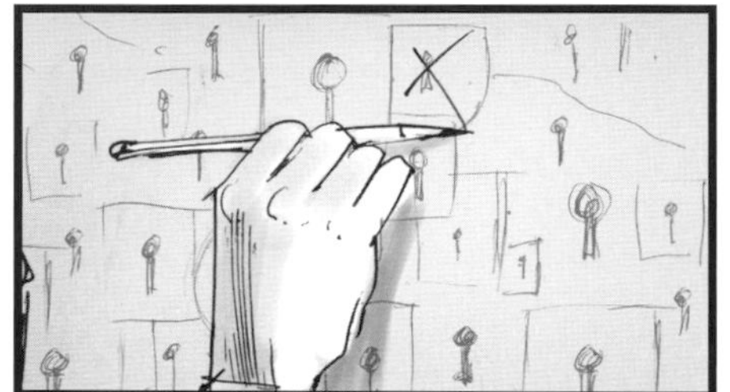

With a pencil he crosses out the keyhole with an X across it.

INT. DARK PALACE. PRINCESS HELENA'S BEDROOM – NIGHT.

HELENA is brushing her hair with slow, repetitive movements.

She looks in the mirror above the mantle.
Her face shimmers and swims for a moment. She still smiles.

INT. BORDERLANDS. THE DOME – NIGHT.

VALENTINE pulls a key out of a keyhole.

He makes a cross over the place where the keyhole was. Pull back to see hundreds of keyholes X'd out. Hundreds still to go.

He sighs.

Tries another. It clicks.

VALENTINE grins like a fox.

The song comes to an end.

He pulls the key – a drawer comes out and inside the drawer is a white box. It's long and flat. A perfect box for a mask.

VALENTINE
Presenting . . . the MirrorMask.

VALENTINE opens the box.

It's empty – at least, it contains only a folded sheet of paper. VALENTINE takes the letter and unfolds it.

He sees a message, written in a childish handwriting.

VALENTINE (CONT'D)
(begins to read)

ANTI-HELENA (V.O.)
To my mother, as even if it is not she who finds this, I have no doubt that it will get to her eventually, as everything always does:

Dearest Mama, as by now you must be aware, I have found the MirrorMask. I shall use it to go away. There are other places. I'll find one with another girl like me in it, a life I can take.

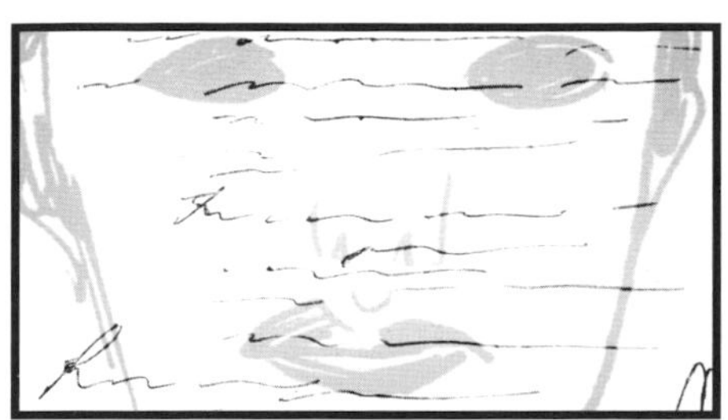

She'll not be as clever as me, of course. I can't live in your world. I have to grow up. I'm going to run away and join real life.

Of course, if I use the MirrorMask it may upset things a bit. But you can't run away from home without destroying somebody's world.

VALENTINE
You stupid little cow.

He sits down, suddenly. Reaches up and pulls off his mask, of him scowling, and flings it away from him. His face now has a huge smile on it. He peels that face off as well.

So he's holding a mask-face in each hand, one smiling, one scowling. He holds one face in each hand, and does the voices for each of them.

VALENTINE (CONT'D)
Well, now what?

VALENTINE 2
(grinning)
It can't be that bad.

VALENTINE
The princess got the MirrorMask thingie. She got out. All that stuff Helena was saying about windows was true.

VALENTINE 3
(scowling)
Did you doubt her?

VALENTINE
Yes. No. I don't – maybe.

VALENTINE 3
So what idiot thing are you going to do now?

VALENTINE 2
It's not what he'll do. It's where he'll go. Up, out. He's rich, he's devastatingly attractive. He's got style . . .

VALENTINE
(modestly)
I wouldn't know about that. But I do have to get out.

VALENTINE 2
Come on. You don't believe all that stuff about the world being destroyed?

VALENTINE
Well. . . When you eliminate the impossible, whatever remains, however unlikely, must be –

VALENTINE 3
A fish. Must be a fish. I never trusted those fish. They're always smiling.

VALENTINE
No. Must be the truth.

He looks at the two masks, and lets them drop to the floor. He realises he's trying to joke his way out of the situation. He made a big mistake. This is the moment when VALENTINE's conscience wakes up.

He looks down. By the wall he sees the red cover of the Really Useful Book.

INT. DARK PALACE. GREAT HALL – NIGHT.

A long table. At one end, the DARK QUEEN. At the other, HELENA. A BLACK GUARD butler takes food from one end of the table to the other.

DARK QUEEN
Have some more ice-cream, Princess.

HELENA
No thank you, dearest Mama. I believe I have had sufficient.

DARK QUEEN
Well, your manners are much improved, anyway.

There is a jarring sort of shudder, like a distant earthquake.

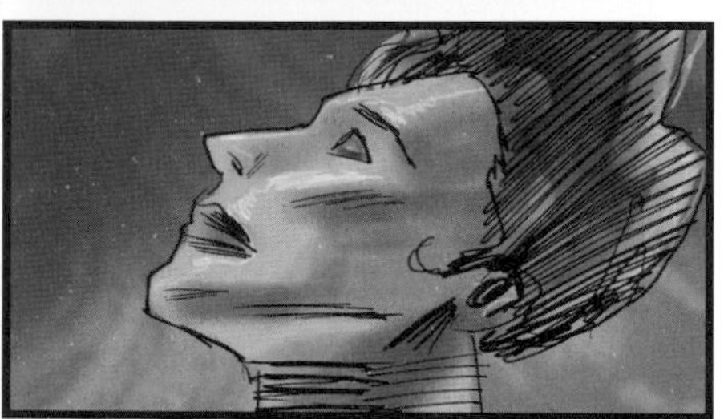

The DARK QUEEN looks around angrily.

DARK QUEEN (CONT'D)
What was that?

HELENA
I have no idea.

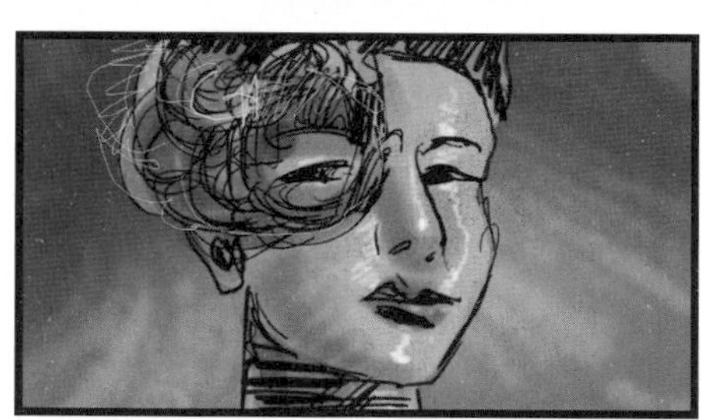

DARK QUEEN frowns.

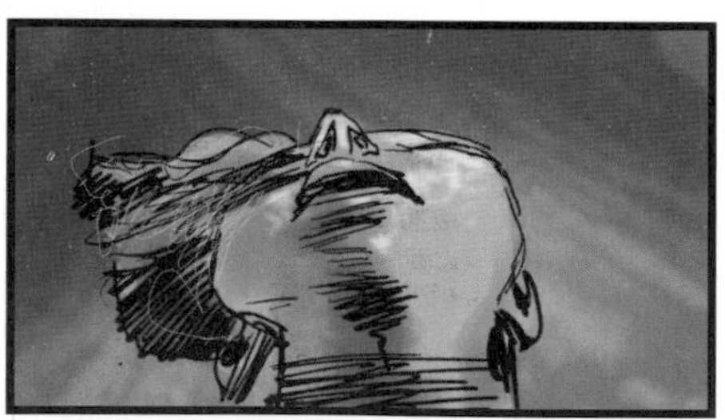

Then she opens her mouth wide and throws her head back. Two black bird shapes emerge.

DARK QUEEN
Go. Be my eyes. Find out what's happening.

HELENA's still a doll, and passively she says:

HELENA
You know what's happening. She's going to destroy everything. Your real daughter. When she left, she threw this whole world out of balance, and now it's falling apart.

DARK QUEEN
You will not talk to me like that!

A beat.

Then a smile from HELENA, doll-like and compliant.

HELENA
No, Mama. Sorry, Mama. Can I have some more ice-cream, please?

Another beat then . . .

DARK QUEEN
Good girl. Just one scoop, though.

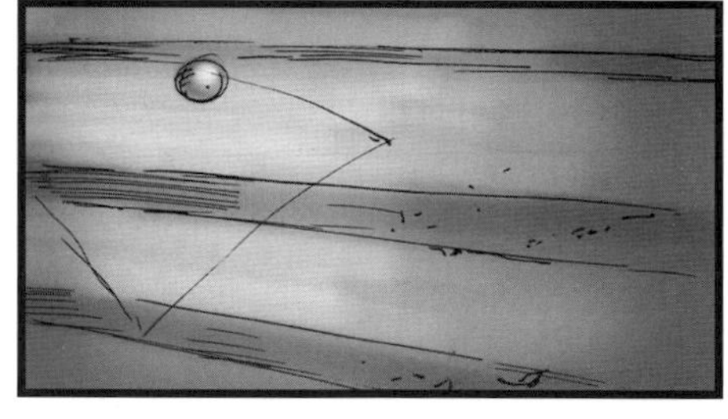

EXT. DARK PALACE. STEPS – NIGHT.

By the steps, HELENA plays with a black ball, bouncing it against the wall, a regular beat. Her face is blank.

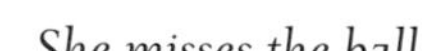

She misses the ball.

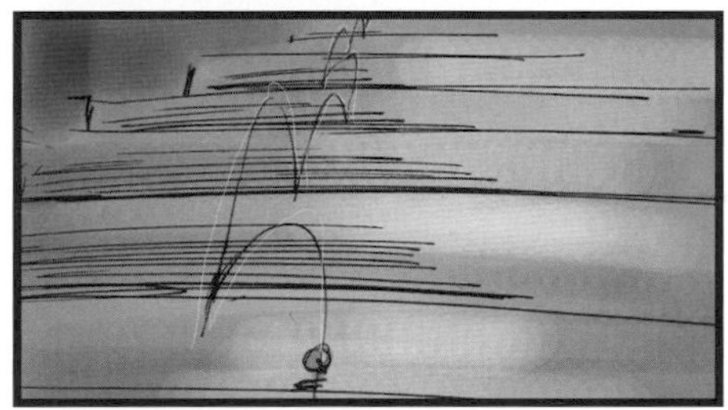

It bounces down the many steps. She seems confused for a moment, then she runs after it.
When she gets to the bottom of the steps she looks down. The ball is nowhere to be seen.
She stands there, looking puzzled.

VALENTINE
Um. Right. I suppose that an "oops and I promise not to do it again" isn't actually going to cut the mustard.

VALENTINE steps into shot. She stares at him blankly. He's holding her ball.

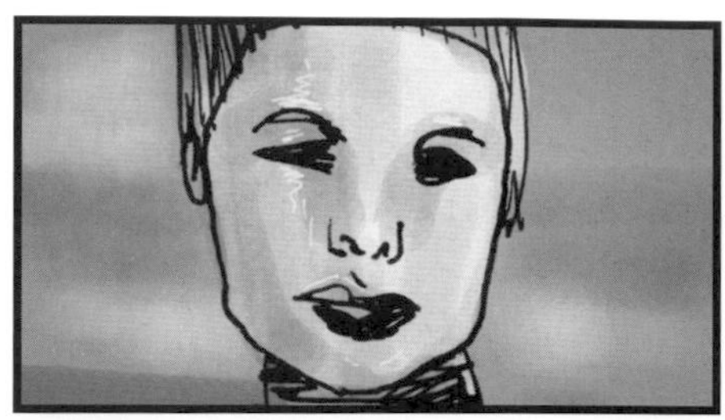

VALENTINE (CONT'D)
Helena?
I really am s . . . I'm . . . if I were to say sor . . . say something apologetic, it would reflect my feelings in this matter. Accurately.

He tosses the ball from one hand to the other. Then he joins it with a glowing light and another light.

VALENTINE (CONT'D)
And you were right and I was . . . not as right as you were. About everything. The MirrorMask. The windows. The world ending. The whole bit. And you probably hate me. I mean, I'd hate me, too.

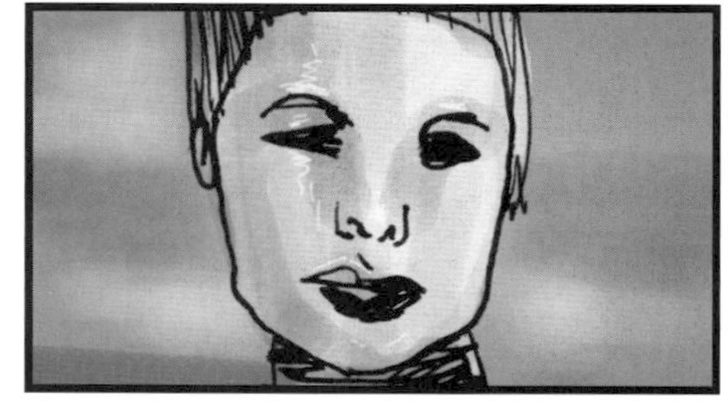

No emotion crosses her face.

VALENTINE (CONT'D)
Look, whatever she's done to you . . . I know you're still in there.

No reaction.

Nothing. He sighs.

And gives up. VALENTINE tosses her the black ball –

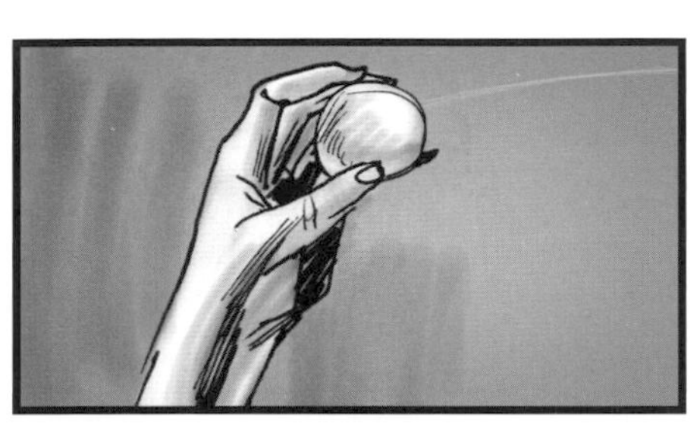

and automatically she catches and tosses it back to him, as any juggler would.

He throws her the other balls,

and they stand there juggling balls of light.

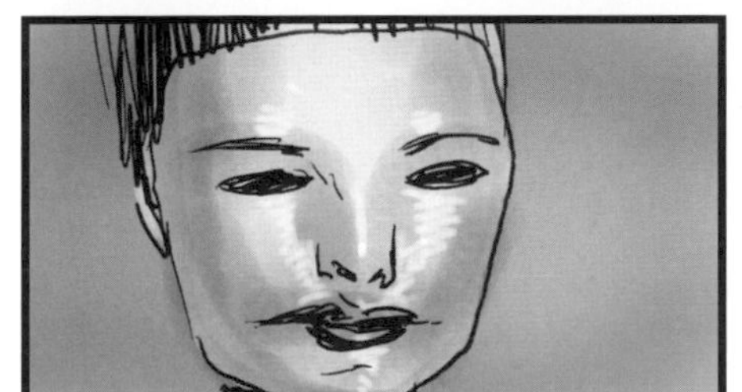

HELENA blinks – she's waking up.

VALENTINE changes the rhythm of the juggling and adds in a few more balls.

HELENA's smiling. And it's not a doll smile any longer.

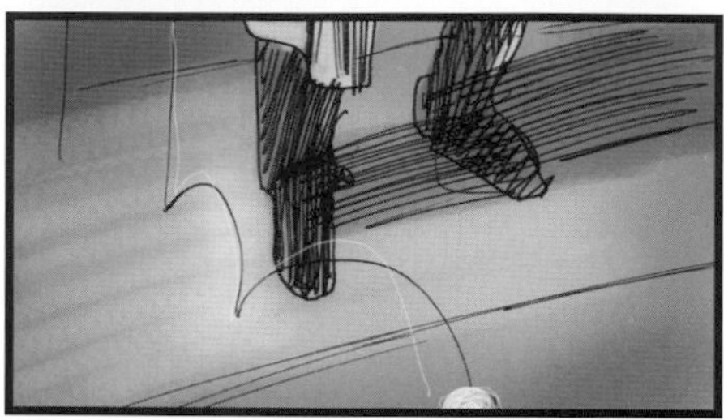

VALENTINE drops a ball.

And HELENA – and it's HELENA, with human eyes, not the doll-girl any longer – says:

HELENA
Butterfingers.

INT. DARK PALACE. PRINCESS HELENA'S BEDROOM – NIGHT.

HELENA
Well, if it was me, and I wanted to hide something, like a MirrorMask or something . . . I'd hide it in my bedroom.

VALENTINE
It's not here, we've looked all over the place.

HELENA
Well that's what I'd do.

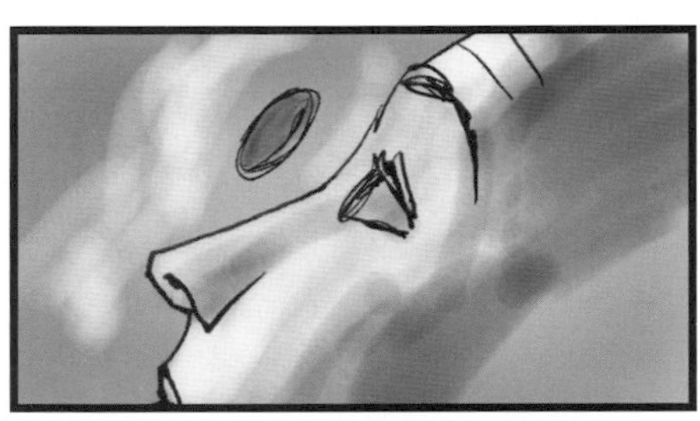

HELENA's face, reflected. She pulls her face back, and we see she's on the bed, with her face pressed up against the mirror over the mantelpiece. She is looking into the room next door, with her eyes against the mirror's eyeholes.

Through the eyehole we can see . . .

INT. DARK PALACE. THRONE ROOM – NIGHT.

The DARK QUEEN in her throne room. There are several grotesques, who have come to complain about what's going on.

DARK QUEEN
What are you saying?

OGRE
Something destroyed the Pit of Despair.

BOGGART
The Swamp of Doom simply isn't there any more. It was a lovely swamp. You can't get them like that these days.

DARK QUEEN
I'm afraid somebody is actually doing this.

OGRE
Who?

DARK QUEEN
Somebody who hates me.

BOGGART
Nobody hates you, Majesty. We love you.

DARK QUEEN
Crawler. But you have a point. I must call a council.

She bangs a gong.

And we go back to the portrait on the wall, and through an eye-hole, into . . .

INT. DARK PALACE. PRINCESS HELENA'S BEDROOM – NIGHT.

HELENA gets down from the chair.

HELENA
It's all falling apart. It's all her fault. That girl. Let me see her note again.

VALENTINE
(handing it to her)
She found the MirrorMask. That's how she got out of here. It's the only way out.

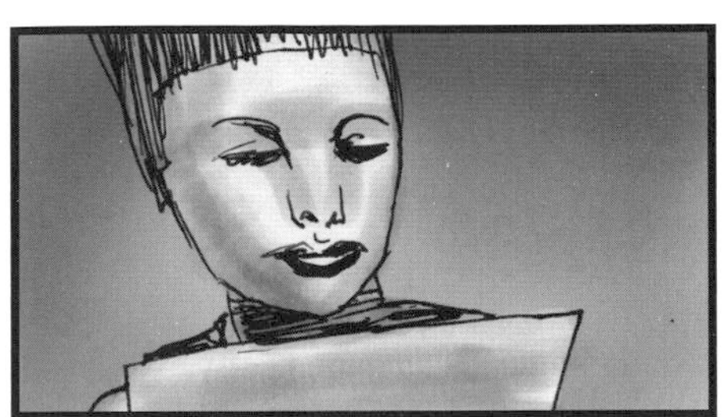

HELENA
We looked everywhere. We looked all over the place. We could keep looking until the end of the world.

There's a knock on the door.

The door is pushed open by a SMALL HAIRY creature, carrying a tray with some food on it on its head.
VALENTINE is nowhere to be seen.

HELENA is sitting primly on the chair with the doll-smile on her face.

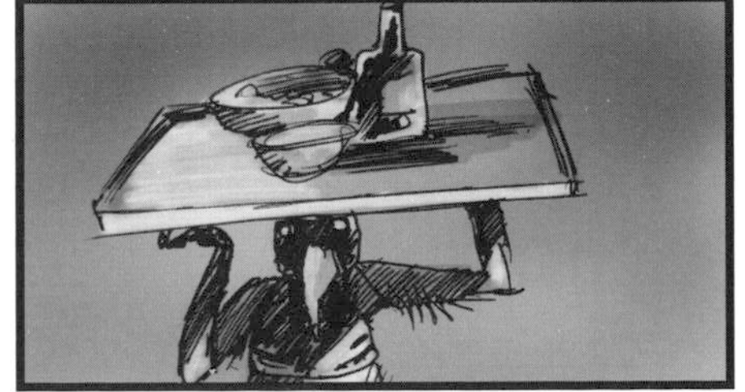

SMALL HAIRY
Message from Her Majesty. 'hem. Affairs of state mean she's very busy, and you'll be eating in your room tonight.

HELENA
Mama is too kind. Please thank Her Majesty for me.

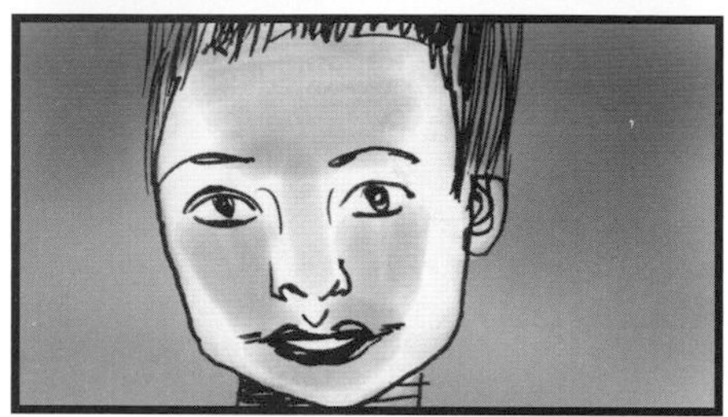

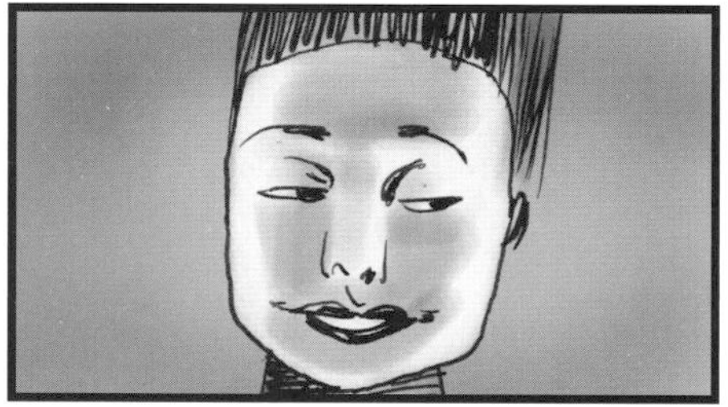

And then she spots VALENTINE's foot sticking out from under the bed.

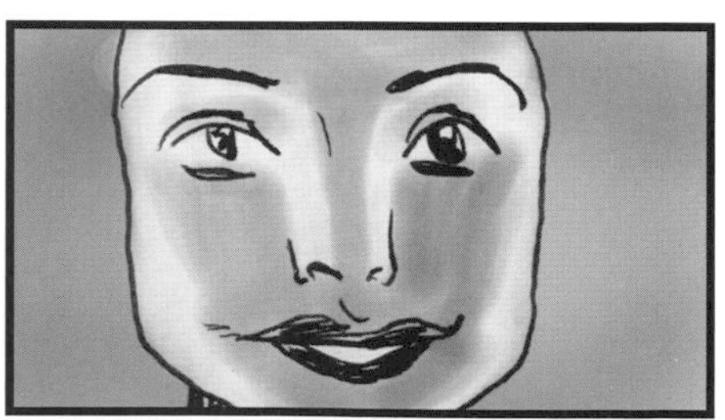

She looks at the SMALL HAIRY creature – it's putting her food down on the table, and hasn't noticed VALENTINE.

HELENA quickly gets up and walks over to the bed so, when the SMALL HAIRY creature turns around, her dress covers VALENTINE's foot.

SMALL HAIRY
Right. Well, bon appetit.

HELENA
You are too kind.

The door is closed as the SMALL HAIRY creature goes out. VALENTINE comes out from under the bed.
He immediately makes for the plate of food and begins to devour it.

HELENA (CONT'D)
We've wasted so many opportunities. We don't even have the Really Useful Book . . .

VALENTINE takes the battered remains of the Really Useful Book out and tosses it to her, without turning around. It flaps a couple of times and glides into her hand.

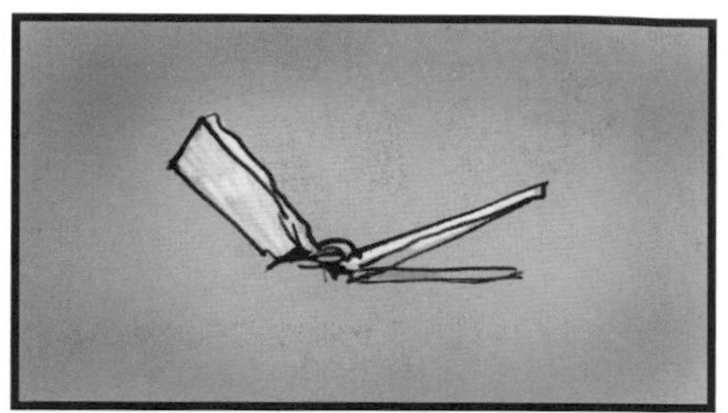

HELENA (CONT'D)
There's just one page left. What if it's the wrong page?

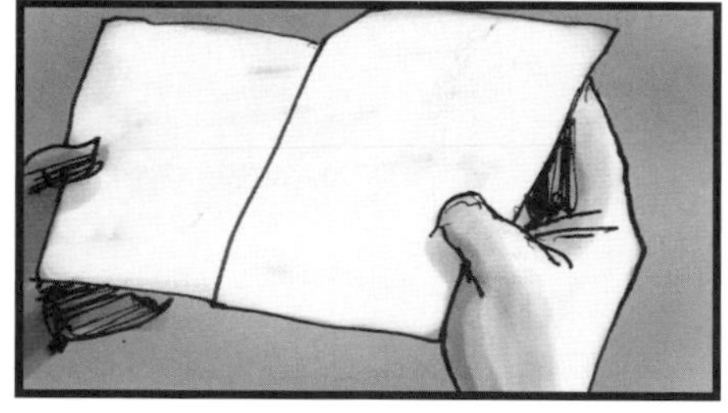

Looking over her shoulder – it says "Remember what your mother told you."

HELENA (CONT'D)
Remember what your mother told you.

VALENTINE
Mine said, it's a dog-eat-dog world, you get them before they get you, eat your greens, please don't do that, don't embarrass me in front of the neighbours, I think it will be better for everyone if you leave home and please don't ever come back.

HELENA
Really?

VALENTINE
She wasn't actually my mum, either. She bought me from a man.

HELENA
I miss my mum. She'd always have advice. It's like when you lose something, she'd say . . . "Don't give up. Most of the time it's staring you right in the face."

She looks up at the mirror over the mantelpiece. Her face is reflected in it.

The mirror with the eyeholes.

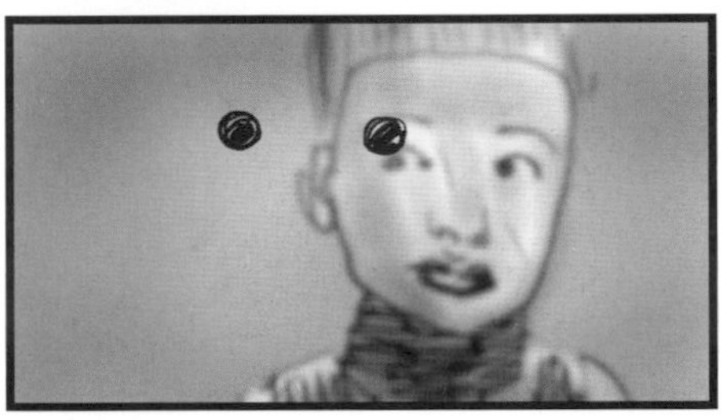

The eyeholes sit exactly over her eyes.

Just like a mask.

HELENA (CONT'D)
This was her bedroom. The other girl. The Princess.

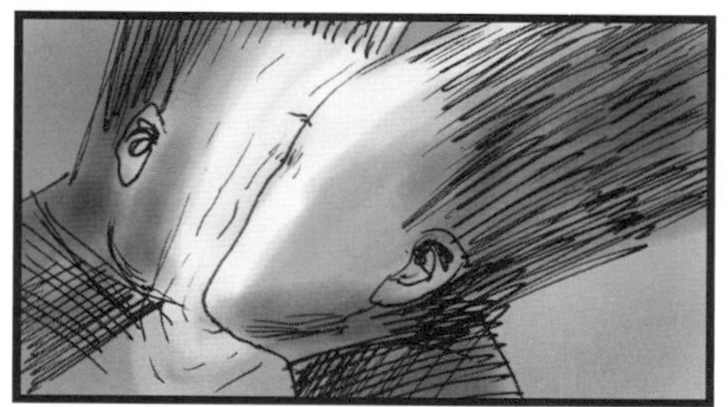

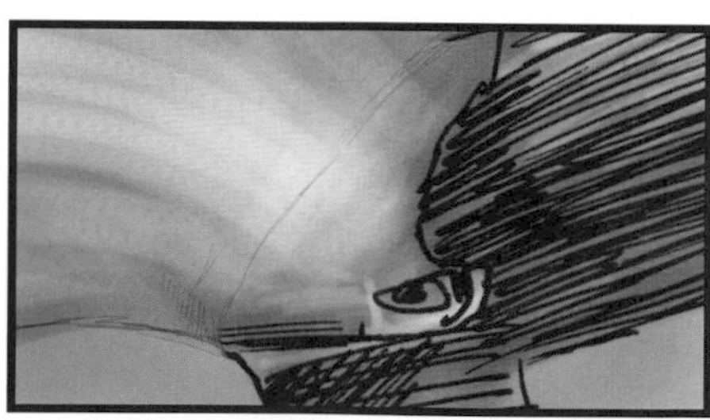

VALENTINE looks up at it, too.

HELENA (CONT'D)
Are you thinking what I'm thinking?

VALENTINE
Absolutely! If we put little wheels on the bottoms of our shoes, we could just roll around.

HELENA
No, silly. What's the best place to hide a mirror?

In the mirror their eyes meet.

Then we go out of focus – we're looking at the frame, at the mirror itself.

HELENA stands up.

The palace shakes and rumbles. Somewhere something bad is happening.

Helena pushes her face into the mirror on the wall, her eyes lining up with the holes. She pulls her face back.

The mirror pulls away from the frame, like rubber. In the frame now is a painting of the princess in a posh frock.

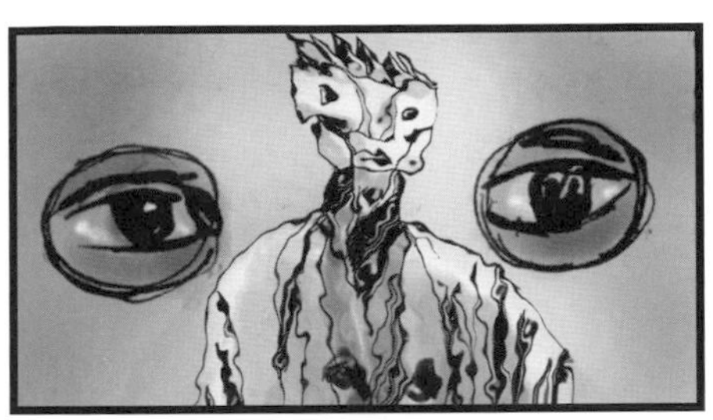

VALENTINE
Don't touch it. It might be dangerous.

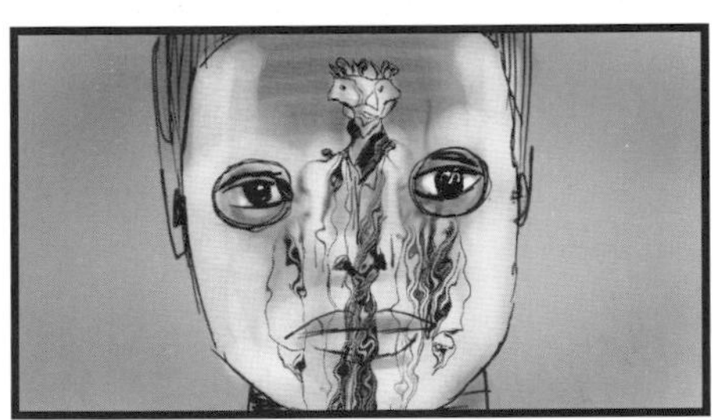

We're looking at VALENTINE reflected as he says this. Then we pull back a little to see HELENA's eyes staring at us through the holes in the mirrored surface.

Her face is now a mirror. Only the eyes are her own.

The world shakes.

And then she pulls it off. She looks around, and grabs a black velvet bag. She puts the MirrorMask into the bag.
A distant rumble.

HELENA
We've got to find a window.

VALENTINE
Before or after dinner?

HELENA
Tt! Valentine.

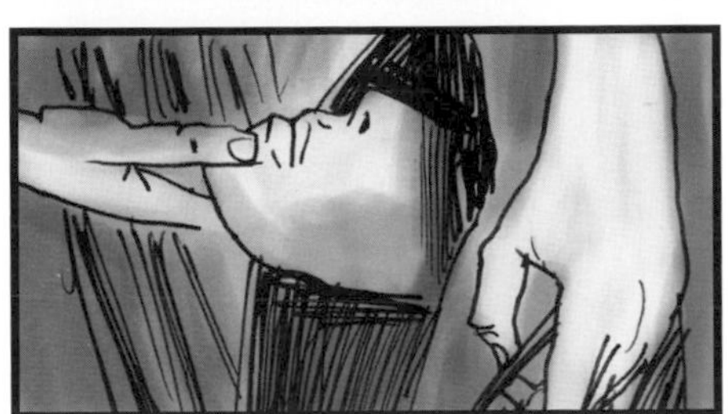

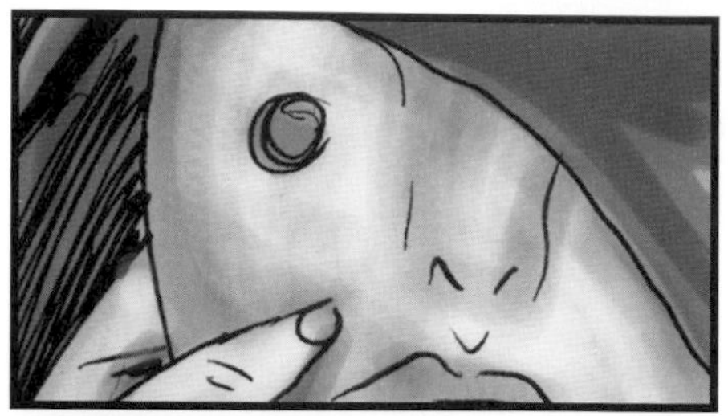

EXT. DARK PALACE. STEPS – NIGHT.

VALENTINE and HELENA come out of the door and go barrelling down the stairs.

At the bottom of the steps the SMALL HAIRY creature looks at them, blinks, and calls:

SMALL HAIRY
Princess! Princess!
(to himself)
Oh, not again.

He begins, laboriously, to climb the steps.

EXT. DARK FOREST – NIGHT.

VALENTINE and HELENA are running through the forest.

VALENTINE
Run. Keep running. Towards the fog, the fog's okay. Stay on the path. Run. Go on. Run. Don't let anything distract you.

There's a clearing up ahead of them and a tree in it – with one branch, upon which grows an enormous fruit, like a gigantic lychee.

VALENTINE (CONT'D)
Food!

HELENA
Valentine, we have to keep going. There's honestly no time!

VALENTINE
You're absolutely right.
(pause)
Right –

He runs over to the tree, hauls off the fruit and begins to peel it.

A SMALL WOMAN, asleep at the foot of the tree wakes up and walks over to HELENA.

SMALL WOMAN
Is he very holy, my love?

HELENA
Holy? I don't think so. Why?

SMALL WOMAN
Usually, it's only very holy people who come here.

HELENA
I'm afraid we got here by accident.

SMALL WOMAN
The holy people. They eat the future fruit, and they come back with words of wisdom. Sometimes they write whole books. It's wonderful. Takes one fruit three hundred years to grow, my petal.

VALENTINE has finished peeling the fruit, which means he is left with a huge amount of peel and a little fruit, and has taken his first exploratory bite.

VALENTINE
Not bad. Rather yummy actually. Why do they call it a future fruit?

SMALL WOMAN
Because that's where you go when you eat it, my ducks.

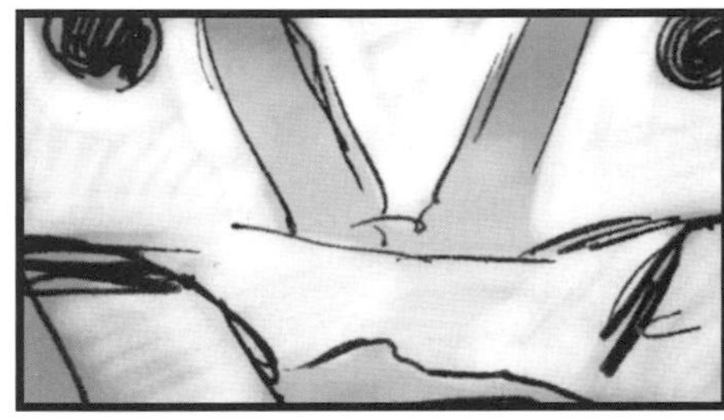

VALENTINE looks shocked and stunned. And then things go swimmy.

INT. BORDERLANDS. VALENTINE'S TOWER – DAY.

HELENA and VALENTINE are in a white room, with a window in, through which we can see our world.

HELENA
There's only one way out –

VALENTINE
And I'm taking it. Goodbye.

He snatches the MirrorMask from her. It forms itself to the shape of his face.

We hurtle in on him as he – pushes through his mind into . . .

EXT. LONDON. STREET – DAY.

It's a grey, wet day in London.

We see a bedraggled-looking VALENTINE, maskless and human, his hat on the ground in front of him, juggling, dispiritedly.
Several people walk by without stopping.

Then a POLICEMAN stops and begins to talk to him. VALENTINE looks sick.

And we –

CUT TO:

INT. LONDON. RESTAURANT – NIGHT.

Now VALENTINE has a proper job – he's a waiter, walking through a crowded restaurant balancing several plates. As he goes, people start to shout at him.

He puts the plates down on a table –

as more and more customers start to shout orders at him, looming at him in crazy angles. At first he nods, and then he runs back towards the kitchen, shaking his head, unable to cope –

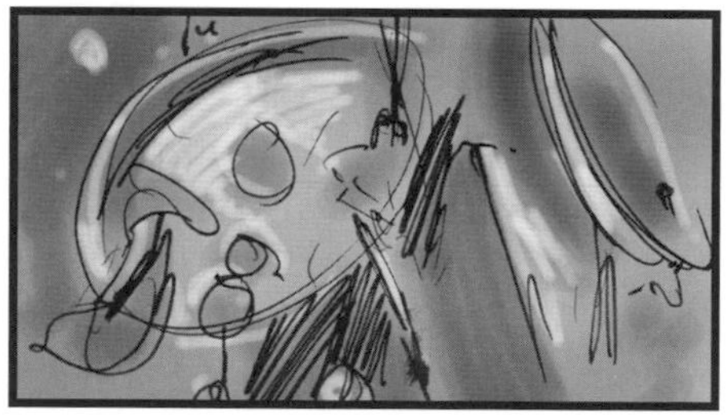

He drops plates of food that crash to the ground.

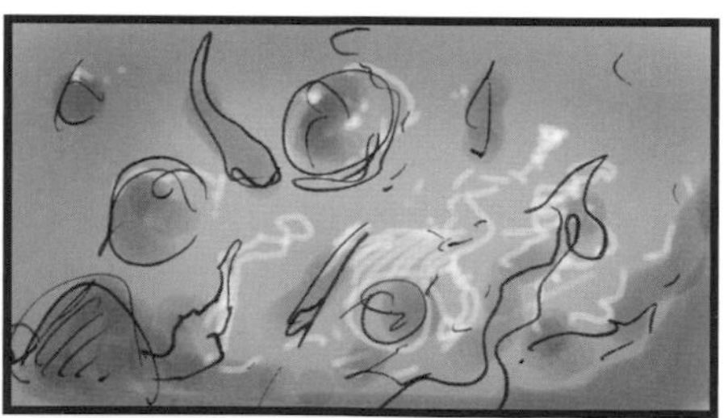

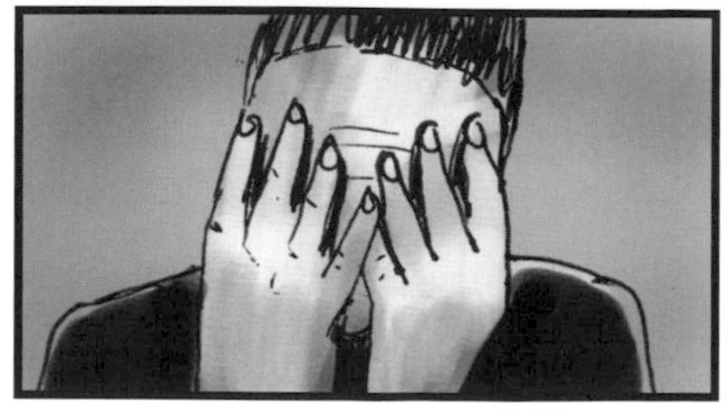

And we close in on his face and –

slam back to the future fruit tree –

EXT. DARK FOREST – NIGHT.

VALENTINE opens his eyes very wide.

VALENTINE
No! I don't want to be a waiter!

HELENA
Are you okay?

VALENTINE
Of course I'm not okay, you stupid girl. I stole the mask from you, and I went to your world.

HELENA
Really?

VALENTINE
Why would I lie about something so, so monstrous, the policeman
(mimes)
I go
(mimes)
then everything goes sorry sir here's your ratatouille, oh it'll come out, it's just food, there's not even a rat in it, help, fire, volcanos!

SMALL WOMAN
(interrupting)
Excuse me, my flower?

VALENTINE
What?

SMALL WOMAN
If you don't mind, I ought to plant the seed.

VALENTINE passes her the fruit seed. As they walk away, the SMALL WOMAN takes out a little trowel and begins to dig a little hole to plant the seed.

SMALL WOMAN (CONT'D)
Three hundred years, and what do we get? "I don't want to be a waiter." I was hoping for something with a bit more meat to it, like "Love one another".

INT. DARK PALACE. THRONE ROOM – NIGHT.

The SMALL HAIRY creature pushes open the door to the throne room. The Council sits around a huge table, arguing: a strange and motley bunch of nightmare creatures.

OVID
I think a retaliatory strike against the White City is really the only way to go on this.

HORACE
You are talking through your hat! With respect, Majesty, I think this entire end-of-the-world scenario is grossly overexaggerated. We are wildly overreacting to a minor series of –

BOGGART
Minor? You try living in a swamp that isn't there any more, mate. You come and tell me that that's minor.

During this the SMALL HAIRY creature has walked around the table, very nervously, and is now standing next to the DARK QUEEN. Very, very, very quietly it's going:

SMALL HAIRY
Ahem.

SWINBURNE
Look. The question is not "Is the World Ending?" But far more realistically, "In today's fast-moving world, is there a place for – "

OGRE
Total world destruction?

SWINBURNE
Well, all right, "is there a place for total world destruction" vis-a-vis —

SMALL HAIRY
Ahem. Ahem. Ahem.

And the DARK QUEEN notices him.

DARK QUEEN
Yes?

OVID
A scenario which is simply not feasible –

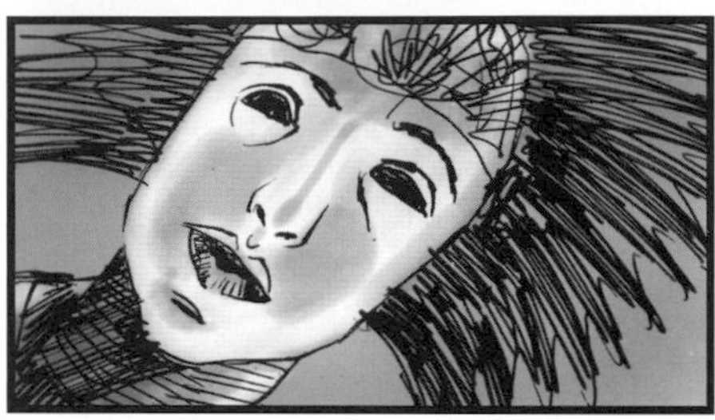

DARK QUEEN
Quiet!

(to Small Hairy)
What?

SMALL HAIRY
It's the Princess. . . .

DARK QUEEN
What. About. The Princess.

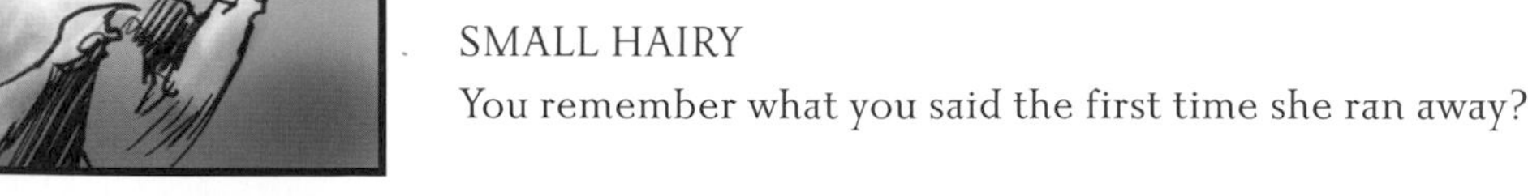

SMALL HAIRY
You remember what you said the first time she ran away?

DARK QUEEN
(sweetly and dangerously)
The first time?

SMALL HAIRY creature squinches up its face and prepares for something bad to happen.

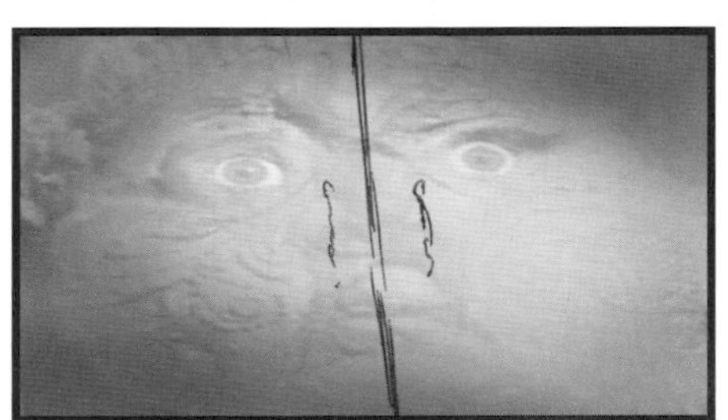

EXT. DARK PALACE. STEPS – NIGHT (ALL CGI).

We hear the DARK QUEEN roar.
Down the steps come hordes of creatures. Everything that the budget will run to. Thousands upon thousands of Orcs and mighty Uruk-hai, their weapons glinting as they prepare to do the bidding of the evil Saruman. . . Sorry. Got a bit carried away there. Wrong movie. No budget.
Whatever we've got comes down the stairs.
Black birds come out of the windows.
Black tendrils and tentacles explode out of the door.

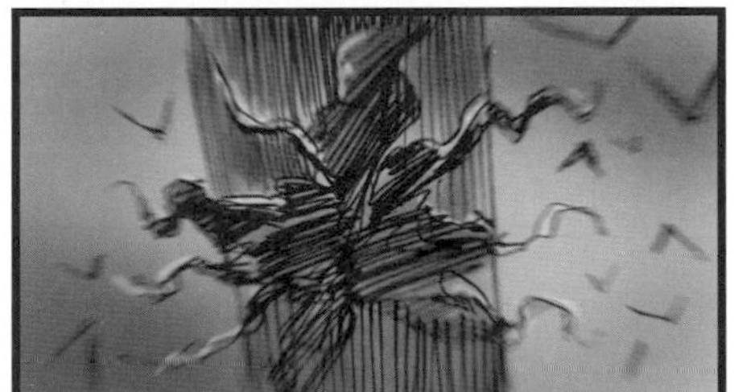

EXT. DARK FOREST – NIGHT.

VALENTINE and HELENA are still on the run through the forest. The lampposts are getting wilder and stranger.

VALENTINE
So this MirrorMask . . . there must be a way to use it to get us out of here.

HELENA
I think we have to find a window. If I can see her I bet I can get to her.

VALENTINE
We won't find any windows here in the forest.

HELENA
I have to see what she's doing.

VALENTINE
We know what she's doing. Whether she means to or not, she's destroying the world.

HELENA
And snogging boys and eating chips and smoking and everything!

EXT. DARK LANDS – NIGHT.

The DARK QUEEN's birds are flooding through the skies. Along the ground, blackness flows like a tidal wave, destroying all in its path.

EXT. BORDERLANDS – NIGHT.

VALENTINE and HELENA come out of the forest.

Ahead of them we can see the White City, the Day Lands. Behind them are the Dark Lands.
They are in a wasteland. A border zone.
They run.

VALENTINE
We're nearly there, Helena.

She trips on the now ragged hem of her dress.

HELENA
Why do people wear these stupid dresses?

She rips off the bottom of it. The black birds come down from the sky like something from a very blobby Hitchcock movie and form a moving wall in front of VALENTINE and HELENA. VALENTINE and HELENA stop and look around.

The tidal wave of darkness is coming towards them.

EXT. BORDERLANDS – NIGHT.

It stops a few hundred feet away, and it forms itself into a huge face.

A face the size of a house. It's the DARK QUEEN. She looks at them.

DARK QUEEN
I should have known you'd be involved in this, Valentine.

VALENTINE
Ah.

HELENA
Listen to me. Your daughter is going to destroy everything. I need to find a window and get back there. Please, let us go.

DARK QUEEN
You are my daughter.

HELENA
You know that's not true.

DARK QUEEN
I am a reasonable woman. You come back with me. I'll execute Valentine humanely. And we'll say no more about it.

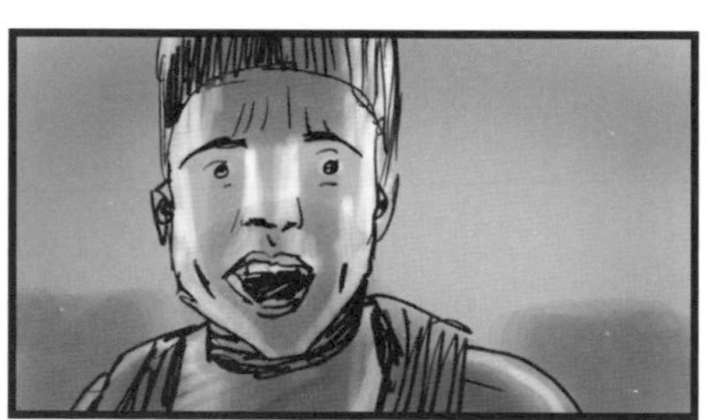

HELENA
She's not a pet. She's not even a child any more. You have to let her grow up.

DARK QUEEN
(reasonably, as if she's finally getting it)
You mean . . . let her choose her own clothes. Her own food. Make her own mistakes. Love her, but don't try to possess her.

HELENA
Yes. That's exactly what I mean.

DARK QUEEN
Absolutely out of the question.
Now, this will hurt you a lot more than it hurts me.

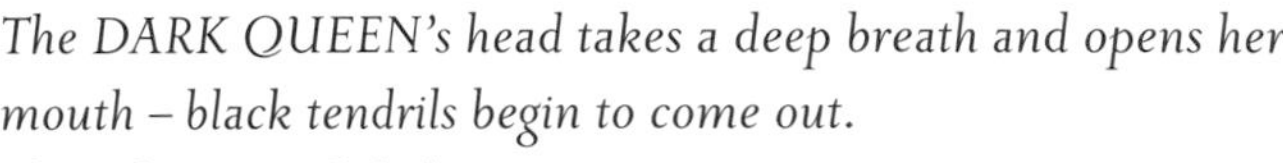

The DARK QUEEN's head takes a deep breath and opens her mouth – black tendrils begin to come out.
Then the ground shakes –

VALENTINE
I don't need this, you know. I'm a very important man.

HELENA
If we can't get away from her, you're a very dead man.

VALENTINE
Light.

HELENA
What?

VALENTINE
The thing you have that makes light. Where is it?

HELENA reaches into her bag and pulls out her torch. VALENTINE snatches it.

VALENTINE (CONT'D)
And the mask. Give me the MirrorMask.

She hesitates.

VALENTINE (CONT'D)
For God's sake. I know what I'm doing!

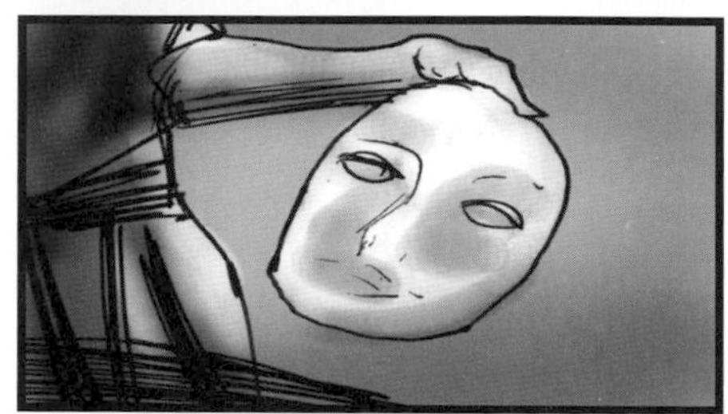

She gives him the mask.

He shines the light of the torch onto the mirror – a glow surrounds them. The darkness retreats, nervously. Then the mirror sends a burning beam of pure white light reflected up into the sky.

DARK QUEEN
Stop them!

VALENTINE looks up desperately, then shakes his head.

VALENTINE
I thought it would be here by now. That was always our signal.

HELENA
Didn't you say you'd had a fight . . .

VALENTINE
Only a difference of opinion. And I was completely in the right.

HELENA
Sometimes you have to say sorry.

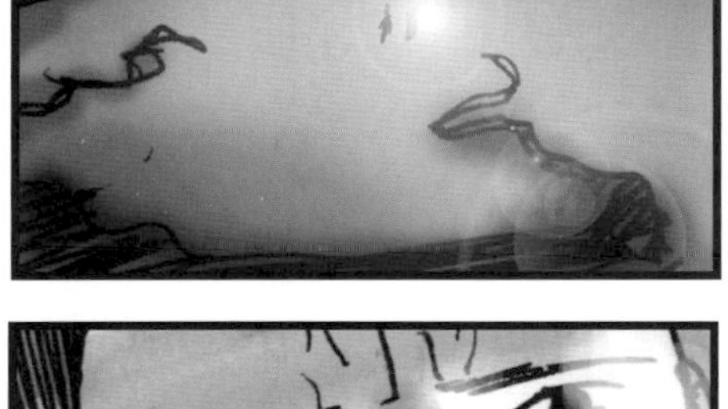

VALENTINE
I'll never say s . . .

(but the DARK QUEEN's shadows move closer)

All right. I'll say it!

(shouts to the sky)

I'm sorry!

And it comes, a huge and flapping tower, like a small skyscraper. Rocketing towards us on tiny wings.

HELENA
It's a real tower. You really did have a tower!

VALENTINE
Well, I'm a very important man.

The tower crashes towards them and then, at the last moment, touches down like a feather.

HELENA and VALENTINE run through the door of the tower.

The blackness realises what's going on, and a curling tentacle of darkness heads for the tower. But too late . . .

the tower's taking off into the sky.

They're already out of reach, and the tentacle falls back.

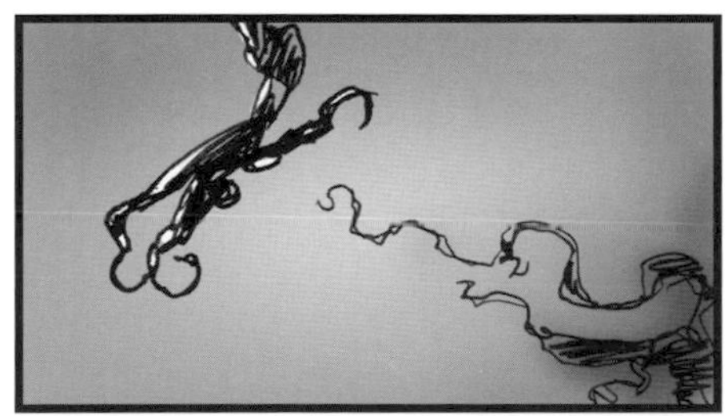

INT. BORDERLANDS. VALENTINE'S TOWER – DAY.

VALENTINE and HELENA inside. The tower is flying in huge flapping movements, swinging from side to side.

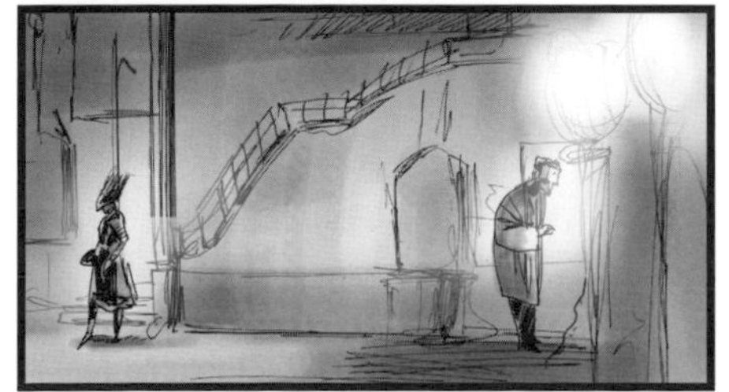

VALENTINE runs over to a window. It's just a window – all he can see is the world outside.

HELENA runs to another window – and finally sees through . . .

INT. TOWER BLOCK. AUNT NAN'S FLAT.
HELENA'S BEDROOM – DAY.

The window: ANTI-HELENA in her bedroom. She's now dressed in a style that a teacher might call "inappropriate". She's already ripped every picture down from the wall. She shuffles through the papers until she sees a piece of paper with a drawing of an odd skyscraper on it.

VALENTINE watches the landscape below.

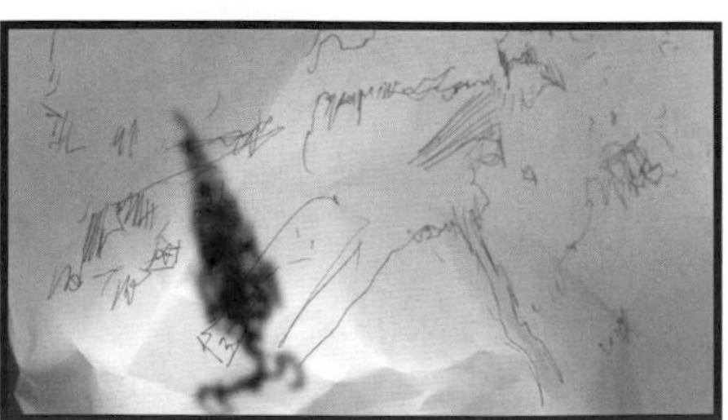

It crumples like paper.

HELENA
The windows, the ones I drew, they're doorways between her world and our world and she's destroying them.

The MirrorMask! Valentine! Give it to me, for heaven's sake –

One moment of recognition. HELENA looks up,

ANTI-HELENA looks down . . . she sees, through a tiny window on the paper, a tiny HELENA staring up at her.

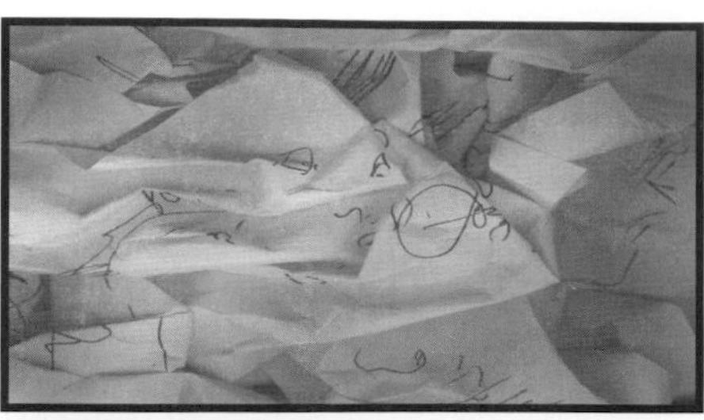

Everything crumples to black.

VALENTINE
What's happening!

HELENA
There are no more windows left.

It's over.

She won.

INT. TOWER BLOCK. AUNT NAN'S FLAT. HELENA'S BEDROOM – DAY.

And we're seeing it now from a different perspective. A ball of paper being scrunched tightly in a girl's hands.

Everything feels very real again.

ANTI-HELENA
(whispers)
I'm never going back.

ANTI-HELENA has gathered together every bit of paper she can find from the bedroom, and she's folded it all over, made a paper ball out of it, so that no windows are visible.

INT. TOWER BLOCK. AUNT NAN'S FLAT. LOUNGE – DAY.

We follow her as she goes into the lounge.

NAN, sitting in her chair, watching TV with the sound low, glances at her with not-quite-suppressed anger, but says nothing.

And ANTI-HELENA grabs a box of matches from the mantel-piece.

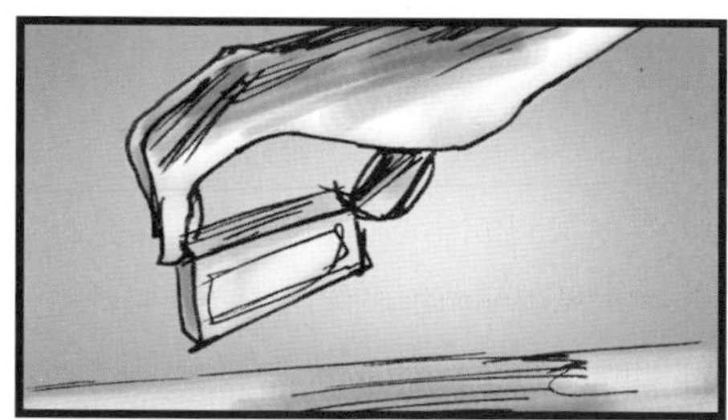

EXT. TOWER BLOCK. ROOFTOP – DAY.

ANTI-HELENA comes out onto the roof of the tower block, through the door. It's a windy day.

Up on the rooftop, she tries to light the matches, but the wind blows them out –

and she burns her fingers.

She walks to the edge of the roof. The city is laid out beneath her. On the roof we can see the remains of HELENA's coloured chalk drawing.
Petulantly, ANTI-HELENA throws the matches away.

Then she starts to tear up the drawings and the wind whips them away like confetti. She's laughing. She's won. Tiny strips of drawings which she tears again and again.

There is a bang from behind her,

as the door on the roof blows closed.

ANTI-HELENA turns and sees . . .

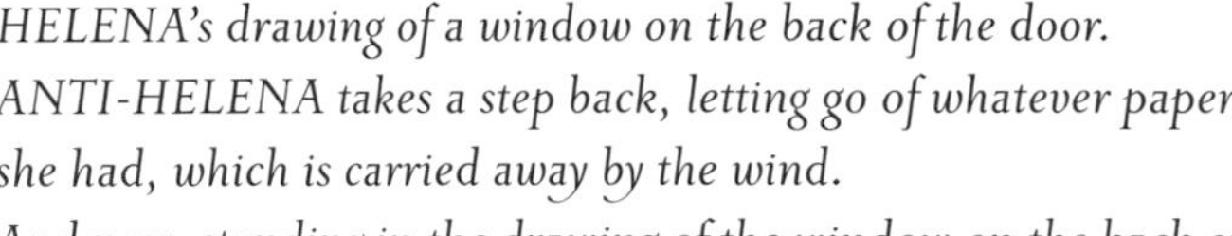

HELENA's drawing of a window on the back of the door.
ANTI-HELENA takes a step back, letting go of whatever paper she had, which is carried away by the wind.
And now, standing in the drawing of the window on the back of the door, is HELENA. She's holding the MirrorMask.

ANTI-HELENA
No, I'm not going back!

HELENA
This is my life. My world. You can't have it.

ANTI-HELENA
Please . . . ? I just wanted a real life.

HELENA
Real life? You couldn't handle real life.

ANTI-HELENA
No. I won't go back! I won't! It was my dream.

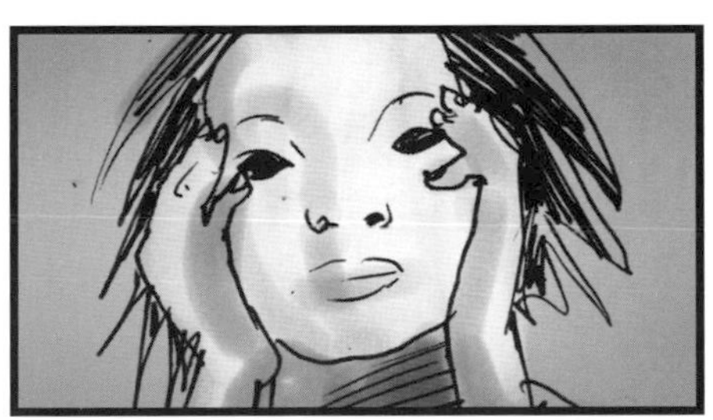

HELENA
It's not your dream. It's my dream. And it's done.

ANTI-HELENA looks around urgently, trying to see somewhere to escape to, somewhere to run, but she's on the top of a tower block.
And it's too late, because HELENA is holding the MirrorMask, and is raising it to her face.
Her face is reflective.
In it we can see the world reflected – and the other HELENA.
HELENA starts to slip through into our world.
The fragments of paper, the confetti, the bits of paper, are blowing towards the window.
It's sucking everything in.
HELENA holds out her hand.

ANTI-HELENA takes a step backward, fighting and resisting the whole way as best she can, but she's being pulled towards the doorway.

The two girls, identical, one with a reflective face, are now nose-to-nose.
They touch . . .

And like two beads of mercury slipping into each other, they begin to merge.

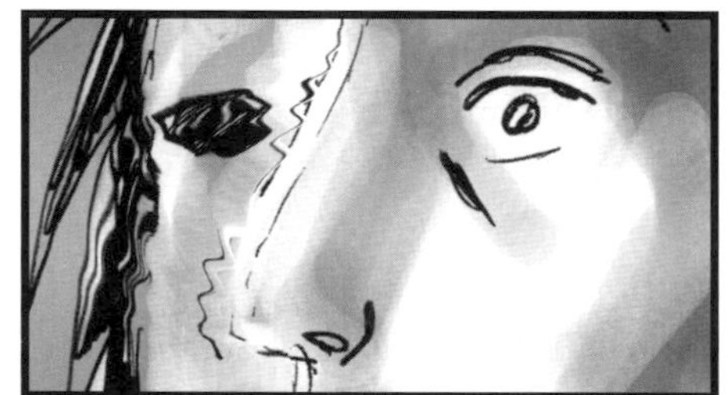

The MirrorMask swallows the ANTI-HELENA's face . . .
The girls dissolve into each other like two beads of mercury . . .

The music becomes transcendental, the montage begins.

HELENA (V.O.) (CONT'D)
And in the days that followed, there were other voids and other lights and other shadows. The MirrorMask she placed beneath the sign of the queen, to show the city that she knew it would never be finished, because the city was her life, and it would live forever.

And we see, as she says this . . .

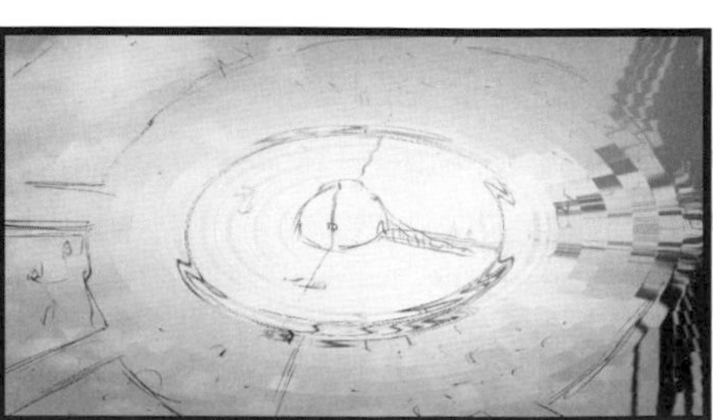

INT. WHITE CITY. WHITE QUEEN'S BEDROOM – DAY.

The White City . . . More elegant than we've ever seen it before. A place of beauty and magic. Not ruined, no longer run-down.

Multicoloured fish swim across the sky as the sun comes up – And we dip to look into the window of the White Palace.

The WHITE QUEEN, who opens her eyes and smiles . . .

Fade to:

EXT. TOWER BLOCK. ROOFTOP – MORNING.

It's 4:00 AM on a summer morning and the sun is just starting to rise. The world is quiet. A couple of birds are starting a tentative few early bars of the dawn chorus. There are puddles on the rooftop from the storms, a few hours ago.
Below us, on the roof of the tower block, a girl is asleep.

We descend. It's HELENA – wearing the T-shirt nightie she was wearing earlier in the film. She's asleep. Barefoot, or in bunny slippers.

A man stands beside her. He crouches and rests his hand on her shoulder. It's her father . . .

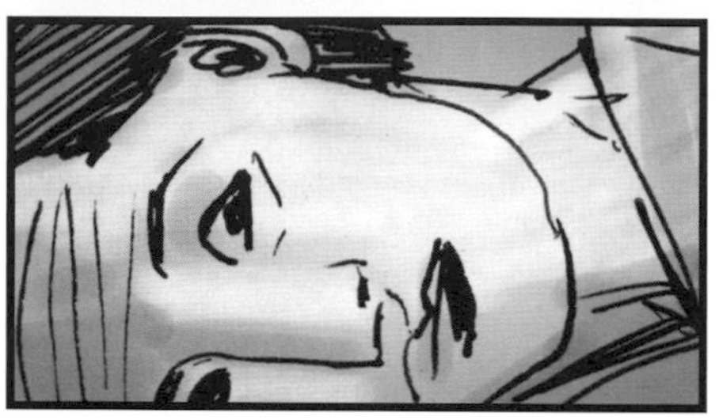

MORRIS
Helena?

She rolls over and opens her eyes.

HELENA
Dad?

She touches her face . . . feeling for the MirrorMask, touching flesh . . .

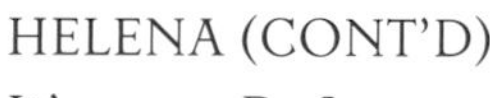

HELENA (CONT'D)
It's gone, Dad.

MORRIS
Funny place to go to sleep, love.

HELENA
I wasn't asleep. . . I was in . . .
(then, remembering)
Mum!

MORRIS
No news yet, love. Let's just keep our fingers crossed. Look at you. You must be frozen . . .

He puts his jacket around her shoulders.

The mobile phone in the jacket pocket rings. HELENA answers it.

HELENA
No. But I'll put him on.

(to Morris)
It's for you. It's the hospital.

She's scared; so's he.

He listens to the message, his face a poker. Then, trying to hold back tears, he says:

MORRIS
No. Thanks for telling me. No, I appreciate it. No. That's . . . I'll make the arrangements.

He looks down at HELENA. Rests his hand on her shoulder.

HELENA
What did they say?

MORRIS
Cup of tea?

HELENA
Dad!

MORRIS
She's fine, love. They got it all. She'll be a bit weak for a little while, but she's going to be fine.

We're going to be fine.

CAPTION
And they were . . .

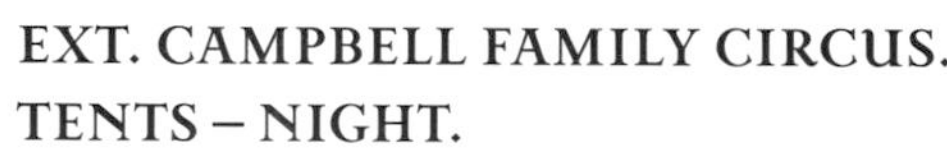

EXT. CAMPBELL FAMILY CIRCUS.
TENTS – NIGHT.

We see a new leaflet/poster incorporating the half sun/half moon image of the city, and in the foreground, it shows the reunion of the DARK QUEEN and her daughter.

It is being walked past by a YOUNG MAN in the foreground. A line of people is queued up to go into the circus. . . We go along the line.
JOANNE is taking tickets, at the end of the line. There's a YOUNG MAN with his back to us . . .

YOUNG MAN
One please. And I was wondering about how I'd go about, er, running away and joining the circus.

JOANNE
(as if she answers this question every day)
You need to be over eighteen. And pass the audition. And mad. Next?

Then JOANNE looks past him and smiles at someone –
– it's HELENA, who is walking along the crowd, juggling as she walks.

HELENA
The greatest little show on earth will be starting in five minutes, so please, ladies and gentlemen, will you take your seats . . . ?

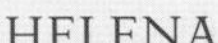

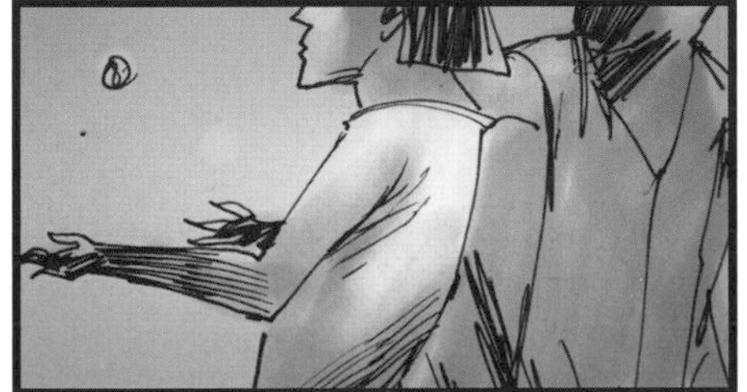

She takes a step back, bumps into someone behind her who is not looking where he's going, and one ball goes flying.

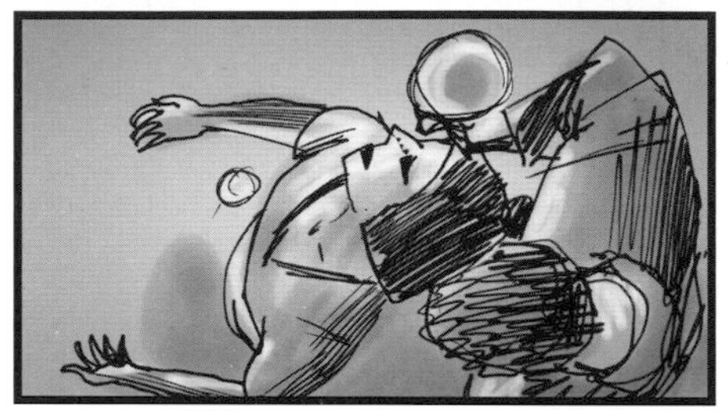

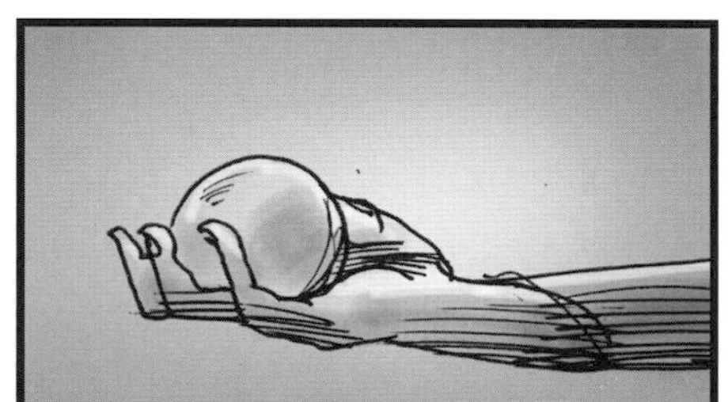

A hand reaches out and the ball slaps down in it.

YOUNG MAN
I'm sorry.

HELENA
It's okay.

It's the young man who was just buying a ticket. It's VALENTINE . . . or at least, VALENTINE's human equivalent. Oddly, HELENA doesn't seem to mind at all. He tosses her the ball.

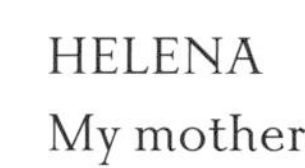

VALENTINE
I was talking to the woman in the window.

HELENA
My mother.

VALENTINE
I was talking to the lovely lady in the window. You know, I've always wanted to work in a circus.

HELENA
Good. You would have made a lousy waiter.
See you after?

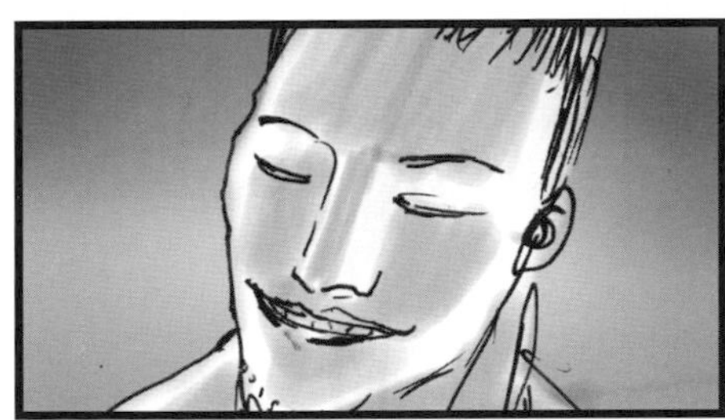

They laugh, in recognition . . . and then:

VALENTINE
What?

Crash cut to black and credits and circus music.

END

APPENDIX A – The Origins of MirrorMask

From: Neil Gaiman
To: Dave McKean

Date: 09/06/01 8:11 PM

RE: early neil notes

Dave –
Dump or keep anything you like . . .
n

THE MIRROR AND THE MASK

A tale of urban magic and the imagination.

There was a girl called Lenore Wilkins. She was fifteen, and she didn't fit in. Her parents had been two of the last travelling players in England, part of a troupe giving performances of Shakespeare and Jonson and Marlowe in country theatres and hedgerows and village halls, and Lenore was, she was told, born in a trunk.

This is not actually true. But her parents thought it was.

Then her mother got sick, and nobody said the word cancer aloud, and she faded. Her father took to the bottle, and nursed his wife as best he could, until it was beyond his skill, and the troupe, who had only been held together with spit and cobwebs and dreams, fell apart.

Lenore, who had been acting with the troupe since she was a tiny child, was sent to stay with her mother's sister, Aunt Kallie.

Sometimes she would go, on the bus, to the hospice, where her mother was. There was a photo on her mother's bedside table of Lenore and her mother and father.

When you are on the road, your education is a strange thing. She'd rarely be anywhere long enough to go to school. Her parents were meant to teach her out of books, but as long as she was reading they were happy.

Which meant that, when she went to school, Lenore Wilkins could perform any of Shakespeare's heroines, and most of the minor parts. She knew them word-perfect, and she knew what they were saying. She didn't know where America was, or Bohemia, or the Forest of Arden, or Switzerland. She didn't know about the EEC, although she had argued the merits of Marlowe and Sheridan with her father, and could run rings around the English teachers.

She dressed weird. She was liable to fly off the handle and into an explosive temper, if teased. She did not play well with others. The other kids said she was a witch, and that made her angrier still.

And she was being haunted.

Life in her new home was not good. A tower block, built in the 1960s, now ripe for demolition, smelling of piss and damp concrete. Most of the people have been moved out, but Aunt Kallie is still there, up endless stairs because the lifts don't work.

She could take that. But not the people in animal masks who stare at her from other stairwells and from down the ends of corridors, spooking her, scaring her. Hanging upside down . . . and never there when she goes to look for them, and to face them head on. They are in the tower block. They are at her home. She is scared that they are in her mind.

And then, sometimes, in the half-light, there was someone in the mirror, who wasn't ever there when she turns around.

And the nightmares, of being imprisoned somewhere beneath the ground.

At school, Midsummer Night's Dream was being cast. Lenore wanted to play Titania, but her teachers decided she'd be too much trouble, and offered her the prompter job. Lenore stormed out . . .

On top of the tower block she furiously declaimed Titania's big speeches.

Her reflection, in a puddle, stared back at her. And then she saw the same figure she had seen in the mirror, a lithe young man in a brown mask, standing beside her. A glance to her side he's not there, only in the reflection.

She lunged into the puddle . . . And she grabbed the young man. She held him tight. He seemed shocked that she had made it through the reflection into his world. He told her that he was trying to make it into her world, to warn her that she is being hunted.

Who is he? He's a puck.

She sneered, he's not Shakespeare's Puck. No, he said. Just a puck. A willy wisp. There are a hundred of us.

She looked around. They were no longer on top of a tower block . . . Now they were on some strange reflection of a tower block, as a natural formation, inhabited by strange creatures.

This place, Puck told her, is Mirror. It is the most wonderful place in the world, ruled by the Queen of Night . . . a goblin creature who is feared and hated.

But, Puck mentioned, in the garden of the Queen of Night grows a bush with golden fruit on it. Fruit that would cure any disease, any pain.

Even cancer? She asked.

Yes. Even that.

If her mother was well, her father would stop drinking. He would put the troupe together. She would be able to go home. She could stop this horrid school.

In a moment, Lenore was focussed. We're going to get the fruit, she told Puck . . .

In the Palace of the Queen of Night, the Queen herself was on the move. She was beautiful, but cruel, and the creatures in the palace that served her were all of them terrified of her. She was going down to the bottommost cell in the palace.

In the deepest cell, there was a prisoner. Filthy, and scared, and the mirror-image of Lenore, blonde where Lenore was dark.

Where is she? asked the queen. Where is your sister?

I'll never tell you, said the girl.

You don't need to tell me, said the Queen, with a smile. She was on Earth. But we've found her. She's on her way here.

She closed the door on the blonde girl, and went up.

Puck and Lenore travelled through the strange night-world. They met strange goblin-creatures, masked things, weird things like old children, dancers, all manner of entities and people.

Lenore performed for them. They loved that poetry to the goblin kind is as meat and drink and money to us.

She danced with the dancers. These were her people . . .

Lenore found Puck infuriating but good-hearted. As the two of them travelled towards the palace of the Queen of Night, Lenore learned a number of things.

In Mirror, it had been night for fifteen years.

In Mirror there was once a Queen of Day. There was balance. But the last Queen vanished one night, and the Queen of Night grew darker and stranger and more cruel. Tendrils of night crept across the world, covering everything. Morning never came.

The Queen buys things. She wants to own them. If she cannot own them, she will destroy them.

What is important in Mirror is status. The mask you wear says who you are and how important you are. Puck tells Lenore he dreams that he would be allowed to wear the Hunter's Moon Mask, as opposed to his own lowly puck mask.

On the way to the palace, Puck saved Lenore's life.

Lenore, in her turn, saved Puck from a fight that he got himself into.

They were in a hostel, a small inn, and Puck was putting on a show to keep Lenore's spirits up singing, dancing, animating common objects in a chorus, to the delight of Lenore and the people in the inn, when the Queen of Night walked into the hostel, and where her feet passed people fell asleep. All except Puck. He stopped singing, mid-verse.

You will be with us tomorrow, she said. You have done well.

He did not look as pleased with himself as he should. He had done what he was meant to do, but still . . . he was uncomfortable.

Smile, Sir Puck, she said. Tomorrow, you will wear the Hunter's Moon Mask.

When they woke, they set off to the palace of the Queen of Night.

What happened to the Queen of Day? Lenore asked. Is she dead?

Puck shook his head. The Queens cannot die, except by their own hands.

The palace of the Queen of Night was dark and impossible and huge. It looked like it was made of night, and stars twinkled in its fabric: a citadel of darkness. The trees burned with their own cold light, and Chinese lanterns and glow worms and fireflies hung and glowed on its grounds.

The Puck led Lenore to the place behind the palace where the tree grew with glowing golden fruits. She reached up to take one . . .

. . . and the procession began. Clowns and tumblers and stilt-dancers and the rest came in, followed by the Queen of Night in all her awful majesty.

It'd all been a set-up.

The Queen congratulated Puck, who stared down, unhappily. Lenore was horrified. "I saved your life," she said. "I trusted you."

Puck told her to be quiet, unable to look at her or talk to her.

The Queen of Night put her arms around Lenore, and explained to her that Lenore is here to be the new Queen of Night. She was going to be the Queen's protégée. She was one of a pair of twins born fifteen years ago, and she was sent to Earth to hide her from the Queen.

The Queen showed Lenore the mask that would be hers now, a strange and wonderful Titania mask.

Lenore did not want it. But the Queen persuaded her, whispered and beguiled if Lenore wanted a fruit from the Queen's garden, then she would be a good girl and indulge the queen on this one thing . . .

Lenore put on the mask, and was transformed: it made Lenore look like some transcendent butterfly-faced young woman. Her clothes changed, too. She was a princess.

But the moment Lenore put on the mask, she forgot everything. She forgot her mother. She forgot Earth. She was now, simply, the Princess . . .

The Queen triumphantly led the procession away, leaving only Puck holding his new silver Hunter's Moon mask, by the tree that could have saved Lenore's mother's life.

In his new Hunter's Moon mask, the Puck went out, and heard people talk about the brave Puck who had stood up to the queen . . . He realised they were talking about him. Or what they thought he was. He saw things that reminded him of Lenore . . . and of what he did . . . And he was inexpressibly miserable.

In her throne room, the Queen was delighted with her control of Lenore.

She explained to Lenore that there is one more task to do before Lenore can be a full princess. She needed to kill an evil girl who wanted to hurt the Queen . . . an evil criminal.

The Queen went down to the prison, to say her good-bye to the blonde girl who looked like Lenore.

Puck (perhaps he wore a guard's mask, but either way, he was disguised) accompanied her, and realised that Lenore and this girl were, together, the Queen of Day. If Lenore killed the girl, then she would be killing both of them.

He has to snap Lenore out of it.

He breaks into Lenore's quarters and tried to explain to her what was going on. But the brainwashed Lenore simply summoned the guards and the queen, who congratulated her.

In the moonlight, the queen gave Lenore a curved knife, and told her to kill the girl. To prove her loyalty, her fitness for the throne.

And first, she must kill the troublesome Puck.

The bound Puck was lowered from a rope in the sky.

Lenore is meant to cut his throat. Instead she slices his bonds, and drops the knife. Then she takes off the Titania mask. She goes to the blonde princess . . .

I dreamed your dreams, said Lenore. You were imprisoned.

The blonde princess nodded. She held out her arms. Lenore touched them and the bonds fell away . . .

The Queen was going mad. "Stop them!" she was screaming. "Kill them!"

But the two girls touched . . . and melted into one person, like two drops of mercury touching and joining. They became a new person: something like Lenore, something like her sister, but transformed and transcendent, lit by her own light.

Daylight. Morning has broken.

It was the first time in fifteen years daylight had been seen in the world beyond the mirror.

Light revealed: the palace of night was a shadow, a skeleton place, not impressive at all, like a fun-fair by day: everything impressive was lights and reflections.

The Queen was terrified. "What will you do to me?"

"Nothing," said the Queen of Day. "There must be day, as there must be night. But you can never again do anything to touch the balance of the two. Or we will take your power forever."

In a little tavern, Puck was discovered by some strange little creatures. "Sir," they said. "Are you not entitled to wear a Silver Hunter's Moon Mask?"

"I am," said Puck.

"Then why do you not wear it? Why do you wear that old puck mask?"

In reply, he took off his mask entirely, and let it fall, leaving the little creatures scandalised and horrified. And, despite themselves, impressed at his bravery. Perhaps he will start a new trend . . .

In the hospital, Lenore's mother woke from a thin and troubled sleep. There was a smell, coming from the fruit on the bedside table. She tried some. Then she smiled, weakly, but, for the first time in a long time, her colour started coming back.

And she saved a little of it for her husband.

"Where did it come from?" he asked.

"I don't know love," she says. "I think it's a miracle."

"It's a remission," he says. "They happen." And he chews the last of the fruit. "It reminds me of something," he says. "But I can't think what." And then he says, "A remission, eh? Well, that calls for a drink . . . Or maybe it doesn't." Their hands meet.

There's a photo on the bedside table. We saw it before, but it no longer has Lenore in it. Just a man and a woman.

From: Dave McKean
To: Neil Gaiman

Date: 10/14/01 2:00 PM

RE: early neil notes

Hi Neil,
Okay so far I think, is it necessary to talk about faeries?

I've been trying to think of things that could be mirrored, things that we in this world entertain ourselves with that are in fact long-lost representations of the other world. Circus is a good one. And in that world they also have circus but it has acts that caricature and distort our world. Where we have high trapeze that parodies flying creatures and jugglers that mimic telekinesis, they have acts that parody a nuclear family juggling career/babies/cooking (this comes from CIRCUS UMBILICUS that I developed as a film with Django Bates but didn't come of anything). Comics is another one. Also tattoos, ritualistic stuff, even modern art/situationist events/installation art. Also some sports events; boxing/wrestling, fencing, all sorts. I'm thinking of anything that has developed its own characters/rules/language and no one really knows why, and what these things mean. They could be leakage, slippage from that world to this, the connection between the two, the bridge. Also, I find it very helpful to start to hear a film, especially music, it really sets the tone.

I've been listening to ANJA GARBAREK, who I think is just right for this.

From: Dave McKean
To: Neil Gaiman

Date: 10/10/01 11:19 AM

RE: early neil notes

Hi Neil,
Good to talk yesterday.

Having gone to sleep thinking about worlds behind the mirror or wall and tendrils of night, I woke up this morning with an idea, what do you think?

Family and situ as you've got it so far.

You've got the mother unwell, how about something really life changing/threatening, how about cancer. Something that our girl has no power over, and this becomes the theme of the film, the way we create situations for ourselves that we DO have power over, in order to distract us from the reality that we don't have power over the big stuff.

The news that her mum has cancer is enough to push our girl into retreat into a fantasy world. In the real world she's like every kid, sometimes kind and understanding, sometimes spiteful and bolshy. I like the use of mirrors etc, but I'm not sure about the "seeing reflections of other people" stuff, I saw the trailer for THE OTHERS yesterday and that was all mirrors and ghosts reflected in them, and it's been done so many times, the greatest being ORPHEE. How about she wakes up in the night. Silent and dark, wind blowing. Maybe she hears something to get her out of bed, nobody around, her mum's in hospital but her dad isn't in bed either. She looks out the window, no one around, the front door is open, she wanders out into the street, we move gradually into a slightly changed reality, she walks into the desolate road, turns and her front door has gone. (Is this too close to Coraline for you?) But we start with the audience AND OUR GIRL assuming that this is a dream, confirmed by the fact that early on, she looks through a window on tip-toe and sees herself asleep in bed, she is in one of the drawings on her bedroom wall. But later she looks out of another window and the bed is empty, she is up, it is daylight in her bedroom. She realises that she has split into the good girl, now locked in this world, while her bad side is inhabiting her real body. I don't think we should spend any time with the bad girl, but we should see (but not hear) her arguing with her dad and upsetting him, spending her savings on frivolous things (instead of bus fare to visit her mum) and about halfway through, our girl sees her starting to burn all the photos of her mum she can find, adding urgency to her quest.

In the fantasy city, everyone has deserted apart from a few strange stragglers, it is end-of-the-world type strangeness, mad prophets and lost souls. The reason is the impending endless night, tendrils of night start to drift down the streets. The reason why the queen of night is taking over is the illness of the queen of light. This is obviously a visualisation of her mum's illness. The cancer black tendrils of night warp and rot everything they touch. But here she is not powerless (I like the idea that in order to gain control over the situation with her mum, she has lost control over her real body to her bad side). In fairy tale tradition if she follows a route, or map, or sequence of clues, she begins to loosen the grip of the tendrils (there must be logical reason to this, even if it's an internal logic, the audience must start to see the internal logic and be willing her to realise the next step; these events must not be explained as just "that's the way it is"). It would be good if about two thirds through, the bad girl starts to play a more direct role, ripping drawings off the wall, trying to destroy our girl, or reordering the drawings confusing her, or turning them upside down, so she has to walk on the upside-down surface of water, or on the ceilings of rooms. I like the idea that she has to map her territory at some point to keep track, walking around a building and noting the shape and interior courtyard as a lozenge, maybe an eye. She climbs the highest tower she can find, and the building is an eye within an arrangement of buildings forming an animal, maybe she was trying to find the end of the tail, etc.

The finale should include as you've said already, the good and bad girl melting together, we can only exist with both sides to our nature in balance. She needs to perform one final act as the complete girl in order to wake the queen of light.

At the end, well if this was reality, mum would die, but we should give her something, cancer can go into remission. There should be a completely rational reason for her mother's state of health. Actually, better than that, maybe dad didn't tell her that she was going into the operating theatre that night. Her fantasy was a visualisation of the battle over her mum's body under the surgeon's knife.

I hope this is of use, I don't think it changes much from what we've talked about already. I'm just anxious that the film be about real people in real situations. Fantasy stories rely on cliché too much, fairy stories about fairies I think are pointless, fairy stories about the people who need to believe in fairies can be fascinating.

Let me know.
Cheers
Dave

From: Dave McKean
To: Neil Gaiman

Date: 10/31/01 9:18 AM

Hi Neil,
A couple more thoughts:

1. Opening scene. Two pairs of manky socks waggle with feet in them, bunched at the toes, pointing to the ceiling. They exaggerate the conversation, a completely natural exchange/argument between two girls, something completely mundane, the best boy band, what's "cool" etc. They look like they've been dressing up. We move slowly towards them. Off camera shout, sounds like a parent, Camera continues to move in and then rolls over the top of the sofa where the two girls are lying, upside down, feet in the air, camera comes to rest on head and shoulders of the girls, they are the right way up in camera, but upside down in reality, so their hair falls upwards. Dad shouts name at door, girl answers "coming" gives typical look of boredom to friend, "that's my dad, I'll be back in a minute," camera pans up, upside-down dad at door, "come on petal" and then a gesture indicating "out" (as if to indicate "homework" or something else mundane).

Camera rights itself as we follow her jumping up, pulling on her socks and shoes and heading out the door, camera follows behind her out of the room, into a hallway, out of another door and into a spotlight, surrounded by an audience, into her act.

2. End scene, last-ditch attempt by bad girl to scupper our girl's plans, she tears the drawings off the wall and screws them up. We can see which one our girl is inhabiting, the damage comes closer and closer, as she touches the paper, this is where the two meld together. Could be an exciting scene as we cut between bad girl furious tearing and good girl seeing city in the distance tearing up, folding in on itself, the apocalyptic damage coming closer and closer.

3. Maybe the quest is something that the queen of light has hidden. Something that she has taken with her into her coma. None of her courtiers/advisers know. Our girl would have a logical advantage over everybody. The light queen is a version of her mum, what would her mother have done. Does she use memories of her mum to work out the puzzle. Could we open up more of their relationship/past/love for each other/closeness by using these flashbacks, she regrets not paying more attention, getting to know her mum better.

Let me know.
cheers
Dave

From: Neil Gaiman
To: Dave Mckean

Date: 12/10/01 04:00 AM

Brilliant – I love both ideas. Can we do the city scrunching without it being ruinously expensive?

n

From: Dave McKean
To: Neil Gaiman

Date: 13/10/01 06:32 PM

Hi Neil,
Yes, what you should know is everything I'll suggest to you is possible with the tools I have already and for the super low budgets I've been used to. The only thing that more money will allow is crunching the time factor. More money means more employees and machines to number crunch quicker, but everything COULD be done just with me and Max (or a Max equivalent).
I realise that this is all upside down, but every scene set in a hospital or school or other location, I can see the £ flying by, crew, scouting, getting permission, equipment and set decor, lighting a working hospital, all very time-consuming and money-consuming, but collapsing a city, no sweat.
Having read your e-mail, I understand more where you were coming from with the "swapped kids/prince and pauper" idea, I'll think more about this. Loved the use of fruit, both a fairytale fave and a hospital regular.

Still like the masks running through everything/artifice.

I'll keep thinking.

Dave

From: Dave McKean
To: Neil Gaiman

Date: 26/11/01 10:51 AM

RE: more thoughts

Hi Neil,

Had a great and very inspiring day in London with family yesterday.

Went to British Museum with new Norman Foster roof over reading room, stunning.

Looked around Egyptian and Roman rooms.

Roman rooms full of sculpture you just want to see breathe. Especially an exquisite sphinx, greyhound body, eagle wings, female head, in marble, sitting, not the more familiar lying, life-size. I'd love to see this creature, in marble, walking around.

Went to Cirque du Soleil QUIDAM. Stunning again, basically the template for the film. Little girl loses herself in fantasy world while parents are emotionally absent. Wonderful costumes, humour, playfulness, would love to see some of these acts, which verge on the impossible, they make you believe for a moment that the act of spinning raises them into the air, rather than the wire that actually does the job, I'd love to see animated figures really break that suspension of disbelief. I've just done it a bit with the Sonnet film, which is now finished. These tumblers seemed to almost levitate, the guy in the big metal wheel seemed to have some telepathic control over it. It really was magical. I wrote a little story for Pictures That Tick which involves an actual memory I have of flying, the sensation of relaxing and pushing up off the floor, pushing onto textured air, and swimming/floating into the air, I'd just forgotten how to do it. Should our girl have such a lesson?

Another great moment, when the father figure (just like the one in Goldfish, constantly reading newspaper) is surrounded by 6 identical versions of the daughter. Another was 2 strong people, man and woman, who created extraordinary balances of themselves but very very slowly. You could see the tension in the muscles shift down the body as they slowly moved into the next pose. Wonderful.

Cheers
Dave

From: Dave McKean
To: Neil Gaiman

Date: 08/02/02 3:51 PM

RE: creation myth

CREATION MYTH (written during a very nice calzone at lunchtime)

In the very beginning, our great goddess of the MirrorMask found herself in a new and empty space. And all was white, a sort of off-white which she later found out was called apple-white in the catalogue, and the corners were a bit flaky, and the carpet was a bit manky, but it was a good space. And she sat in the centre of the space, legs crossed, arms folded.
And beheld a void.
A clean white sheet of void.
And she held her mirrormask to her face.
And reflected in the mirrormask was a city.
An endless city of lost horizons and tall stories.
And just as it had been reflected in the mirrormask, so it appeared in the void.
And when there was no more room in the void, she turned it over and continued on the other side.
And so the void was filled from corner to corner on both sides, a city of front and back, a city of light and shadow.
And our goddess rested that first night on her bed, which had just been delivered that afternoon, around teatime, and dreamed of her creation, and the lives that existed there.

And in the days that followed, there were other voids and other lights and other shadows.
And the city sprawled across the space in all of its two dimensions.
And though our great goddess of the mirrormask rested occasionally, and reflected on the world she had created, she knew it would never be finished, because the city was her life, and she would live forever.

APPENDIX B – Dave McKean by Neil Gaiman

I was twenty-six when I first met Dave McKean. I was a working journalist who wanted to write comics. He was twenty-three, in his last year at art college, and he wanted to draw comics. We met in the offices of a telephone sales company, several members of which, we had been told, were going to bankroll an exciting new anthology comic. It was the kind of comic that was so cool that it was only going to employ untried new talent, and we certainly were that.

I liked Dave, who was quiet and bearded and quite obviously the most artistically talented person I had ever encountered.

That mysterious entity which comics artist and writer Eddie Campbell calls "the man at the crossroads", but everyone else knows as Paul Gravett, had been conned into running advertising in his magazine *Escape* for the Exciting New Comic. He came to take a look at it himself. He liked what Dave was drawing, liked what I was writing, asked if we'd like to work together.

We did. We wanted to work together very much.

Somewhere in there we figured out that the reason the Exciting New Comic was only employing untried talent was that no one else would work with the editor. And that he didn't have the money to publish it. And that it was part of history.

Still, we had our graphic novel to be getting on with for Paul Gravett. It was called *Violent Cases.*

We became friends, sharing enthusiasms, and taking pleasure in bringing each other new things. (I gave him Stephen Sondheim, he gave me Jan Svankmayer. He gave me Conlon Nancarrow, I gave him John Cale. It continues.) I met his girlfriend, Clare, who played violin and was starting to think that, as she came up to graduation from university, she probably didn't want to be a chiropodist.

People from DC Comics came to England on a talent scouting expedition. Dave and I went up to their hotel room, and they scouted us. "They don't really want us to do stuff for them," said Dave, as we walked out of the hotel room. "They were probably just being polite."

But we did an outline for *Black Orchid* and gave them that and a number of paintings anyway, and they took them back to New York with them, politely.

That was fifteen years ago. Somewhere in there Dave and I did *Black Orchid* and *Signal to Noise*, and *Mr Punch* and *The Day I Swapped My Dad For Two Goldfish*. And Dave's done book covers and interior work for Jonathan Carroll and Iain Sinclair and John Cale and CD covers for a hundred bands.

This is how we talk on the phone: we talk, and we talk and we talk until we're all talked out, and we're ready to get off the phone. Then the one who called remembers why he called in the first place and we talk about that.

Dave McKean is still bearded. He plays badminton on Monday nights. He has two children, Yolanda and Liam, and he lives with them and with Clare (who teaches violin and runs Dave's life and never became a chiropodist) in a beautiful converted Oast House in the Kent countryside.

When I'm in England I go and stay with them, and I sleep in a perfectly round room.

Dave is friendly and polite. He knows what he likes and what he doesn't like, and will tell you. He has a very gentle sense of humour. He likes Mexican food. He will not eat sushi, but has on several occasions humoured me by sitting and drinking tea and nibbling cooked chicken in Japanese restaurants.

You get to his studio by walking across an improvised log bridge over a pond filled with koi carp. I read an article once in the *Fortean Times* or possibly the *Weekly World News* about koi exploding, and I have warned him several times of the dangers, but he will not listen. Actually, he scoffs.

When I wrote *Sandman* Dave was my best and sharpest critic. He painted, built, or constructed every *Sandman* cover, and his was the face *Sandman* presented to the world.

I never minded Dave being an astonishing artist and visual designer. That never bothered me. That he's a world-class keyboard player and composer bothers me only a little. That he drives amazing cars very fast down tiny Kentish backroads only bothers me if I'm a passenger after a full meal, and much of the time I keep my eyes shut anyway. That he's now becoming a world-class film and video director, that he can write comics as well as I can, if not better, that he subsidises his art (still uncompromised after all these years) with highly paid advertising work which still manages, despite being advertising work, to be witty and heartfelt and beautiful . . . well, frankly, these things bother me. It seems somehow wrong for so much talent to be concentrated in one place, and I am fairly sure the only reason that no one has yet risen up and done something about it is because he's modest, sensible and nice. If it was me, I'd be dead by now.

He likes fine liqueurs. He also likes chocolate. One Christmas my wife and I gave Dave and Clare a hamper of chocolate. Chocolates, and things made of chocolate, and chocolate liqueur and even chocolate glasses to drink the liqueur from. There were chocolate truffles in that hamper and Belgian chocolates, and this was not a small hamper. I'm telling you, there was six months' worth of chocolate in that hamper.

It was empty before New Year's Day.

He's in England, and I'm in America, have been for more than ten years, and I still miss him as much as I miss anyone. Whenever the opportunity to work with Dave comes up, I just say yes.

I was amused, when *Coraline* came out, to find people who only knew Dave for his computer-enhanced multimedia work; they were astonished at the simple elegance of his pen-and-ink drawings. They didn't know he could draw, or they'd forgotten.

Dave has created art styles. Some of what he does is recognisable enough as his that art directors will give young artists samples of Dave McKean work and tell them to do that – often a specific art style that Dave created to solve a specific problem, or a place he went as an artist for a little while, decided that it wasn't where he wanted to be, and moved on.

(For example, I once suggested to him, remembering Arcimbaldo and Josh Kirby's old Alfred Hitchcock paperback cover paintings, that the cover of *Sandman: Brief Lives* could be a face made up of faces. This was before Dave owned a computer, and he laboriously photographed and painted a head made of smaller faces. He's been asked to do similar covers many times since by art directors. And so have other artists. I wonder if they know where it came from.)

People ask me who my favourite artist is, to work with. I've worked with world-class artists, after all, heaps of them. World-class people. And when they ask me about my favourite, I say Dave McKean. And then people ask why. I say, because he surprises me.

He always does. He did it from the first thing we did together, and a couple of weeks ago I looked at the illustrations he's done for our new graphic novel for all ages, *The Wolves in the Walls.* He's combined paintings of people, amazing, funny-scary line drawings of wolves, and photographs of objects (jam, tubas and so on) to create something that is once again not what I expected, nothing like what I had in my head, but better than anything I could have dreamed of, more beautiful and more powerful.

I don't think there's anything Dave McKean cannot do as an artist. (There are certainly things he doesn't want to do, but that's not the same thing at all.)

After sixteen years, some artists are content to rest on their laurels (and Dave has shelves full of laurels, including a World Fantasy Award for best artist). It's a rare artist who is as restless and as enthusiastic as he was when he was still almost a teenager, still questing for the right way to make art.

Neil Gaiman

APPENDIX C – Neil Gaiman by Dave McKean

I'm sitting in a dub suite in London, watching the *MirrorMask* sound editor press buttons and toggle switches as we premix the film. Once in a while I'll say, "louder," or "longer," but that's as exciting as it gets at this stage. Which is fine, actually. It's been a long haul to get to this point, one that started years ago in a series of e-mails between Neil and me.

First, I have to say that making this film has not been a pleasant experience. We were dogged by technical problems and computer glitches. Just about everything that could go wrong did go wrong. There were many times I called home in complete despair and talked to my patient and empathic wife about how impossible it all was, and how we really should just admit it to ourselves, pack up our few remaining marbles, and go home.

In amongst all this chaos, I realised that only Neil could have convinced me to jump off this cliff in the first place (thinking of *Butch and Sundance,* "Don't worry, the fall will probably kill you . . ."), and then only Neil would have given me so much slack in the interpretation and restructuring of his words, always offering fixes and patches where needed, never complaining or demanding. And only Neil could keep me coming back to it all with renewed focus after an encouraging phone call and a bag of sweeties.

I think we trust each other, that's the main thing. Unlike many working partnerships who define themselves in relation to each other, we have always had lives apart which strengthen rather than weaken our desire to work with each other. I think we both like to challenge each other, it's become almost a game of dare. I think we both like to learn new things. There is just no joy in doing the same thing again and again. I think finally that we fill in each other's blanks. Neil understands story and makes sure it is solid; I feel safe to play on Neil's secure foundations. He cares about his audience, he likes to please them, but also to surprise them. He wants them to feel welcome, but not too safe, but most of all he wants them to FEEL.

I can't believe it but 2006 will mark our twentieth year working together. I remember the strange meeting in London working on the never-to-exist *Borderline* magazine and talking to Neil, then a jobbing journalist, for the first time. I certainly remember taking photos of him and his then four-year-old son Mike as reference for our first book together, *Violent*

Cases. And in the intervening years we have had several conversations that have turned into battle plans for the future. Most of these seemed to have worked out, and *MirrorMask* is the result of our last five-year plan to get a movie made. Neil would write scripts in Hollywood and get a little clout, I would make my short films and get a little experience and a visual point of view, and we'd meet up sometime around 2004 and make a film together.

I guess we'll see where we go from here, but even without the benefit of eating a future fruit, I can foresee phone calls at four A.M.: "Hi it's me, I'm in Ireland/Las Vegas/Norway/Rekjavik/The Bahamas. . ."

"The BAHAMAS?" I will say as After Effects crashes again on the screen in front of me.

"Yes," he will say. "I'm in the Bahamas by accident. I've thought of a great idea for a version of Snow White with goblins and anteaters, we don't have to call them goblins, but I think they need the ears, and apples that fall up and I'm sure we can get some cats and Venice in there somewhere, but it's set in Shepton Mallet. Or Barcelona. And it's going to be funny and scary and strange. . ."

And I will be in midair, the cliff edge behind me, the water (and rocks) approaching from below, thinking of Butch and Sundance . . . again . . .

Dave McKean
In a dub theatre in Camden
November 2004

APPENDIX D – The Apology Song

"The Apology Song"

One day, in early 2004, Dave phoned me and said, "I need a song for the end title credits – do me some lyrics." I remembered something I'd written when I was fifteen, which I thought at first might fit, but it didn't quite, and so I wrote "The Apology Song" instead. It was written and sent to Dave on January 5, 2004.

.....

From: Neil Gaiman

To: Dave McKean

Sent: Monday, January 05, 2004 7:40 PM

Subject: more lyrics

In case you didn't like the 30-year-old lyric, I thought I'd write one today.

n

.....

If I apologised
it wouldn't make it all unhappen
wouldn't make the darkness go away

If I apologised
it wouldn't mean I was forgiven
wouldn't mean you wanted me to stay

But
it's a dream
when you seem
to be walking into the sun
we're on first
unrehearsed
and we still don't know what we've done
so we don't say anything . . .

If I apologised
I don't suppose you'd even notice
even though I'd whisper it inside

If I apologised
we could be the perfect couple
Well we could, but only in my mind

but
if you ask
for the mask
then we're stumbling on through the dark
But we wait
it's too late
And we only had to be asked
so we don't say anything . . .

It couldn't hurt to try it
It couldn't hurt too much to try
It's there beyond the quiet
It couldn't hurt too much to fly . . .

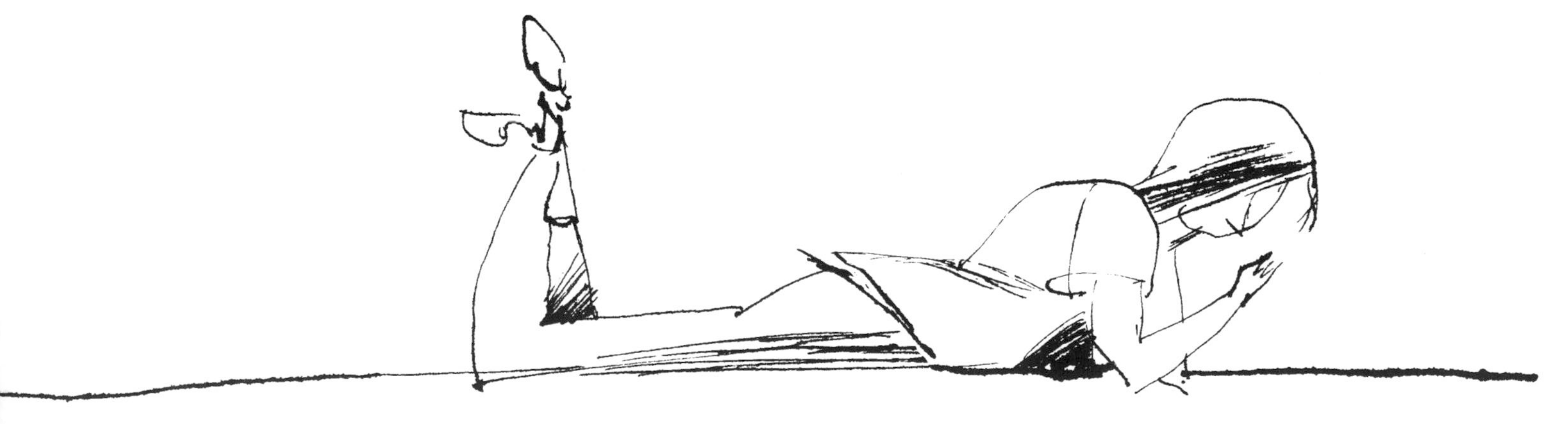